Yesterday Once More

A tale of one boy's journey growing up to the soundtrack of the sixties.

BY

Alan Mumby

Copyright © 2016 Alan Mumby

All rights reserved, including the right to reproduce this book, or portions thereof in any form. No part of this text may be reproduced, transmitted, downloaded, decompiled, reverse engineered, or stored, in any form or introduced into any information storage and retrieval system, in any form or by any means, whether electronic or mechanical without the express written permission of the author.
.

ISBN: 978-1-326-55153-7

PublishNation
www.publishnation.co.uk

For Ellen and Anna-Clare

CONTENTS

	Page
Introduction	1
Chapter One 1960	4
Chapter Two 1961	21
Chapter Three 1962	42
Chapter Four 1963	63
Chapter Five 1964	88
Chapter Six 1965	110
Chapter Seven 1966	134
Chapter Eight 1967	167
Chapter Nine 1968	196
Chapter Ten 1969	230
Epilogue	261

INTRODUCTION

"The past is a different country; they do things differently there." The opening line of the novel "The Go Between" by L.P. Hartley.

Looking back, I often wish that I had talked more to my grandparents and, indeed, my parents about what life was like for them when they were growing up during their formative years. What did they get up to? What social pleasures did they really enjoy? What was it really like for them in the early part of the century or just before the start of the second world war? Nowadays, life is fully documented by all sorts of media, so the adults of tomorrow will have ample information available to them about what life was like for their own parents in the early part of this century. They should still ask, though, whilst there is still time as every individual has his or her own unique story to tell. The inspiration for this book originally came from my desire to set down in words for my daughter what life was like for me growing up in the sixties. A decade that I believe to have been one of the most important decades of the last seventy years and, from a cultural point of view, probably one of the most important ever. But as the book developed, it brought back memories that I thought had long since vanished and made me think, when recounting those memories, that this may be a book which others might possibly find interesting, from a general social point of view. After all, apart from the odd documentary or Pathe News film, there is not such a wealth of material showing what life was really like for young people such as me growing up in the sixties and anyway, we all have our own different stories to tell and experiences to relate.

At the start of this historic decade, I was a 10 year old boy living in a mining village on the borders of Nottinghamshire and Derbyshire whose main interests were football, trainspotting, playing with my mates in the great outdoors and all the other usual activities that a pre-teenage boy enjoyed at that time. At the end of the decade

I was a 20 year old law student at Liverpool University whose main interests were football and all the other activities an adolescent who had experienced growing up in the sixties enjoyed, not least, an abiding love of, and obsession with, the music of that decade. Needless to say, by the close of the decade, trainspotting had long since departed as being a matter of interest to be replaced by, shall we say, pursuits of a more hedonistic nature. This, for anybody who may be interested, is the story of some of my remembrances of that decade. A decade which still divides opinion on whether it has changed society for good or ill, being associated forever with the introduction of the pill which enabled women to have control of their own bodies and also a decade in which young people in this and other countries of the western world started questioning the attitudes and beliefs of their parents and elders. Whatever opinion you may have of that decade and its legacy, I know one thing, I count myself lucky to have lived through my formative years experiencing the sights and the sounds of that exciting period which will undoubtedly never be repeated. I suspect I am not alone in that thought.

For anyone waking up on Friday the 1st of January 1960 not one of them could possibly have envisaged the events which would unfold in the course of the next vibrant 10 years which culminated with man leaving our planet for the first time to set foot on the moon; an era in which four young men from Liverpool would change the face of popular music for ever and would end with the number one single on the 31st of December 1969 belonging to one Rolf Harris entitled Two Little Boys. Not a record, incidentally, that I will be urging you to lend an ear to if you have not already had that dubious pleasure. Having said that, it must have appealed to a good number of people who were willing to spend their hard earned cash on such a "novelty" record enabling it to become top of the pops. I wonder what those same buyers think of it now? Then again no, life's too short. It just goes to show that not all the popular music recorded and released in that golden decade was ground breaking and immortal. It also shows that music, like most aspects of art and literature, appeals on different levels to different people and long may that be so. My remembrances of this decade, and particularly my opinion of its music, will, therefore, be subjective through necessity and will not appeal to everyone and nor would I have any belief that it should do so. My intention is merely to share and possibly, if I may be so bold as to say, to enlighten. It is therefore my intention to finish each chapter with a brief list of my own favourite songs of that year coupled with a mention of some of the notable films released during that year.

For any of you reading this who are old enough to have lived through that memorable decade, I hope that my retelling of some of the events which affected me jogs some memories and for those of you who were unlucky enough to have missed it, then all I can say is that I hope my memories give you some flavour of what life was like for me and countless others growing up in the sixties. Perhaps you might even give a listen, if only once, to some of the music which I will be recommending and which still resonates with and influences people to this day. So let me take you back to the days of black and white TV with a choice of just two channels to watch; to a time when popular music was still in it's infancy, struggling to find an identity after the brief early flourish of rock and roll; to an era when a child of ten or eleven was free to wander wherever he or she wanted without parents worrying what their child was up to; to a time when we were on the verge of leaving behind the dour fifties and entering on what would become the vibrant and colourful era that was the sixties.

CHAPTER ONE
1960

"Is it a book that you would even wish your wife or your servants to read?" Question posed by the Prosecuting Counsel, Mervyn Griffith-Jones, to the jury at the Lady Chatterley novel obscenity trial held at the Old Bailey in 1960.

Nothing seems to me to sum up the prevailing class differences existing in 1960 more than the above question addressed by the prosecuting counsel in the Lady Chatterley obscenity trial to those ordinary members of the public who made up the jury in that trial. Just how many members of that jury did the upper middle class barrister think actually employed servants? Had he any idea how ordinary people lived their lives and what they thought? What is certain, however, is that by the end of 1969 no barrister would dream of asking any such question to members of a jury so great would be the social changes which would occur in that momentous decade.

Some people would no doubt argue that the moral decline of our nation started with the reduction in censorship which occurred late in 1960 with the conclusion of the obscenity trial at the Old Bailey of Penguin Books for wanting to print D H Lawrence's novel, Lady Chatterley's lover, which had originally been published in Italy in 1928 but banned from being printed in full in this country prior to the obscenity trial being held. The resultant publicity of the trial meant that when the book eventually went on sale immediately following the outcome of the trial, there were queues of people wanting to read a book by a novelist of whom the majority had probably never heard of up to that date and involving a plot centering around a class system and social conflict in the early part of the 20th century, which, I suspect, is a subject of which most of the novel's buyers would have had but a vague notion and not a great deal of interest.

No, what the majority of the book's buyers were really interested in reading about were the rude bits and they knew there must have been some in the novel for it to have been banned previously and for it's publication to have been so vehemently opposed by the establishment. Cue the start of the great social upheaval launching, amongst other things, the permissive society (whatever that was) and heralding the prelude to "the swinging sixties", of which more later.

Personally, as a 10 year old in 1960, I didn't have a clue what all the fuss was about, nor did I much care. If I had heard the words Lady Chatterley uttered I would have thought this was probably referring to a relative of the Queen and I certainly would not have known why a gamekeeper would have been interested in a lady garden. I didn't like gardens then anyway and would only venture in to them to retrieve my wayward football. I have come to appreciate all sorts of gardens since then though. Ah the innocence of being a child in 1960 in Britain. No mobile phones, internet, ipods, ipads, game consoles, facebook, twitter and all the other paraphernalia of our modern society which has robbed today's children of such innocent pleasures as knocking on a friend's door to see if they wanted to come out to play at football, cricket, fishing for tadpoles and sticklebacks, scrumping, playing Cowboys and Indians, bird nesting and generally having a good time in the great outdoors with your mates. Funny that you didn't see many fat (sorry overweight) kids then. Now why could that be?

As Friday the 1st of January ushered in the sixties decade, I was living on a small housing estate built for and rented by mining families in the North East Derbyshire village of Creswell. Our modest house was a basic two up, plus box room, and two down with coal fires and no central heating. Nor did we have such a thing as a fridge, telephone or car, something we had in common with most other families but our house did have an indoor toilet, unlike my paternal grandmother's house in the neighbouring village of Clowne, where the toilet was at the bottom of the garden and there was no bathroom inside their house either, but again more of that later. My father worked as an electrician at nearby Whitwell Colliery in the South Yorkshire/Nottinghamshire coalfield and my mother was a typical housewife of the time, looking after the home, myself and my little brother, Philip, who was then 5 years old and (through no fault of his) a source of occasional irritance to me as little brothers can be when you are growing up and you think that everything should revolve around you. Well I did anyway, but I have come to appreciate him since then and in fact he has been a source of inspiration for me writing this book, having himself already written about his exploits with his scooter gang in the early 1970's. Money was tight for our family back then, as it was with all mining families and indeed working class families generally, but we were all in the same boat and I don't remember any feelings of envy towards others as we did not have to suffer a media obsessing about vacuous celebrities, their meaningless lifestyles and trying to make you feel inadequate if you didn't aspire to, or have, their indulgent lifestyles and material goods. At my age, in 1960, as long as you were warm, didn't go hungry and had your mates to play with then nothing much else mattered.

For Christmas the previous year, I had been given a two wheeler bike as my main present and this was a source of great enjoyment as it gave me the freedom to go riding off either on my own or with my mates. I must say that Santa did a great job getting that down our chimney. Dynamo eat your heart out. Traffic was not a problem in our village as hardly anyone could afford a car so the streets were safe for children to play in. So much so that our games of street football or cricket were generally only interrupted by the arrival of Manfredi's ice cream van at which point all the kids vanished in the blink of an eye to rush indoors to beg threepence or sixpence (in old money that is, i.e 1.5p or 2.5 p nowadays) for a lolly or ice cream cone with raspberry juice. They were delicious and I am sure they tasted better than today's ice cream, or am I just looking at this through a kid's eyes? Anyway, I was so proud of my bike that I went in for the Cycling Proficiency Test which was held in our school yard and I achieved the grand total of 100% in the test which meant that I was rewarded with a Knights of the Road badge, which I still have somewhere.

As 1960 started, I was in the third year of my junior school and life basically revolved around school and playing out with my mates. Junior school life in 1960 was very regimented and probably differed little from school to school. We sat at desks which seated two children at a time and in my school a boy would have to sit next to a girl. Yuck! I suspect this was to stop the girls from talking to each other, which seemed to be their favourite pastime and one in which my future wife excelled, so I understand. Anyway, I was not too taken with this idea, I mean, what self respecting 10 year old wanted to sit next to a girl in class. I should have made the most of it back then though as my attitude to the fairer sex certainly altered, unsurprisingly, as this decade wore on and I would soon find the company of girls in short supply. For now, I just put up with it and although I enjoyed the school work, the highlight of my school week was Wednesday games which in Autumn and Winter was football and in summer, it was cricket. I had just been picked, at the start of my third year the previous September, for the school football first team, even though it was mainly made up of boys from the year above and I thoroughly enjoyed it.

It is, however, interesting to read my school report for this year, which I still have, as it is remarked in my yearly report that I needed to take more care in English, my arithmetic was excellent, general subjects was very good except for practical work and for printing it was noted that I was "untidy". That last comment would crop up again with some frequency as my school career proceeded. Furthermore, in that regard, I have not improved, unlike a good wine, with age. I did finish 1st out of a class of 42 so it wasn't all bad. Yes, those were the days of class positions where you knew exactly where you stood amongst your peers. Very important for someone as ultra competitive as I was.

At Junior School, in addition to our academic work, we also had the weekly trips to the local swimming baths where we were taught... to swim. Well, it wouldn't have been fencing, would it? Creswell

Baths were situated in a fairly old building with a relatively small freshwater pool. The depth of the pool started at three foot and gradually went up to six foot at the deep end. There was also a small tiered wooden diving board affair at the deep end for the older boys and teenagers to dive off and generally show off to their mates. I enjoyed visiting the baths and soon learned to swim and became quite proficient at the breaststroke but for some reason I always found the front crawl quite difficult. It was a good venue to visit on a hot summer's day to cool off and lark about.

So far as TV was concerned, there were only two television stations, BBC and ITV, in 1960 and there was not a great deal of choice on what you could watch on your small black and white TV but as a child my favourites included "The Lone Ranger" - who was a masked cowboy who rode a white horse called Silver and was particularly fond of shouting "Hi ho Silver, away!" generally at the end of each episode, when he headed off to his next adventure accompanied by his loyal companion, a red Indian (was there any other colour?) called Tonto, who could tell how many men they were chasing, what they were riding and their birth sign just by looking at the footprints in the dirt, though I may be exaggerating about the birth signs. He also had a gun that fired silver bullets, The Lone Ranger that is, which I always thought was a bit showy but a great idea. Silver obviously being in plentiful supply though I can't remember where he bought them from, though I have a vague recollection he had his own silver mine, but that may just be senility setting in and playing tricks with my memory.

Another of my favourites was William Tell who was, as far as I can recall, a folk hero from Switzerland in the 14th century and who was very handy with a crossbow, to such an extent that he split an apple on someone's head with his crossbow arrow, although quite why he would want to do so and, more to the point, why anyone would stand as volunteer for such a stunt now escapes me. I can't imagine there would have been much of a queue for volunteers, but then again life was probably not that exciting in 14th century Switzerland and having this done to you may just have been their version of bungee jumping. Who knows? Anyway, he was forever fighting evil aristocrats particularly a fat villain known as Landburger Gessler who bore a passing resemblance to the Michelin Man and looked like he had eaten all the cheeses in the nearby country and each episode seemed to consist of William Tell thwarting Gessler's evil schemes. Trust me, you had to be there to appreciate the programme.

Robin Hood was another favourite (well, we are talking kids programmes here) on the ITV channel and as you should be familiar with his story I will not elaborate much but it had a great theme song "Robin Hood, Robin Hood riding through the glen..." sung by one Dick James who would later achieve some prominence and much riches as a music publisher for a couple of budding songwriters who you may have heard of called Lennon and McCartney, of whom more, in fact much more, later. Great programme though, and a source of inspiration for me and my mates if we wanted to go out and play outlaws in the neighbouring woods. Without a Maid Marian, I hasten to add. We were much too young to be bothering with girls, so that was a firm no no.

BBC had a programme on that amused me called "Whack-o" which starred Jimmy Edwards as a drunken, gambling, cane-swishing headmaster of a public school who always seemed to be trying to swindle kids out of their pocket money. Now I know you are probably thinking that this politically incorrect material does not seem much like comedy but I thought it was quite funny, although I doubt it has worn well. Must try to find an episode on Youtube to view. It was certainly not as funny, however, as Sergeant Bilko in an American import called "The Phil Silvers Show" which involved a sergeant and his platoon in the American army and each episode involved Bilko trying a scheme to make money which always backfired. This show can still be caught on one of the rerun channels and has lasted quite well I think.

Programmes shown for all the family which I enjoyed included "Bonanza", a cowboy show revolving around the Cartwright family, and which ran for 14 seasons, such was its popularity. "Rawhide", another cowboy show starring the inimitable Clint Eastwood as Rowdy Yates and generally involving a cattle drive when the cowboys would have to fight off rustlers and Injuns to get the cattle to market. I seem to remember that cattle stampedes featured quite regularly and again this programme was a source of inspiration for the games me and my mates would play, minus the cattle obviously. Whilst living in a rural area did have its benefits, borrowing some farmer's cattle for this type of game would not have gone down well so imagination had to be actively used.

Intellectual stimulation was provided by my favourite quiz show which was "Junior Criss Cross Quiz" and which involved two kids trying to answer questions to gain a nought or cross on a board and to win you had to get a line of one or other and you were then rewarded with a prize, although I cannot now recall what they were. "Crackerjack", which was a children's variety show, originally shown on a Thursday teatime but eventually moved to a regular slot on each Friday teatime, also had a quiz section called "Double or drop" which involved two kids answering general knowledge questions and being given a prize to hold each time they got a correct answer and a cabbage (heaven knows why) each time they answered incorrectly and whoever either dropped an item or received a third cabbage was then declared the loser. Exciting eh! The long winter evenings positively flew by, to borrow a line from a later comedy sitcom.

Whilst choice of evening viewing was somewhat restricted for a 10 year old, there were some adult programmes which I could enjoy, such as "Double your money", a general knowledge quiz hosted by Hughie Greene and I mean that most sincerely folks. "Take your pick" (nothing whatsoever to do with DIY) was another quiz show which involved contestants having to pick a closed box in which there was either a good prize or a booby prize and for which the host, Michael Miles, would offer the contestant a sum of money to see if they would either take the money or open the box.

Crime shows were not as prevalent then as now but my favourite was "No Hiding Place", which was a metropolitan detective programme and Saturday nights would not be complete without George Dixon as "Dixon of Dock Green", greeting all viewers with his familiar "Evenin' all" whilst standing under the Police lamp of his station and then regaling us with a recent moralistic tale. Comedy came in the form of "The Army Game" which involved recruits undergoing national service and the exploits they had during that time and the programme had as cast members some famous names who would later go on to star in the Carry On films, such as Charles Hawtry, William Hartnell (who later became the first Doctor Who), Bernard Bresslaw and Alfie Bass. Eric Sykes had a show called "Sykes and a .." which focused on a different topic each week and was a programme I thoroughly enjoyed, but my favourite, which I think ended in 1960, was "Hancock's Half Hour" starring Tony Hancock and which I found hilarious. I believe that this show has stood the test of time, which is a real testament to it's talented writers, Galton and Simpson, who went on to write "Steptoe and Son".

Variety shows came in the form of "Sunday Night at the London Palladium" hosted by Bruce Forsyth, who seemed to have less hair then than he had when hosting "Strictly Come Dancing" but a show which I found totally boring was called "The Black and White Minstrel Show" which involved white male singers being blacked up, Al Jolson style. Now why they couldn't just have used black singers is a puzzle to me and I hated this show but unfortunately my parents thought it was entertaining and they wouldn't generally miss it. Now that was one time an Ipad would have come in useful.

Sport was somewhat rare on the TV and was mainly catered for by "Grandstand" on Saturday afternoons which showed various sports, but strictly no live football league games, and on Saturday evenings there was Sports Special which would show brief highlights of one or two of the day's football matches. The only live football shown was restricted to the occasional International Match and the European Cup Final, this year played between the then great Real

Madrid side and the West German team Eintracht Frankfurt, which resulted in a thrilling game won by Madrid by 7 goals to 3. Probably one of the best European finals ever played.

Domestically, however, the main event and the most important match of the year, was the Cup Final. A match which I longed to go to, but doubted that I ever would have the chance. However, I am glad to say that I can now count myself lucky that I have had that chance and pleasure (mostly) on no less than seven occasions. How times have changed and whilst you can now see any number of live league games, the Cup Final, thanks to the Premier League and it's paymaster in chief, Sky Sports, has been consigned to the status of an also-ran, although any real football fan will still say that it is a dream to go to Wembley to support your team and long may that be so. I can certainly say that, speaking personally, nothing matches the magic of going to support your own team on Cup Final day. Particularly if they win.

Finally, to conclude my reminiscences of TV programmes, I come to the music section. There was no MTV around, of course, in those long lost days and we had, as the main event, a programme called "Juke Box Jury" which was hosted by David Jacobs and each week had a different panel of four celebrities reviewing the latest record releases and voting whether each record reviewed would be a Hit or a Miss. If the panel voted that a record would be a hit, the host would ring a bell and, if a miss, he would sound a horn. Now for those of our younger readers I have referred to a record release as the song itself would be on a 7" black vinyl piece of plastic called, you guessed it, a record and which you could place on your Dansette record player, or whatever player you were lucky enough to have, and listen to it to your heart's content. Whilst I remember enjoying the programme, I was not really interested greatly in the popular music of that time and my family did not possess a record player in any event.

My moment of revelation, so far as music was concerned, only arrived one spring evening in 1963, of which more in a later chapter.

Music on the radio was available through the BBC's Light Programme and on Saturday morning my age group was catered for by a programme called "Children's Favourites", hosted, initially I think, by Peter Brough and his ventriloquist's dummy called Archie Andrews. Ah, I can hear you thinking, how does a ventriloquist act work on radio? Well, you can't see his lips move for a start! I thank you, I'm here all week. Peter Brough was very good on the radio. His problem came when he ventured on to TV and, surprise surprise, the audience could now see his lips move. The mystique was broken.

The main source of popular music on the radio came in the form of "Two Way Family Favourites" which was broadcast every Sunday lunch time and was hosted by Jean Metcalf, who played record requests for troops and their families. That programme will, for me, forever be associated with the smell of the Sunday roast cooking. No ready meals in those days, of course, and we didn't obsess over fat or sugar content in our meals as all the food we ate was fresh and cooked within days of being bought. Sunday lunch at our house was always a small joint, usually roast pork including the crackling, which I adored, together with home made apple sauce, roast potatoes and one or two vegetables followed by a pudding such as apple pie with Bird's custard. The pudding was always freshly baked, of course. I hated vegetables though, and even now my dislike of them can generally bring a word of reproach from my patient and long suffering wife, Ellen, when she tries to encourage me to have them, generally with little success. I've always liked baked beans though. Do they count? Yes, chips and beans was a firm favourite with me back then.

Let me tell you something about my village, Creswell, which was a small mining village with one main street on which stood a picture house called "Regors Cinema" and which was the main source of entertainment for the village. Creswell has, however, now achieved an element of fame because, situated just outside the village, is Creswell Crags, which is a limestone gorge and the site of habitation of early man some 50,000 years or so ago. It is, in fact, one of the earliest known sites of human habitation in this country, but as a child, while I was vaguely aware that it had some historic importance in those days, it was merely just a great place for me and my mates to go and play. In 1960 not all the caves were boarded up and you could, if you dared, venture inside some of the caves although they were quite dark and a little scary to a 10 year old. I am sure we used to mess around with old bones which used to lie on the floor so apologies to any anthropologists if we damaged some of the old relics, but it was fun and what did we know anyway? The site is now designated as a Site of Special Scientific Interest so definitely not a playground now for 10 year olds, but I think it is well worth a visit.

Another place where me and my mates went to play was quite near to our mining estate and was known locally as "The Grips", actually, to give it it's proper name, it was Markland Grips. This, like Creswell Crags, was a dolomite limestone gorge and a great place to play cowboys and indians and climb trees, although we never found any caves there. There was also a small stream running through the wooded gorge where you could take your fishing net and jamjar and fish for sticklebacks. On summer days we could spend most of the day there, particularly if we took a picnic with us. Two of my favourite picnic sandwiches were banana sandwiches and cheese with tomato sauce. Very Heston Blumenthal!

Anyway, back to the Cinema. As there was nothing on TV on Saturday mornings for kids in 1960, the weekly ritual every Saturday morning for kids such as myself was a visit to the cinema where there was always a special film showing to keep us entertained and in fact most of the village kids would go to this where mayhem would ensue. You can imagine the scene of about 200 or so pre-teen kids wanting to let off steam and generally have a good time and possibly even watch the film. Some hope. Think of that scene from "Gremlins" when they have all gone to the cinema to watch Snow White and that should give you a pretty good idea of what the audience would have looked like and how they behaved. Well, in truth, the Gremlins were better behaved than we were.

Adults ventured to the Saturday morning flicks, as they were known, at their peril as kids would be running round, fighting, shouting, messing around and also someone would inevitably let off stink bombs which was just so gross. Audience participation at its very best and no encouragement needed. The mayhem would generally reach a crescendo after half an hour or so of the first film starting and would then result in the owner of the cinema marching on to the stage, stopping the film, holding his hands up and threatening to clear the cinema unless we all behaved. Cue obedient silence and cherubic faces from the audience for 10 minutes or so until the general level of mayhem gradually returned, although this would often die down when the weekly serial came on, which was usually a cowboy which would always finish with a cliffhanger of an ending tempting you to go back next week to see how the hero extricated himself from certain death. Which he always did. At the end of the serial, 200 or so kids exited the cinema quickly and we often acted out scenes from the serial all the way home for our Saturday lunch. Kids of today have no idea of the fun they are missing.

Summer in our village ushered in one of the most exciting events of the year, the annual visit of the travelling fair with it's rides such as the Waltzer and the dodgems. There would be prize stalls where you could win a goldfish or some other prize as well as a Noah's ark ride, which was a roundabout type affair having animals as its theme on which you rode in a similar manner to a merry-go-round. This was a time when you pestered parents for pocket money to go on the rides and I can still picture the scene when approaching the fair, which was always set up on the local rec (recreation ground), you first heard the humming of the generators powering the rides, the screams of kids on the rides, the smell of the hot dogs and fried onions and the sounds of the latest records blaring out from the loud sound system at each ride.

As a 10 year old boy in a small village this was pleasure at its most extreme and my first introduction to good pop music. Needless to say, although the fair would last for a few days, you always blew all your pocket money on the first night. The Waltzer was always my favourite ride, particularly if one of the fairground men kept twirling your Waltzer car around in between his death defying scrambling between the respective cars, but if he saw any girls in a car then that was the end of any attention you would receive from him and you then had to rely solely on gravity to twirl your car round after that. The film "That'll be the Day" captured the essence of this very well.

I have to say that even though I may have blown all my money on the first night, it did not stop me and my mates going back each night to the fair to lark about and listen to the music being played. As it was the summer of 1960, the big hit of the summer was "Cathy's Clown" by the Everly Brothers, a golden classic to coin a phrase, and each time I hear that record it immediately evokes those long last golden moments of that summer. It's strange how strong an association of a song with a particular memory can be.

Disaster did, however, lurk on one particular night when we visited the fair in our penniless state. We noticed that one of the empty flat bed fair lorries used to transport the rides was situated a few feet away from some stacked bales of hay and one of my small gang thought that a good game would be to climb on the lorry, run full pelt along it and jump off the lorry on to the stack of hay. The rest of us weren't too sure about this so we decided to let him go first. He set off from one end of the lorry like Usain Bolt with a firecracker up his arse but failed to spot that the lorry had a horizontal bar at the end of it, at a height equivalent to his nose. Whack! Metal met bone. His legs kept going when he hit the bar like one of those cartoon characters (think Tom and Jerry) whist his head and upper body stayed firmly behind the bar and he then came crashing down on the ground. After a brief moment of hilarity, we all rushed to him to see if he had survived and, despite him being momentarily knocked out, I'm pleased to say that he did recover, but I don't think his nose was ever the same again and the 30 yard flat bed lorry dash and long jump was consigned to history. A pity really, as I always thought that it would have made a great Olympic sport. Particularly with an iron bar in place!

Summer holiday this year was particularly memorable for me as it was spent in Blackpool where we stayed at my maternal grandmother's fish and chip shop in North Shore. Now, for any 10 year old the prospect of going on holiday to Britain's premier seaside resort was exciting enough in itself, but couple that with the fact that we would be staying in a fish and chip shop and you had a kid's Utopia and although I may be biased, from my memory, those fish and chips were the best I had ever tasted.

What you also have to realise is, that if you asked most people in the late 1950's and early 1960's where they would most like to holiday, then Blackpool would have been the choice of most people. Outside of London, it had the most entertainment venues at which all the big stars of the day would perform and a great many of the stars would be in town for each summer season, appearing at venues such as the Opera House, Winter Gardens, Queens Theatre, Palace Theatre and, of course, the three piers.

Appearing in the resort this summer were Bruce Forsyth and Pearl Carr and Teddy Johnson (early entrants in the Eurovision song contest), the Central Pier had "The Peter Webster Show" (a talent contest for kids) and for adults, "Let's have fun" starring some really obscure folk like Zio Angels, Parnell and Ashton, Roy Earl and Mike and Bernie Winters, who will crop up later in this book. The now long gone Palace Theatre (once situated on the Promenade near to the Tower) had Harry Secombe and Harry Worth and the soon to be demolished Hippodrome (later replaced by the just demolished at the time of writing, ABC Theatre) featured a starry cast of current, for then, pop stars such as Adam Faith, Emile Ford, Morton Fraser's Harmonica Gang and the Lana Sisters. Yes, that one was certainly for the youngsters!

In addition to the above attractions, well everything is relative, there was the brilliant Pleasure Beach which was a top attraction in itself and a fantastic place to visit with such rides as the Big Dipper, Grand National, Crazy Mouse, Log Flume and many more including the Fun House, outside of which stood the iconic laughing clown, until the Fun House was burnt down some years later. Bet the clown wasn't laughing then, mind. There was also the Golden Mile with it's numerous arcades with machines of all varieties including the slot machines and what would become my favourite, the pinball machines. Last, but not least, was of course the extensive beach and the big attraction to me of going in the sea to paddle and swim. Funny that you didn't notice the temperature much as a kid. Yes, I know that nowadays the sea is not much of an attraction and that you could either die of hypothermia or contact some nasty infection from it, although in fairness they are trying to improve the sea water quality now, but trust me, as a 10 year old coming from an inland village, this was in fact El Dorado. No package holidays for us back then. If you wanted a fun-filled beach holiday then Blackpool was the place to be. Little did I know that just under 2 years later I would be moving here permanently. But more of that in due course.

After the summer, the new school term beckoned which would mean my final year at Junior School and at it's end the taking of the 11 plus exam which I will cover in the next chapter. Exciting eh? Just like the cowboy serial mentioned above. Bet you can't wait. At this same time, over in Arnhem in the Netherlands, an unknown budding beat group from Liverpool, who had recently settled on a name for their band and decided to call themselves "The Beatles", whilst on their way to Hamburg where they were due to perform, made a brief stopover at Arnhem cemetery for some reason and had their photo taken in front of a memorial on which were inscribed the words "Their name liveth for evermore" which was somewhat prophetic, don't you think? Little did they know.

The final event of this year which I can recall was the news of the election of a new American President, namely John F Kennedy, who even to someone of my small years looked quite charismatic and not at all like the politicians I had been used to seeing on the TV such as our then current Prime Minister, Harold MacMillan. The new American President looked young and a bit like a Hollywood film star and his election victory seemed to herald in a new era. So 1960 draws to a close. Thank goodness for that, I hear you say. Do I have to read through another 9 years? Will the writer have enough stories to fill those remaining years? Yes, it's just like the cowboy serial. Turn over the page folks for the next exciting adventure of a boy's tale growing up in the sixties, or not.

Actually it is not quite the end of the chapter as I just want to recommend some of the music of that year which, in retrospect mainly, has appealed to me and at the end of each chapter I will list those records which are my favourite from that year and which I think have still stood the test of time and can be enjoyed today so here goes:-

1. The Drifters - Dance with me.

2. Eddie Cochran - Three steps to heaven

3. Everly Brothers - Cathy's Clown

4. Johnny Kidd and the Pirates - Shakin' all over

5. The Shadows - Apache

6. The Drifters - Save the last dance for me

7. Maurice Williams and the Zodiacs - Stay

8. Roy Orbison - Only the lonely

9. Sam Cooke - Chain Gang

10. Ray Charles - Georgia

I will also have a feature listing some of the films which I enjoyed during the year. For 1960, I cannot claim to have seen all of these at the time, but they are noteworthy for having been released during that year:-

Spartacus - the epic historical drama directed by Stanley Kubrick with an all star cast featuring Kirk Douglas, Laurence Olivier, Jean Simmons, Charles Laughton, Peter Ustinov and Tony Curtis.

Psycho - (one I definitely didn't see until I was much older!) directed by Alfred Hitchcock and starring Anthony Perkins (who played one of the creepiest screen characters ever in this film) and Janet Leigh and featured both the famous shower scene and also the brilliant twist at the end of the film. Probably one of my favourite horror films.

The Alamo - the epic tale of the 1836 Battle of the Alamo featuring that perennial cowboy John Wayne as Davy Crockett with Richard Widmark and Laurence Harvey.

The Magnificent Seven - based on the Japanese film, "The Seven Samurai", and probably one of the best westerns ever made, with a great cast including Yul Brinner and, a particular favourite of mine, the great Steve McQueen, as well as Charles Bronson and James Coburn.

Saturday Night and Sunday Morning - one of the first realistic films portraying the working class and filmed in Nottingham, near to where my maternal grandparents had their fish and chip shop prior to moving to Blackpool, and starring a young Albert Finney. A fine period film of the early sixties and totally evocative of working class life at that time.

CHAPTER TWO
1961

"Have you got that record "My Bonnie" by The Beatles?"
Question posed by one Raymond Jones to the store manager of
NEMS record shop in Liverpool, a certain Brian Epstein.

As 1961 arrived I had reached the age of 11 and found myself in the final year of my junior school with the 11 plus looming in the not too distant future. In the early sixties, if you were a child in a working class family, the only way that you could escape the prospect of a manual job such as a miner, which was the prevalent occupation for most men in my village, was by education to enable you to obtain possibly a white collar job in an office or bank or, if you were really ambitious and worked hard, a professional job such as an architect, surveyor, doctor, chemist or solicitor, but the latter jobs were only available to graduates and as an 11 year old no such thoughts entered my head, even though my academic record was good and I was fortunate enough to be generally in the top three or four of my class at each year end.

No, what I really wanted to be at age 11 was a footballer. Nothing else. Football then was my obsession and I played every minute that I could, which would get me into some hot water during this year. I played for the school first team and had done so since the previous year and my school team had managed to go 2 years unbeaten against neighbouring village sides, whilst also winning the annual cup competition 2 years on the run. If I couldn't find anyone to play with outside school, which was somewhat rare, I would take a tennis ball down the road on my estate to a tarmacked area on which stood a line of garages with iron doors and I would kick a ball endlessly against the garage doors, practising shots and passes with right foot and left foot. It must have been a trifle noisy for neighbours, although no one ever complained. If I wasn't playing, then during the football season I would go to watch either Nottingham Forest or Sheffield Wednesday, who were both in the first division (what Sky have kindly renamed the "Premier League", when they invented football in 1992, or so they like to think).

If I was going to see Nottingham Forest play, this would mean me and a few mates catching the 11.40am train from Creswell to Nottingham, allowing us sufficient time to call at a chippy on the way to the ground for chips and mushy peas and then racing to the ground to get in first so that we could stand right at the front on the side near to the Kop end of the ground. Well, we were small so we needed to have an unobstructed view. Imagine today allowing 11 year old boys to head off on their own to a city to watch a football match with no adult accompaniment. How lucky were we to be able to do so safely! Those were the days when you didn't need to take out a small mortgage to see a game as it was cheap to get into the ground and nor did you have to try to get tickets for a game as it was always first come first served at the league matches. It was, after all, the working man's game and whilst ground conditions were admittedly somewhat primitive, especially the toilet facilities, it had a certain atmosphere and you felt a real attachment to the game and the players, who were themselves ordinary people, not the out of touch, self-important posing superstars of today. A pity we can't have the comfort of the stadiums today with the attitude and commitment of the players of yesterday. Being near to the front of the stand also meant that you could, if you wanted and dared, run on to the pitch to pat a player on the back at the end of the game. Don't ask me why you would want to do that, though. I think it's just something kids liked to do and would probably do so nowadays given the chance, although nowadays they would be probably be banned from going to the game ever again. I do remember once running on to the pitch at Nottingham at the end of the game to pat Bobby Charlton on the back when Manchester United visited, though I doubt he remembers. After the end of the game it would then be a race back to the station to catch the train home.

It was during this year that I visited Wembley for the first time to see a schoolboy match - England vs. Wales and the whole experience was magical for a football mad kid like me. My paternal grandfather from the nearby village of Clowne had managed to get tickets so he took me down on the train, direct to Wembley, and the noise of 60,000 or so school kids yelling their heads off was somewhat surreal, think of a horde of eunuchs cheering their team on and you may get some idea of the high pitched shouting which occurred. Quite unlike a normal football crowd! Anyway, I had visited the mecca of football to see a match for myself and it would not be the last time I would do so either.

Before leaving the topic of football (sorry to you non-football liking readers such as my wife for going on a bit) but I did say that playing football got me into trouble. Well, on two occasions actually. The first was when me and a group of other kids were found playing football in the schoolyard at break time which was, as we all well knew, strictly prohibited but one of my classmates turned up with a tennis ball so we just had to have a kickabout and were caught by a teacher. Straight to the headmaster we were sent and lined up in a row. After the usual pep talk by him about the dangers of playing football in the schoolyard (as opposed to playing in the street, which was our usual venue!) he asked us all to hold out a hand and he then walked along the line with his cane, administering one hefty whack on each kid's palm as he passed. Boy did it sting, but we never played football in the schoolyard again. There must be a moral there somewhere, do you think? Needless to say we did not breathe a word about this punishment to our parents as we did not want a second beating. Those were the days when, if you complained you had received any punishment at school, the reaction you got from your parents was to the effect of "Well you must have been doing something wrong to have deserved it so you will behave next time, won't you?"). Imagine that. Parents supporting their child being punished and not wanting to complain or sue a teacher for assault. How primitive must they have been?

The other occasion on which I found myself in trouble involved me and my mates taking a shortcut from the street on our estate to the nearest football field. What could be wrong about that I hear you say? Nothing, apart from the fact that the shortcut involved trespassing over two sets of railway lines, one of which was the main Worksop to Nottingham line, in order to save a bit of time and energy for the game. What was worse was that on one occasion when we did so, there was actually a standing coal train on the first line which ran at the bottom of our street which was waiting for a signal to change. Well, we didn't know how long it would be stood there and time was getting on so we each crawled between the coal wagons over the railway line and then legged it as fast as we could over the waste ground and on to the next obstacle, which was the main line. Looking back I am, of course, horrified by this but we were gung-ho 11 year olds who had no fear. No sense either, I can hear you say! Heaven knows what our parents would have said had they known. I know I would have been in for a belting from my father if he had found out and I can't say now that I would have blamed him.

Anyway, we eventually tried the trespassing game once too often and were spotted by a nearby signalman who shouted something unintelligible at us from his signal box (though it may have included the words "off" and "little buggers" somewhere in there) and must then have duly reported us to the headmaster of our school. The next day at morning assembly the headmaster asked to see those boys who had been guilty of the trespassing offence to come forward. Well, me and the others glanced at each other, tried to control bowel movements and then meekly stepped forward. I think he probably knew who we were anyway as he knew where we all lived and could reasonably guess, given where the offence occurred, that it would be us. So, we shuffled forwards expecting the worst and that either our palms or our bottoms would once again become best of acquaintances with Mr. Cane but no, to our surprise, he just lectured us on the velocity of steam engines and how long it would take a Stanier tank engine, with which I am sure you are most familiar, pulling three coaches at 45 miles per hour to stop and how long we would have to cross the line once we saw said engine. We thought for a moment but decided not to ask the audience or phone a friend and just stayed silent, muttering our don't knows, but we were all extremely grateful for this physics lesson and duly nodded obedience when asked to confirm that we would not transgress again, being mightily relieved to have palms and bottoms intact. Again, not a word was breathed about this at home as retribution for this offence would have been dire, although undoubtedly deserved.

Talking of trains, I must now tell you something about the joys (yes joys!) of trainspotting for an 11 year old in 1961. (Stop laughing Anna when you read this - Anna is my daughter who has, over the years, ribbed me mercilessly over this hobby e.g. "What, you actually sit at a train station to wait for an engine and then take down it's number? Gripper!"). In those days steam was still in it's glory, although soon to decline. Every so often, mainly on a Saturday outside the football season, I would take myself off to Retford station which was situated on the main East Coast line - King's Cross to Edinburgh route, that is - about an hour's journey by bus and train from my house, armed with my notebook, pen and enough sandwiches to last the week (banana sandwiches, of course, to the fore). Bet you can't get them at Subway! If the holy grail of an A4 Pacific engine (such as Mallard, which held the speed record and which I saw on many an occasion) heading one of the famous express trains was spotted by another boy approaching the station from afar, the cry of "Streak" would go up and we all became anxious to see if it was one of the engines we had not seen before so that we could then mark it off in our spotter's bible, namely the Ian Allan ABC book of steam locomotives.

The main aim of trainspotting was to spot as many different engines as you could. Now I can just imagine you, on reading this, thinking how riveting and fully understanding where my daughter is coming from in her attitude of mirth to this innocent hobby, but trainspotting was popular with most boys at this time and you really had to have been there to appreciate it's appeal. If you ever visit the York Railway museum and get up close to some of these magnificent engines which are on display there, you will get some idea of the beauty and awe that these engines inspired. Anyway, I was in good company back then as I believe even Michael Palin used to go to Retford station himself occasionally when he would go trainspotting. So there. I could spend pages extolling the joys of trainspotting all the various steam engines but suspect I may lose readers who could lose the will to live if I were to do so.

As we are on the subject of Michael Palin, "And now for something completely different", as he might have said. In addition to the TV programmes mentioned in the last chapter, those which attracted my attention this year included yet more cowboy shows (I am still 11 at this stage remember) such as "The Range Rider", (similar to the Lone Ranger but without a mask and silver bullets, so not quite as glamorous); "Wells Fargo", starring Dale Robertson as Agent Hardie, the left handed gun, tracking down the robbers of stage coaches; "Laramie"; "Bronco"; "Cheyenne" and "Wagon Train", the latter of which was my favourite and starred Ward Bond as Major Seth Adams. He was the leader in charge of a wagon train of settlers and pioneers heading from Missouri to California and the programme highlighted the adventures they had during their long journey, which inevitably involved being attacked by Indians who were, unsurprisingly, not partial to their lands being invaded by white men from the East. (A bit similar to what's happening here near the Channel Tunnel as the invaders are also from the East but the only wagons they use are generally the 40 ton sort). Anyway, on the programme, after cries of "circle the wagons" and the usual gunfight the wagon train always managed to hold the Indians off. Well, the series would have ended pretty sharpish if the Indians had wiped them out in the first skirmish wouldn't it? Those TV producers weren't daft.

Cartoons were now beginning to come to the fore in the form of "The Huckleberry Hound Show" which featured a dog of indeterminate breed known, of course, as Huckleberry Hound and who spoke with a southern American drawl and whose trademark was singing "Oh my darling Clementine" for some reason, but always out of tune. It was ok, but the main reason I watched this programme was for the section starring Yogi Bear and his sidekick Boo Boo bear. This featured their antics in Jellystone Park and usually comprised of Yogi trying to devise various schemes to pinch the "pic-a-nic baskets" of tourists to the park whilst avoiding the park ranger. Trust me, it was funny to an 11 year old, although I doubt it would be sophisticated enough for today's 11 year olds who, sadly, are far more worldly wise than we were. Pixie and Dixie and Mr. Jinks were another feature of the show and a bit similar to the cartoons of Tom and Jerry in that they had as the main plot, Mr. Jinks, the cat, trying to catch Pixie and Dixie who were two cute mice and he was always foiled in his plans at the outcome of which he would utter his catchphrase of "I hate those meeces to pieces" but don't ask me why.

"Popeye" was another favourite and involved, as you probably know, a sailor who was always getting into scrapes with his arch enemy, Bluto, and was generally losing until at the very last moment he just managed to locate a tin of spinach and on eating the same he was somehow given miraculous strength and then managed to defeat Bluto. Why spinach, I have no idea, but even as a kid I was not tempted to try the stuff, although I must admit I do now occasionally come across small amounts in my food unless I can wheedle it out, but I haven't noticed it making any significant difference in my muscle power. Popeye also had a girlfriend called Olive Oil who was somewhat on the thin side (think Kate Moss or Cheryl unpronounceable second name and you get the idea, although Olive in fairness was not quite as glamorous) and Bluto was always trying to get fresh with her much to Popeye's displeasure.

The absolute favourite of mine, though, was "The Flintstones" featuring the antics of Fred Flintstone and Barney Rubble and their wives Wilma and Betty. Now this cartoon, if you didn't know, was set in the stone age and the running gags involved stone age items such as their car which had no engine or brakes and a dinosaur which hoovered all the mess up by sucking it up. The cartoon series was hilarious and kept me entertained, as I am sure it did most kids.

Another children's TV show which I enjoyed, and I think was first shown in this year, was a comedy called "Mr. Ed" which featured a talking horse but the trick was that it only spoke to it's owner, Wilbur Smith, and despite Wilbur's best efforts it would not speak to anyone else, which led to a lot of confusion, particularly with the Addisons, who were neighbours of Wilbur. Now I know this sounds less than hilarious but if you ever speak to anyone who was a child at this time I am sure they will back me up in stating that it was funny and very watchable.

Adult shows which I enjoyed this year included "What's My Line" where a panel had to try to guess someone's job from that person miming part of his job at the start and was hosted by Eamon Andrews, who also hosted "This Is Your Life" with which you will probably be most familiar. Comedy was supplied by "The Harry Worth Show" featuring the hapless adventures of Harry Worth which was mildly amusing but certainly not in the Frank Spencer class. An American import was "I love Lucy", featuring Lucille Ball, which I thought was ok but not great, although it was immensely popular in the USA, apparently. "The Rag Trade", which was set in a small clothing workshop and seemed to revolve around the female workers and their shop steward whose catchphrase was "Everybody out" if anything happened which annoyed her and led her to call a strike. No industrial ballots at that workshop!

I have to say that my favourite comedy show at this time, though, was "Candid Camera" hosted by David Nixon and featuring Jonathan Routh as the main prankster and it was often side-splittingly funny. One of the best pranks I recall that appealed to my somewhat warped sense of humour was the one where, unbeknown to the public, Jonathan Routh had put some cut up slices of carrots in a goldfish bowl in a store and when a member of the public approached the bowl Jonathan bent over it and said that the goldfish looked tasty and then he dipped his hand in the bowl and quickly ate one. The reaction of the public was priceless. There was also the "car with no engine" prank which involved two of the cast members pushing a car into a garage and complaining to the garage mechanic that it had broken down. Cue very puzzled look from the mechanic when he opened the bonnet of the car and saw that there was no engine.

Music was still being provided by "Juke Box Jury" at this time but a newcomer, unbeknown to me at the time, was a programme which had started on ITV called "Thank Your Lucky Stars" which would soon become a favourite of mine once I discovered music properly in 1963 and a programme which would eventually feature all the top groups and solo artists of the time. As at this time, 1961, it featured the likes of The Dale Sisters (Who?), Adam Faith, Johnny Leyton and The Brook Brothers (no I haven't a clue either) and you may understand why my interest in music at this time was zero. That would all change in due course. Definitely not featured at this time were The Beatles who, on the 9th of February of this year, performed for the very first time at a small venue in Liverpool called "The Cavern", but were yet to have either a proper manager or a record deal. They did, however, actually appear on record for the first time this year backing Tony Sheridan on a few tracks, one of which was a traditional song called "My Bonnie" and which was recorded in Hamburg in June of this year and subsequently released as a single. Little did they know the train of events that that record would set in motion.

As this part of my life revolved around either school or games with my mates, I think that I had better educate you in the types of games that we played. Remember that for an 11 year old in 1961, there was virtually no daytime TV to watch, no internet, mobile phones, playstations or computers and so you were left to your own devices to amuse yourselves. We naturally had the usual staples of football and cricket but in addition we enjoyed playing other games such as marbles. I am sure you are all familiar with the glass marbles with a strand of colour running through the middle. Well, in addition to those coloured marbles, we also had ball-bearings which were steel balls of varying sizes and in our currency were worth more than marbles. A big silver ball-bearing could be exchanged for six marbles. The game would generally be played on a small patch of flat ground at the bottom of our street and a small round hole would be dug in the dirt into which you had to aim to push all the marbles being used in the game by the various boys then taking part. You each took turns flicking the marbles towards the hole. Your turn ended when you missed the hole and the winner, and keeper of all the marbles used in the game, was the last one to successfully hole the final marble. I often returned home from these games with bulging pockets of marbles and some very dirty hands.

It was also possible to play hopscotch in the road (yes I know that it is a bit of a girly game, but we did play it from time to time) owing to the lack of cars on the roads on our estate. Indeed, cars were so rare on our small road that if one parked on the road, it generally drew a crowd of small boys anxious to see what type of car it was. Our small road was effectively our playground and in summer we would stand a metal dustbin lid up against a row of bricks and we had our wicket. We then chalked out the batting crease and further down the road we chalked the bowling crease and hey presto, we were ready for our game of cricket. No grass needed. You learned pretty quick to hit the ball straight back down the road as if you hit it sideways into a garden this was treated as being out of bounds and you were instantly declared "out". Often followed by some choice words from the neighbour as you went into his garden to retrieve your wayward tennis ball. (Proper cricket balls, or "corkies" as we called them, were too lethal on a tarmacked road, to say nothing of what would have happened if this type of ball had hit a neighbour's window! Or us, as we didn't wear protection either!)

Conkers was another very popular game for us to play but this was restricted to a time of year when conkers were in plentiful supply and this occurred every Autumn. For those of you not familiar with the game, the rules were that you had to drill a hole in the centre of the conker and then thread a piece of string through the hole. You would then challenge another boy and take turns in hitting his conker with your own until the winner was the one whose conker had shattered the other one. In our village the victorious conker would then be given the number of victories that the other boy's conker had previously achieved before it was shattered e.g. if his conker was a fiver (meaning it had beaten other conkers with a total value of five) then that five score would be added to your own conker's current number. Various devious methods were used to harden your conker and the ones that I used included baking the conker in the oven (with your mother's permission, obviously) and soaking the conker in vinegar to harden the conker up before battle. You had to be careful about the hand you used to hold your conker as it was not unusual for your hand to be hit when the other boy swung his conker at yours and that would certainly smart if you were caught. I managed to hit quite a few boys' hands when I swung my conker so some were a little bit wary about playing me at this game. What a surprise!

Finally, there were the rarer forms of games that were probably more local to our area such as "tin-can-a-lurky". I bet this one has you guessing. Well, this game involved chalking a circle in the road of about one foot in diameter and in the middle of the circle you had to place three empty tin cans of varying sizes. The biggest one was placed first and then you balanced the other two tin cans on top of the first one, effectively creating a tin can tower. You then had to chalk a line about fifteen feet away from the circle from where the person who was "it" first had to throw a tennis ball at the cans in order to scatter them as far as he could. The other players in the game then had to try to collect the cans and restack them in the circle whilst at the same time dodging the tennis ball which the first player was frantically hurling at whoever had picked up a can and if you were hit you were out of the game. In more ways than one, as if the ball caught you in a certain delicate area you knew about it. The winner was either the player who remained unharmed and stacked the tin cans correctly or the thrower, if he had managed to hit all the other players before the tin cans could be stacked successfully. It was great fun if you avoided the ball, but could sometimes result in the odd bruise.

Back in the world of grown ups, space exploration took off (see what I've done there!) this year with the launch of a Russian, Yuri Gagarin, into space who orbited the earth on the 12th of April, followed shortly after by Alan Shepherd from the USA, who basically just went up and down, though very much not a full orbit, on the 5th of May. The space race had begun in earnest and on the 25th of May President Kennedy made his famous speech about America's aim of landing a man on the moon and bringing him safely back to earth by the end of the decade. Now that did catch this 11 year old's imagination and I followed all the various rocket launches with avid interest for the rest of the decade.

What about me and my exploits I hear you ask? Go on ask. Well, as you do ask, my most momentous event of this year was the sitting of my 11 plus which I suspect must have been around early spring and whilst I may be mistaken, I seem to think it involved going to school one Saturday morning to take the test, which I have to say I thoroughly enjoyed. I did actually like taking these type of tests so did not view it as any big deal, unlike most kids' parents throughout the land. Over the years since I took the test there have been arguments and counter-arguments over whether it is right for children of 11 to be graded on ability at this age by taking one test and to have their academic lives and, indeed, their futures then mapped out at such an early age. I can't speak for other kids but can only say that as a child from a not very well off working class family, it provided me with an escape route from my background and the chance to achieve a decent career. I disagree with those who say that failing to pass the exam consigned a child to an educational wilderness. There were many good secondary schools in existence in those days and some of my future schoolmates in sixth form eventually came from those schools, where they had managed to obtain good GCE results.

I was a competitive child and needed to be in an environment which would not only test me but make me work hard to either keep up with the others or, if possible, be better than them. This could be achieved for children of my background by attending a non-fee paying grammar school where academic standards were high. It gave a kid like me the chance to compete against children from better off families, who could afford to send their children to the fee paying schools. I was successful in passing the 11 plus along with three other boys and about seven girls in our class of 42 pupils. The 11 plus worked for children such as me as eventually I was able to go on to University and I remember in my first year in hall of residence that the student who occupied the room immediately below mine had been to Eton. A bit of a difference eh, between our respective backgrounds, but at University I was now at the same educational level as him and without a penny spent by my parents on my education, so I have to say that the existence of grammar schools benefited me considerably, and I am sure many more like me, and enabled me to pursue a professional career from fairly humble beginnings.

This was, of course, in an era when there were not many Universities and to gain admittance to one was a feat which caused not a little family pride. It also meant that a grant was available to see you through University without having to land yourself with a huge debt. I think it was a sad day when our beloved politicians closed the grammar schools as this did not affect one jot the children who came from more affluent backgrounds, but did deprive children like me of a high class education and I note that politicians of all hues have not been slow in sending their offspring to the best schools that they can afford. A touch of hypocrisy there don't you think, but then again we should not be surprised about hypocrisy and politicians after what they have been involved in over the years!

This summer of 1961 I would spend my last holiday in Blackpool as a visitor, although I was not aware of this at the time, and it proved to be a little eventful. We stayed as usual at my maternal grandparents fish and chip shop and did the usual holiday activities such as the Pleasure Beach, Golden Mile, piers and playing games on the beach and going in the sea. It's interesting that looking back the weather always seemed to be good, but I am sure there must have been wet days although I can't remember what we did on those days. Probably headed for the Tower or the amusement arcades I should think. We could, of course, have taken advantage of the summer season shows which this summer included "Showtime" at the North

Pier featuring Michael Holliday (a typical early sixties crooner) and Terry Hall with Lenny the Lion (a popular kids ventriloquist with a soft hearted lion as his dummy), "The Tommy Trinder Show" on Central Pier, "Putting on the Donegan" at the Winter Gardens featuring that hero of many a fifties skiffle group (budding Beatles amongst them) Lonnie Donegan, "The Big Show of 1961" at the Opera House which was split between Shirley Bassey and Cliff Richard and the Shadows, Arthur Askey at the Grand, "Rose Marie" at the Hippodrome with David Whitfield and finally Al Read and Yana (you must remember her song "Climb up the wall", no? Me neither, although I probably would have climbed up the wall to avoid hearing it) at the Queens Theatre. Needless to say I was not a member of the audience for any of these shows, no, not even "Rose Marie"!

I do remember with some cause that one day we visited Lytham and for some reason decided to have a game of tennis on a court there. I had not played tennis before and was not a particular fan of the game but was willing to give it a try. My father was on the other side of the net and our game was progressing in a fashion when he served a ball at me which I missed and it hit me squarely in the right eye. Ouch. Let me tell you that it stung somewhat and certainly brought considerable tears to my eye. Not only that, after a moment or two I found that my vision had blurred and that I could not see properly out of my right eye. Cue my first visit to A & E at Blackpool's Victoria Hospital where they examined me fully, prescribed some drops and advised me to see an eye specialist as soon as I could.

I think it was a day or so later that we visited the specialist who said that he didn't think any permanent damage had been done but wanted me to have a check up at home when we returned from holiday. The sting in the tail was, however, that he advised that I would have to wear an eye-patch over my right eye for a while and that I must not indulge in any football, in order to protect my eye from any further damage. Now the eye-patch was bad enough, well whoever heard of an 11 year old pirate (although Short John would have been an apt name don't you think?), and I had to put up with the usual jibes of shall we get you a parrot to go with your new look, but to be deprived of my beloved football was truly purgatory and whilst the pirate impression would fortunately cease before I was due to start grammar school, the ban on football would remain until late in the year.

August brought the building of the Berlin Wall, well not in Creswell obviously, but it did not impact much on me living in Derbyshire as I was waiting with a little trepidation for September and the start of my education at grammar school. The school I would be attending was Shirebrook Grammar School, a mixed grammar school situated in the nearby small town of Shirebrook, which was some 5 miles or so from my village so to get there would mean a walk of about three quarters of a mile from my house to the station and then a train to Shirebrook where the school was within easy walking distance of the town's station. However, an older boy at the school who lived opposite had warned me that new boys would have to undergo some sort of initiation rite and it would be as well to accept it in good grace but he would not elaborate on what form this would take.

The first day of term duly arrived and there was I kitted out in my brand new school uniform, including the dreaded ridiculous looking school cap, and my brand new leather satchel complete with pens, pencils etc., and everything I would need for the new school. I arrived at the station and noticed there were a number of much bigger boys larking around waiting for the train to arrive when one of them spied me and a few of them wandered over and just as the train was pulling into the station one of the boys snatched my satchel and flung it on the line, right in front of the train. They all fell about laughing and I was left asking the guard to retrieve my satchel please from between the train's wheels which he did to much grateful thanks from me. Amazingly, the satchel was still in one piece with just a few scratches on it and I thought I had escaped the initiation rite relatively easily. Well at least they hadn't thrown me on the line which was a plus (tough village ours) but that would probably have been taking things a bit too far.

I thought that I could now relax and enjoy the ride to school. Wrong. The train in those distant days had some carriages which did not access directly on to a corridor. Once you were in your little separate closed compartment there was nowhere to go. I got in one such compartment only to be followed by 5 or 6 second years who were on a mission to wreak revenge for what they had suffered the year before. They politely explained that when the train started they would be all standing on the seats facing the wall of the compartment and that I would have to race from one end of the compartment to the other and back while they banged their bums against each other, bizarre yes I know, and tried to knock me over. (Wot larks Pip, as my fellow author (!) Charles Dickens might have said!). This was not too bad as only a few bruises resulted. The worst was later in the week when I was on a train which had corridor compartments. Then the lark was that as the train arrived at Shirebrook, the older boys grabbed you and threw you into the toilet area and held the toilet door closed as long as they could i.e. until the train started out of the station and they would then jump off leaving you just a few milliseconds to leap from the train behind them before there was no platform left to jump onto. Tom Cruise and Mission Impossible pah, no comparison. And I did all my own stunts. Once the first week was over, the initiation rite ceased and the only other hazard left was the local Shirebrook secondary school pupils who, on their way to their own school, would delight in lobbing stones from the bridge overlooking the station at us posh (!) grammar school boys as we tried to exit the station. Dodging the missiles helped me develop a sidestep which would prove useful when I started playing rugby, of which more later.

Having overcome the Bear Grylls survival Challenge I was in for a culture shock at school as not only was I a small, lowly first year but there were kids in my class who were actually much brighter than me. I was always used to coming top, or near to the top, of the class and found junior school subjects easy. This was a whole new ball game as I was introduced to the joys of languages, such as French and Latin; the mildly interesting lessons of geography and history and the complete mysteries (well to me anyway) of the science subjects. All of a sudden I found myself struggling to keep up in a lot of the subjects and found my interest in schoolwork waning fast. Not only that, but I soon realised that the "fagging" system was still alive and kicking in this school, as I found out one day when I was collared by a prefect shouting "Fag, bring some coals up to our study". I mean, what the f..., they had a coal fire going in their study! Now we are hardly talking Tom Brown's Schooldays in this remote working class part of Derbyshire but the public school system seemed to have found it's way here quite happily. The one saving grace for me was that this school played football and as soon as I was able to start playing again, I was picked for the Under 13's football team which was the school team for the first and second year boys. We were not wildly successful as we were generally playing teams from much bigger schools but I enjoyed it immensely.

Meanwhile, back in the world of popular music, one of the most important events in music history took place in a record shop in Liverpool when, on the 28th of October, a young man by the name of Raymond Jones went into NEMS record shop owned by the Epstein family and asked for a record called "My Bonnie" by a little known group called The Beatles. The store manager, one Brian Epstein, did not have that record in the store and neither had he ever heard of the group but he prided himself on tracking down a customer's request and eventually located the record which had been recorded in Germany by Tony Sheridan and The Beat Brothers (actually, The Beatles, but not designated as such on the Polydor record) so he was able to satisfy the customer's request and this piqued his interest in the group. More was to follow, but this was the somewhat inauspicious start of the rise and rise of the greatest band in popular music history. (Sorry any One Direction fans out there but they actually were).

Coincidentally this year also saw another important event in pop music history when, on the 17th of October at Dartford railway station, a certain Michael Jagger recognised an old school classmate by the name of Keith Richards carrying some long playing records, including one by Chuck Berry, an artist they both admired, and thus began a conversation which would subsequently lead to them both joining Brian Jones in forming a band by the name of "The Rolling Stones" who have, over the years, produced some memorable music, actually some great music, but overall not quite in the same league as The Beatles. Now there's a topic for disagreement. Thank goodness musical tastes are subjective. Imagine what the world would be like if we all liked the Spice Girls or The Bay City Rollers. Pass me the shotgun now please.

As an 11 or indeed a 12 year old, as I became on the 29th of October of this year, music was still not greatly appealing to me but Guy Fawkes night this year was quite eventful. This was a night that all the local kids looked forward to and it was the tradition for me and a lot of the other boys on the estate where I lived to collect wood in the weeks leading up to the 5th of November and build a big bonfire on a nearby field and make up a dummy Guy Fawkes to sit on top of it. It was also a tradition to try to rob another gang's bonfire of their wood as this was a damn sight easier than finding your own but could result in gang warfare and possibly revenge attacks on your own bonfire so it could be a bit hazardous. You picked your targets carefully.

Well this particular year we had managed to build a fairly good size bonfire but were struggling with a guy and were also a bit light in the firework department, as money had run out. What could we do? Someone, I don't recollect who though it may well have been me, hit upon the bright idea of one of us (certainly not me!) dressing up in old clothes and wearing a balaclava with a mask and pretending to be Guy Fawkes. Good so far but how do we get it to people's houses to ask for a penny for the guy? The Guy Fawkes impersonator could hardly amble up to the door with us as this would immediately give the game away we not unreasonably thought, although a walking Guy Fawkes would no doubt have been a novelty. Well, we hit on the bright idea of "borrowing" a wheel barrow into which said fake Guy would climb and we could then push him round the estate requesting our pennies from unsuspecting residents. Lovely jubbly, everyone's a winner. What could go wrong? It did work for a very short while until we knocked on the door of one canny old woman who looked mightily suspiciously at our dummy. "It's breathing", she said. "No missis, it's a dummy", we said. "Have you got a penny for it", we enquired? "Well", said the canny old woman, "if it's a real dummy then it won't mind if I stub my cigarette out on it will it?" she said with some menace as she motioned towards it with a burning cigarette end in hand. Exit dummy from wheelbarrow at breakneck speed to cries of "sod this for a lark, I'm off" and bringing to an end his brief career as a Guy Fawkes impressionist. We then just had to make the best of what we had managed to beg, but the bonfire was great.

The year was gradually drawing to a close but before it did so a DJ by the name of Alan Freeman, unbeknown to me, started presenting a programme called "Pick of the Pops" which was the weekly chart show transmitted at 11pm every Sunday on the radio so way too late for me to hear, even if I had wanted to listen to it. It would, however, become required listening for my generation in the years to come.

Meanwhile, in Liverpool, Brian Epstein visited The Cavern at lunchtime on the 9th of November to see what all the fuss was about involving this group known as The Beatles. He was suitably impressed with the four leather jacketed lads and the music and excitement they were generating in that dark, dank cellar. So much so, that he offered to manage them and find them a record deal. As their music career was not exactly taking off at that time they duly accepted his offer, although none of them could have anticipated how difficult it would subsequently prove to obtain a record deal. Brian Epstein did, however, manage to secure, through his record store contacts with Decca, an audition for them in London for the 1st of January 1962 which hopefully would lead to a record deal so as the year came to an end on New Year's Eve in Creswell I was spending a quiet evening in the house watching the TV while somewhere on the roads of England a four piece band was heading down to London for their big break, or so they thought.

The competition for my would be heroes in the charts this year came, amongst other songs of course, from my following choices which I have enjoyed since that time and are still well worth a listen today but are in no particular order:-

1. Stand by me - Ben E. King

2. Runaway - Del Shannon

3. At last - Etta James

4. Walk right back - The Everly Brothers

5. Crying - Roy Orbison

6. Runaround Sue - Dion

7. Blue Moon - The Marcels

8. Hit the road Jack - Ray Charles

9. Cupid - Sam Cooke

10. Will you love me tomorrow - The Shirelles

Cinema going for me was mainly restricted still to the Saturday morning flicks but the grown ups this year were enjoying the following;-

West Side Story - iconic musical based roughly on the Romeo and Juliet play starring Natalie Wood and George Chakiris amongst others.

The Guns of Navarone - terrific second world war film with Gregory Peck, Anthony Quinn and David Niven.

El Cid - epic historical drama with Charlton Heston and the sultry Sophia Loren (not that I knew what sultry was as an 11 year old.)

101 Dalmatians - classic Disney cartoon.

Breakfast at Tiffany's - brilliant romantic comedy with the stunning Audrey Hepburn and George Peppard.

A Taste of Honey - a very daring, for the time, gritty drama set in Manchester starring a young Rita Tushingham and Dora Bryan.

Whistle Down the Wind - about three children discovering a fugitive in a barn and thinking that he was Jesus. Very evocative of the times, particularly the way the kids dressed and behaved.

CHAPTER THREE
1962

"Groups with guitars are on the way out". Comment made by a Decca representative to Brain Epstein when rejecting The Beatles following the group's audition with that record company.

This was the year which was to prove life changing for both myself and The Beatles and whilst I certainly had no idea how much my life would change, I suspect that neither did The Beatles. Monday New Year's Day saw John, Paul and George, plus their drummer Pete Best, auditioning for Decca records in front of the A & R man, Mike Smith, at the company's London studio, desperately hoping for the longed for record deal and a chance to hit the big time. Some weeks after the audition their manager, Brian Epstein, was duly informed by Smith that they were not being signed up as, in his opinion, groups with guitars were on the way out. Instead Decca signed ...Brian Poole and The Tremeloes who were, yes, a group with guitars! So much for Decca's excuse.

It later became known that Mike Smith could only sign one of the two groups being auditioned that day so he naturally chose Brian Poole's group! He would thereafter forever be labelled as the man who turned down The Beatles. Some label. A bit like choosing a Ford Fiesta when you could have had a Rolls Royce. Not a decision I am sure the record company regretted for one single moment! I have often thought since then how fortunate this decision actually was for the group as if they had been signed up at that time to Decca they would not then have subsequently had the considerable benefit of having George Martin as their record producer in the following years. A producer who would allow and encourage them to blossom and fulfil their considerable talent. Would they have been as successful at Decca without him assisting them, well who can say? A classic case of sliding doors, if ever there was one.

I, in common with the rest of the country, was of course totally oblivious to all of this. The Beatles? Never heard of them. I didn't know that groups with guitars were on their way out. In fact at my age, as a 12 year old, I didn't even know they had been in. It's easy for anyone to look back over these past 50 years and wonder what on earth Decca were thinking of in rejecting The Beatles but we have the benefit of hindsight and all the incredible songs The Beatles have produced logged in our memories. Looking back at the Top 20 at around this time you can perhaps see why Decca were taking this attitude. "Stranger on the Shore", an instrumental record featuring Acker Bilk, was top of the charts (it would go on to be the first British record to top the American charts later in the year) and The Springfields (a folk trio with Dusty Springfield in their midst) was the only group to feature in the charts. Don Mclean would not be far off the mark when he later sang in American Pie (so memorably covered by Madonna, hmm!) about the day the music died following the death of Buddy Holly in 1959.

The budding of popular music, which started in the mid-fifties with such artists as Elvis Presley, Jerry Lee Lewis, Eddie Cochran, Chuck Berry, Little Richard and indeed Buddy himself, came to an abrupt end with the demise of that decade. Rock and roll seemed to have burst on the scene like a firework and then fizzled out in the space of a few short years. Apart from the odd decent record or two which, in my humble opinion, I have listed at the end of the first two chapters of this book and also at the end of this chapter, we appeared to be in a pop music wilderness but all that would very soon change thanks to the soon to be Fab Four. But more of that later.

As spring term started for me and my fellow pupils at Shirebrook Grammar School, I found myself drifting somewhat in the majority of my lessons. For some reason I enjoyed Latin but I struggled with most of the other subjects, particularly History, where unfortunately the teacher could not control his class of bored 11 and 12 year old pupils. Now in those far off days school kids were, on the whole, fairly obedient and reasonably well behaved. There was, of course, an incentive for this behaviour called the blackboard rubber or, if that didn't work, the ultimate punishment, namely the cane.

Many's the time I have felt the whoosh of air as a blackboard rubber whistled past my ear on its way, thankfully, to it's destination further down the class. You had to keep fairly awake to be able to duck said missile and not become an unintended victim. If it hit you then you certainly knew about it. Can you imagine? A disruptive, unruly pupil actually being chastised in this way! But you know what, it worked. It was amazing how much more attentive we became as a result of the missile throwing. Now for some reason the History teacher, as we all knew full well, did not use such methods (he was probably the Jeremy Corbyn of his day) and, kids being very perceptive in this regard, we soon took advantage and became a very disruptive class and I am ashamed to say that I was one of the worst. I realised that I had a bit of an aptitude for making the rest of the class laugh so I regret to say that I played on this quite a bit, particularly with comments I would make during class and as a result my attention in History went downhill fast. So much so that I achieved a grand total of 29% in the end of year exam. Yes, we actually had class positions not only in each subject but overall as well. I achieved an overall class position of 11th out of 24 so nothing to write home about. A far cry from being around top of the class at Junior School every year and it seemed at the time that I was on a slippery downward path so far as my education was concerned.

However, regardless of my boredom and lazy attitude to school work, my year brightened considerably when, sometime in Spring of this year I think it was, my parents announced that in summer we were going to leave Creswell for good to go and live in Blackpool. My maternal grandparents (you know, the ones with the chippy) had asked my mother to help them with their business as it had become extremely busy and also my father could not wait to leave his job as an electrician working down the mine. Now, given what miners had to endure in getting to their place of work (taking a lift down some

900 feet or more in the pitch black to reach the level of the workings), coupled with the danger of the job itself and the extremely hazardous working conditions such as tunnel collapse, the risk of fire and, not that they knew too much at the time, the possibility of suffering pneumoconiosis in later years from breathing coal dust and you have to say who could blame him. Indeed, Creswell pit had had it's own disaster the year after I was born when a conveyor belt in one of the deep level passageways caught fire trapping 80 men who subsequently died from inhalation of the smoke and fumes. My grandfather, who was working there at the time, was one of the lucky survivors. You can perhaps realise why the chance to go and live in Blackpool so appealed to my parents. It certainly appealed to me. The thought of living in what was then the best seaside resort in Britain as opposed to a small mining village was enticing to say the least. As a 12 year old which would you have chosen? The only blot on the landscape was having to wait until summer to move. I was impatient, I couldn't wait to leave, but wait I had to.

As I was now growing up a bit (apart from my classroom behaviour), I was losing a bit of interest in the TV cowboy shows and I had reached the start of that awkward age when you are not really a child and you haven't attained the dreaded (for most parents I now realise!) teenage years. In fact, there were not many TV shows for children, other than the cowboys and cartoons, which I enjoyed. "Crackerjack" was still entertaining but there were two shows which I did enjoy one of which was called "Circus Boy", which was an American show featuring Micky Dolenz (later of The Monkees fame) as a young boy living in a circus and who travelled about with the circus from town to town. His Uncle Noah looked after him and he was in charge of an elephant called Bimbo and no, it was not named after a footballer's girlfriend. The other show was "Just Dennis" and was another American import featuring a young boy called Dennis who would get into scrapes but mainly terrorised his neighbour, Mr. Wilson, and it was, looking back, very funny although whether it still is can only be a matter of conjecture. Must look it up on You Tube sometime.

The cartoon shows which I enjoyed included "The Bugs Bunny Show" featuring not only the rabbit himself but also Daffy Duck and my favourite one, Sylvester and Tweety Pie, which involved Sylvester's long running attempts to catch and eat the little bird Tweety Pie, which always resulted in the cat being foiled. It was very violent and hilarious. The other show which was extremely funny was "Top Cat", featuring a group of New York alley cats headed by Top Cat himself with Choo Choo, Beny the Ball, Brain, Fancy Fancy and Officer Dibble the latter of whom was generally on the receiving end of all their schemes.

There was another American programme, which I didn't care for myself but was popular with some kids, called "Lassie" featuring a collie dog of that name who, I seem to recall, was always finding people trapped down mineshafts upon which Lassie would then run home to tell his best friend, young Timmy, where the accident occurred, what injuries had been sustained and what type of rescue equipment would be needed, all communicated just by a few barks. Well, that's how it seemed to me. The other programme which again was not my idea of fun was a home grown programme called "Tuesday Rendezvous" and was hosted by Wally Whyton and Muriel Young and featured some glove puppets and also some upcoming singers and groups, most notably on the 4th of December this year an upcoming group called The Beatles performing their current single "Love Me Do". I have to say that, sadly, I don't remember it at all. The programme that is.

Adult programmes which I enjoyed included "77 Sunset Strip" (an American detective show), "Gunsmoke" (a western featuring Matt Dillon), "The Flying Doctor" (featuring a doctor in the Australian outback who visited his patients by aeroplane, now that's something you don't see with the NHS), "The Avengers" with Patrick MacNee as John Steed and a leather clad Honor Blackman as Cathy Gale, although being only 12 years old at this time I could not really appreciate why that apparel was so popular with the adult male population. I would find out more about this in later years. Oh the innocence of youth.

Comedy was provided by "The Arthur Haynes Show" which featured sketches involving Arthur Haynes, and I particularly enjoyed the one where he would appear as a tramp. Benny Hill also had his own show which did not rely as much on scantily clad girls then as it did later. What I particularly didn't enjoy, in fact hated with a passion, were programmes like "The White Heather Club" featuring Andy Stewart (no I can't be bothered describing it, it was beyond description, think of kilts and Scottish reels and you get the picture), "The Good Old Days" which was old time music hall variety from a theatre in Leeds where all the audience would dress up in Victorian costume (you had to see it to believe it) and "The Billy Cotton Band Show" featuring those awful Black and White Minstrels again. TV to set the pulses racing eh? Don't complain too much now about all the reality TV rubbish we have on these days. It wasn't all TV gold back then. Even big brother celebrity big bake off in the jungle get me out of here would be more entertaining than the last three shows that I have listed, but that is not saying much.

However, there were two adult programmes which did start this year and were excellent entertainment in their own right. The first was a weekly police drama called "Z Cars" featuring policemen out on patrol in their squad cars, a relatively recent innovation for police forces up and down the country. This programme was set in the fictional town of Seaport which stood in for a thinly disguised Liverpool and even the Police themselves considered it realistic. Far more so than the paternal George Dixon "Dixon of Dock Green" fame and this programme was really the start of realistic gritty TV drama. The other programme was a comedy called "Steptoe and Son" featuring the magnificent writing of Galton and Simpson and starring Wilfred Brambell as Steptoe senior and Harry H. Corbett as his long suffering son. The programme was hilarious and even now, when repeated on TV today, it is still extremely funny. One that has definitely stood the test of time.

Finally, while I am on the subject of TV programmes, a new Saturday night programme had started this year revolving around popular music called "Thank Your Lucky stars" which would run for some 5 years and be hosted by Brian Matthew. It would later prove to be required viewing for me as I grew up, but not just yet. I managed to locate a synopsis for the programme broadcast on the 10th February of this year which featured such greats as Tony Orlando, The Karl Denver Trio, The Viscounts, Don Charles, Barbara Kay and Gene Pitney. Now that line up would keep you from going out on a Saturday night, wouldn't it? No, really? The most interesting bit in the synopsis was, however, the part of the programme called "Spin-a-disc" involving a panel of teenagers and a DJ by the name of Jimmy Saville (a recipe for disaster if ever I saw one) reviewing the latest record releases, when he could free his hands for long enough to put a record on the turntable that is. Although that last bit was not actually included in the publicity blurb for the show, naturally. Radio programmes were the same as previously listed apart from the fact that Alan Freemen's "Pick of the Pops" was now broadcast at 4pm on a Sunday, not that it grabbed my attention, yet.

Talking of music, on the 6th of June my heroes visited EMI studios, as they were then known, on Abbey Road in north London for the very first time to record their first single, or so they hoped, for the Parlophone record label. Apparently George Martin, the producer, was not actually in attendance at first as he had left the session in the hands of his assistant Ron Richards and was only called up to listen at the behest of Norman Smith, the sound engineer, once the group started playing "Love Me Do" as Smith thought that it was somewhat unusual. It was. Most certainly for the times. It was subsequently redone a few months later by the group and it's release would prove to be a pivotal moment in music history. Furthermore, George Martin was to stay at the side of the group for the rest of their career.

Summer was at last approaching for this boy (good link eh?) but I was not overly happy when I was told that my parents and brother would be going to Blackpool permanently at the end of June but that they didn't want to disrupt my school work (that was a laugh, I was making a perfectly good job of that myself without any outside assistance) and wanted me to stay and see out the academic year. This would mean going to live with my paternal grandparents who lived in the neighbouring village of Clowne. I was not best pleased. Not that I didn't like my grandparents. Quite the contrary. My grandad, a retired miner, always liked to come and watch me play football for the school team as he had been a useful footballer himself in his youth and they were both always very welcoming to me whenever I visited. No, it was not the prospect of staying with them that caused my resentment, it was having to stay behind while the rest of my family went off to Blackpool but what could I do? Just grin and bear it.

My grandparents rented a small terraced house which had neither an indoor bathroom nor indoor toilet, although this was not totally unusual in a mining community in this era, but it was not what I had been used to by any means. Our own rented house in Creswell was small but at least it had indoor facilities. Furthermore, the WC at my grandparents' house was situated at the bottom of the garden so if you had to go after dark then you needed a torch to get there and back and when you did get there you anxiously looked round for spiders on the whitewashed walls and you were not often disappointed. Thankfully my time there was in summer, heaven knows what it must have been like in the depths of winter. I should think you would have needed a blow torch to defrost the seat. Frostbite must have been a real danger!

How did you manage when it came to taking a bath I hear you ask? Good question. The answer is that in the scullery adjacent to the living room there hung on the wall a large tin bath. For your weekly bath (well it was a weekly one for me) down would come the bath and into the living room it would be brought, right in front of the TV and the coal fire. It would then be filled up with hot water and you could relax in the bath whilst watching the TV. Provided you were on you own that is. I didn't want an audience thank you. Sheer luxury. I must say that when I see these five star hotels today with the TV in the bathroom and think about the cost of the rooms visitors incur for such facilities, I think back to those past times and muse that we were way ahead of the game then when it came to luxuriating in a bath in front of the TV at much less cost. I have to say, however, that the modern bathrooms do have one facility we lacked. A plug with an outfall drain. Bit of a draw back as at the end of your bath at my grandparents you had to empty the water by hand, well actually with the aid of a saucepan which could take some time. Ah well, it was different. You youngsters today, you've no idea how easy you have it. A comment which echoes down the generations and always will.

Talking of TV, again, although we were still in the primitive age in 1962 so far as TV broadcasting was concerned (all programmes being in black and white remember, a positive boon to "The Billy Cotton Band Show" and their minstrels), a glimpse of the future was had on the 11th of July of this year when a satellite called Telstar relayed it's first television pictures and the first transatlantic pictures also on the 23rd of July. I remember the broadcast and the excitement generated but little did I know what would follow from that and how satellite broadcasting would develop. Elsewhere, on the 12th of July, a group called the Rolling Stones would perform together for the first time at London's Marquee Club without causing any scandal or, indeed, any notice at all amongst the wider public. That would soon change.

At last, for me, came the end of the school summer term and I could now look forward to my exit from Derbyshire to the glamour and excitement of Blackpool (remember that we are talking 1962, of course, when Blackpool was in it's heyday and far removed from the sad resort you see today, there really is no comparison whatsoever). Consider, for example, the summer shows held in town that year which included Tommy Cooper at the Queens Theatre, Ken Dodd at the Opera House, Tommy Trinder (ok, not a great draw at the time but he had been very popular in the past and indeed still was for the older generation), Jimmy Jewel and Ben Warriss (think of a poor man's version of Morecambe and Wise if you can), Harry Worth at North Pier and, of course, the Tower Circus with Charlie Cairoli. In those days this was a pretty impressive line-up and would certainly have beaten any other seaside resort's summer entertainment. This was, of course, without even considering all the other attractions of Blackpool which I have mentioned previously.

My journey to Blackpool came courtesy of my uncle Malcolm, my mother's brother, who was working in Nottingham in a bank and would go home at weekends to his parents, my grandparents, (keep up) and he offered to call at Clowne on his way to collect me in his car and transport me to Blackpool. Grateful though I was to my paternal grandparents for looking after me, I really couldn't wait to leave the mining community of Clowne and settle in to life in my new home. I can still recall after all these years the excitement of glimpsing the Tower as we approached the Town at the end of our journey and I did wonder then how life would change for me.

The first thing to be tackled was my new school. I had been accepted at Blackpool Grammar School. This was an all boys school situated on the outskirts of Blackpool which in those days had a fine reputation as an academic institution with very high standards and also a reputation for turning out good sports teams. There was, however, one major problem. It was a rugby playing school. No football teams whatsoever. As a football mad kid I was devastated and enquired whether or not my parents couldn't choose a school that played football, but to no avail. I was told that I should count myself lucky that I had got in at such a good school. I didn't quite see it that way as in my eyes a school was a school and the only thing that mattered was whether or not I could play football. I was not looking forward to it at all.

Indeed, it was in a mood of early teenage obstreperousness that I accompanied my mother to an interview at school with the headmaster before term started at which he would assess which class would be most suited for me. He studied my end of year report from Shirebrook Grammar and noticed my poor showing in History. "I see you are not very good at History. Why do you think that is?" he asked. Quick as a shot I replied "It wasn't me, it was the teacher, he was useless". Now whilst that might be a reply that would not elicit much surprise these days, in fact these days there would probably be an expletive or two in the pupil's reply, in those days this was a fairly bold statement for a 12 year old to make to a headmaster who, at this school, was only one step down from God (in this case this was literally true as the headmaster was in fact a reverend, the Reverend H Luft) and whose word was law. I could see that not only was he somewhat taken aback by my comment but my mother also nearly fell off her chair and I am sure I heard the headmaster mutter something to the effect of "We'll have to see about that".

Two events of a very different kind occurred on the 5th of August of this year with the mysterious death of Marilyn Monroe and the arrest of Nelson Mandela. I do, however, understand that the two events were not linked in any way, well he was several thousand miles away for a start and was standing up for his own people against the iniquitous apartheid regime. She was a fading, but still glamorous, film star who was embroiled with the Kennedy clan and whose death has always been the subject of much conjecture ever since. Whilst I was aware of who Marilyn Monroe was, sadly I cannot claim to have known who Nelson Mandela was at that time as my interests, not unsurprisingly, did not cover South African politics. It does not need saying which of these events was the more important and had the most lasting effect on the world.

Meanwhile back on Merseyside three of The Beatles had decided that it was time to part company with their drummer Pete Best, which proved to be somewhat controversial for some of the group's fans. The reason for their decision has been delved into by many an author without any clear cut answer being arrived at. George Martin has always said that he didn't rate Best as a drummer and in fact was already considering in his own mind having a professional session drummer for the group's next recording session. Paul McCartney has said in the past that Best didn't fit in with the rest of them and it is not hard to see what he meant when you read any of the biographies covering their early pre-fame days. The drummer they did like, and who they all wanted, was a certain Ringo Starr and so they told their manager to sack Best, which he did on the 16th of August. Ringo was, at the time, playing in another group performing at a holiday camp for the summer and he duly joined the other three two days later and so they became the Fab Four, known forever to all in future as John, Paul, George and Ringo. Fame would not long be coming for them but they had to wait a short time longer yet. The one ironic twist to my tale at this point is that, unknown to me, on the 25th of August, just one week after Ringo joined the group, they performed at the Marine Hall Fleetwood just some three or four miles up the coast from where I was living. Now if only I had access to the Tardis that is a day above all others I would like to revisit. Catch a tram up to the venue and see the group in the days just before the fame and the incessant screaming started. If only.

Two momentous events occurred on Tuesday the 4th of September. The Beatles on this day recorded the version of Love Me Do which would soon be released as their first single and I started the autumn term at my new school. A new start for both of us on the same day. Would this portend any future coincidences? Who can say, just wait and see. For now, I was as oblivious of what they were up to as they would be of me. Well, I am pretty sure that was the case but Paul can correct me if I'm wrong.

Anyway, while they were on the verge of changing popular music forever, I was kitted out in my second new smart school uniform plus the dreaded school cap, which no boy liked wearing and ditched as soon as he could, and set off on foot from my grandparents fish and chip shop, where we were still living, to the old Bus Station on Talbot Road in Blackpool to get the number 14 bus to Highfurlong, which is were the Grammar School was situated. I was a little wary as a new boy as I didn't know what to expect and wondered whether they had any initiation rites for new boys similar to the ones that I had experienced at Shirebrook. Oh well, at least there was no train journey and stone throwing secondary schoolboys to avoid.

I needn't have worried. There were no initiation rites at all, not even for first years, so far as I could tell. I have to say that the last bit was a disappointment to me given what I had had to put up with the previous year. I was looking forward to a bit of retribution. No, my only problem was my accent. I came from North East Derbyshire and my dialect was quite broad to say the least, similar in fact to a broad Yorkshire accent but with a bit of Nottingham thrown in, "sithee lad" as we would have said. Just a bit different to the way my new fellow pupils spoke.

Indeed, my unfortunate accent caused quite a bit of mirth amongst my fellow pupils who no doubt wondered who this yokel was who had pitched up in their midst, but I could cope with that. As long as the banter didn't get out of hand. However, one bright spark took it too far and started taking the piss mercilessly so I thought a marker had to be laid down. I came from a fairly tough mining estate in Creswell where it was not unknown for kids to settle their differences with their fists. I was no different. A bit primitive I know, but that is how life was in those days. Indeed, I had already had one or two fights at my previous school so was not phased one bit by any physical contact. William Golding, in his book "Lord of the flies", describes so well how violent kids can be, if left to their own devices. The law of the jungle soon takes a hold. I recommend you read it sometime, it will not disappoint.

Anyway, break time arrived and I duly approached bright spark in the school yard and asked what his problem was. He started to mimic my accent and said about two words before he felt my fist in his face. End of mimicry. Not something I am proud of but one blow was all it took and that was the end of any piss taking. Not only that, but I seemed to have gained some respect from the other boys in my form and we were soon happily engaged in a game of football in the lower quadrangle. This was a tarmacked area of about eighty yards by thirty yards in which you would often find six or seven informal games of football taking place simultaneously. It didn't half improve your passing skills when you had to pick out a teammate from amongst all the other kids taking part in their own games. Funny to think back that this was a rugby playing school but the only game we all wanted to play at break time was football. What does that say? Pity the school didn't take heed but there was a certain snobbery then surrounding the rugby playing schools and I always felt that they considered themselves a bit elite and looked down somewhat on the football playing schools.

As for school itself, I had been put in Form 2A, although this did not mean it was the top class, no, the top class was in fact known as 2X for some reason and was where all the brains, weirdos and geeks hung out who just lived for schoolwork, or so it seemed to me (see paragraph on rugby later). You had to be really clever to be in that class where spectacle wearing seemed to be compulsory. They were all destined for University, without question, and I was nowhere near their standard. The subjects I would be studying would be identical to those which I had studied at my previous school with one notable exception, Latin. This had been my best subject at my previous school for some reason which I can't explain, as old though I now am, I was definitely not born in Roman times, but I liked it and found I was reasonably good at it. The reason this was the exception was that at Blackpool Grammar School Latin was not taught to first year boys. Why, I have no idea, but it gave me a head start as we would now cover all the work I had done in my first year and it was all new to the others so here was one subject I could reasonably hope to be better at than the other boys and so it proved.

However, the downside was that the standards at this school were extremely high in all subjects and discipline was fierce. Strangely enough, I found that this was something I needed and adapted to quite quickly. All masters wore gowns, as did the prefects, and you stood up when a master entered the room at the start of a lesson or if the headmaster came in at any time. Prefects, who were drawn from the sixth form and seemed like grown ups to us youngsters, enforced discipline at break times and could issue lines (this was a punishment consisting of writing out a sentence however many times a prefect chose, say 100 lines of "I must not shout/run/swear/smoke/ fight/decapitate another boy (delete as appropriate) whilst in the school building") or an essay of so many sides of paper on any obscure subject of a prefect's choice if a prefect found you misbehaving. Failing to obey the punishment resulted in a visit to the headmaster's study where the cane would inevitably follow.

Games were held on one afternoon a week. Rugby in the autumn and spring terms, cricket in the summer term. Games day rolled round and so my introduction to rugby commenced. I knew nothing much about this game and I think I had just seen glimpses of the odd game on BBC, but not much. All I knew was that you picked this oval ball up (strange shape I thought) and tried to cross the other team's goal line with it, hence the term "try", meaning a score. I hope I'm right on that. My good friend Marshall will correct me if I'm wrong as he is an expert on the game. Anyway, the accomplished boys in the school team in my year all went off to play on their own pitch and being a new boy I was landed with the lads from 2X, who all looked as though they would prefer to have had their heads stuck in some maths or physics book. They certainly did not want to be out on a cold wet muddy field. You know the sort. Kit all haphazard, if they had managed to bring any in the first place that is, and they were generally in possession of a note from their parents asking to be excused from games on the grounds of head cold/pneumonia/bad chest/boil on the bum/suicidal tendencies etc (as before, delete on note as appropriate) which went down like a lead balloon with the games master who was always as fit as a flea in his tracksuit with obligatory whistle hanging round his neck and who classed anyone wanting to miss games as a waste of space and a skiver. Excuse notes were anathema to him. No kit? Go over to that locker and get yourself some from the kit left behind by other boys. Bear in mind that that kit probably hadn't been washed since time immemorial and smelt like the remains of a rotting corpse. Broken leg? Rubbish, get out on that field, you can go on the wing. You'll soon run it off.

Well, imagine my joy when I found out that in this game if another boy from the opposite team got the ball you had licence to flatten him. Legalised violence! This was for me. I took to it like a duck to water. Not only that, I soon realised that if you got the ball you could stick your hand in the face of an opponent if he tried to tackle you, a hand off it was called. I was beginning to enjoy this game. I got hold of the ball and soon found 2X were not that keen on tackling you if you ran directly at them, snarling as you went. They scattered in different directions as this crazed lunatic ran at them with a contorted face breathing fire. (Well, that's probably a little exaggerated, but you get the picture). Physical contact was definitely not on their to do list.

Anyway, after the game had been proceeding for a little while I received the ball and managed to cross the try line and grounded the ball. I knew that was the rule in this game. For you non-rugby afficionados, this meant that your team then had a place kick, as it was called, which meant placing the ball with it's pointed end facing the posts and you then attempted to kick the ball through the upper posts. Rugby rules lesson over. Well, as I had scored the try, I was going to have a go at this. The rest of my 2x teammates could take a breather. No one was taking that ball off me. I was going to take the kick as this was something I was good at, albeit with a different shaped ball. Through the posts it duly sailed and I had found a new game to enjoy.

Now while the games master oversaw the boys who could actually play this game and had their own pitch, my game took place on one of the minor pitches and was refereed by a stand-in teacher whose interest in the game was minimal and whose knowledge of the rules was basic, to say the least. However, when he refereed my game the following week, he obviously saw that I had some aptitude for the game as after a few minutes he stopped the game and told me to go over and join the proper rugby players on their own pitch, much to the relief of 2X, I suspect. I was thrilled. I duly reported to the games master and he let me join in with the players he was coaching. In those days, as a 12 year old, I was quite stockily built and of average height (stop laughing those who know me, it was true. I only became vertically challenged in later years!) so the master told me I would be playing as a wing forward which meant joining the scrum and trying to flatten the opposing scrum half as soon as he got the ball. Again this appealed to my primitive side and I was soon launching into tackles with gusto.

After a week or so of playing with this group I was picked for the school Under 13 side which meant two games a week, one on Wednesday afternoons and the other on Saturday mornings, which were played against other schools in Blackpool and other parts of the north west of the country. This meant that if you were playing against a side such as Cheadle Hulme Grammar in Cheshire for example, then on a Wednesday you would have to leave school late on a Wednesday morning to travel by coach to the match so you would have to miss a number of lessons. Bonus! The only downside to this was that my fledgling football career took a back seat and I would not play in a proper game of football for the next 3 years.

Meanwhile, on the domestic front, me and my family had left my grandparents' chippy and settled into a rented house in Richmond Road just round the corner from the chip shop. This was a small terraced house with two bedrooms, a bathroom with WC and a box room upstairs and a lounge, dining area and lean-to kitchen on the ground floor. No central heating, of course, but it did have indoor facilities so no need for a torch or a book on dangerous spiders to avoid when sitting on a toilet seat. It also had a concrete yard at the rear and this would be my permanent home for the rest of the decade. The house that is, not the yard! I was quite happy in these surroundings which were not too dissimilar from those enjoyed by other working class families.

On the 5th of October The Beatles first single, "Love me do", was released to total ignorance from not only myself but probably from the majority of the population outside those in the know on Merseyside. It is difficult to overstate the importance of this release looking back from today and how it would ultimately lead to the total transformation of popular music over the coming years, but all you have to do is look at the Top 20 for that week to give you some idea of the background against which this record was launched. Whilst the number one record was, in my opinion, a very good instrumental called "Telstar" by The Tornados (which would go on to top the charts in the USA), the majority of the chart for that week contained more than it's fair share of dross which was not untypical of the time.

Mediocre tracks from Elvis and Cliff were interspersed with offerings from Tommy Roe, Frank Ifield, Bobby Darin, Ronnie Carroll and Shirley Bassey. Not a group with guitars to be seen anywhere. A semblance of respectability was, however, provided by Carole King and also a terrific record by Little Eva called "The Locomotion", but otherwise there was no freshness in the chart and not a lot that a youngster could enthuse about. Pop music was definitely drifting along, with nothing to excite.

The whole music scene seemed to be waiting for something new. It had been in the doldrums for some years now. Indeed, you only had to listen to "Love Me Do" to know that here was something totally different and really unusual for the times. It would gradually gain some air time and eventually reach the dizzy heights of 17 in the top twenty at the end of the year. It was a gentle knock against the walls of popular music but it would be the next record which would blow the walls apart. On the 26th of November The Beatles were back in the studio to record a new song called "Please Please Me" and so confident was George Martin of the success of this track that at the end of the recording he told the group that they had just recorded their first number 1. He was not wrong. But that would not occur until the next year and that year very nearly never arrived for me and the rest of the western world.

Why was this I hear you ask? Yes, I do, really. The answer was not blowing in the wind, the answer lay in the unfolding drama of what came to be known as the Cuban Missile Crisis. On the 14th of October an American U2 spy plane had overflown Cuba and took reconnaissance photos showing a number of missile sites. Cuba was then, and at the time of writing still is, a communist country with close ties to the then Soviet Union. President Kennedy and his government were greatly alarmed by this as it meant that there was a possibility of the Soviet Union launching nuclear missile strikes against America with the assistance of the Cuban government which itself owed it's existence to it's much larger partner. The President was advised by his chiefs of staff to launch air strikes against the missile sites, which could have provoked a catastrophic reaction from the Soviet Union and caused a nuclear war, the outcome of which would have been uncertain but would undoubtedly have proved devastating for everyone in the western world.

It is no exaggeration to say that during these two weeks in late October the world held it's breath. There exists some ridiculous government advice films advising kids such as me to hide under a desk to shelter from a nuclear bomb in the event of a nuclear attack. Now they would have had to have been some desks. I don't recall that my desk would have been of much use in that eventuality. No, if the bomb had dropped at that time then I don't think I would now be around today telling my story. I would have been fused into one charcoal desk, I suspect. Thankfully on the 28th of October both protagonists came to their senses and negotiated a tactful withdrawal of the missiles from Cuban soil. The next day I celebrated a new birthday as I had reached the age of 13 and the rest of the world celebrated just being alive. It had been a close run thing. Was I aware of the seriousness of the situation at that time? Yes, I was. It was plastered on the front of our daily paper which caught my attention in no small way but it was only as I grew up that I was to learn how near to disaster we had all come. Anyway, it had safely passed and I was now free to become every parent's nightmare, a teenager!

The end of the year was drawing to it's somewhat eventful close but this one did not go out with a whimper as on the 22nd of December there started what was to become known as the Big Freeze. Temperatures plummeted and whilst this was not unusual for this time of year, we were in winter after all for goodness sake, what was to be unusual was not only how low the temperature would drop but also how long the freezing cold spell would last. But that is a topic for my next chapter. An incentive to read on if ever there was one. I can't let this year end, however, without one last comment on the state of the music scene. To give you an idea of how bad it was at this time, just consider the line up for the end of year's edition of "Thank Your Lucky Stars" which, as you will recall, was one of the few pop programmes then being broadcast. It was shown on the 29th of December and featured Cliff Richard, Kenny Ball and his

Jazzmen, Ronnie Carroll, Petula Clark, The Karl Denver trio, Craig Douglas, Frank Ifield, The Shadows and Helen Shapiro. This was a programme aimed at youngsters like me. I mean, come on, what was there in that line up which could possibly have appealed to my age group? We wanted something new, something fresh, something we could enthuse about. Roll on 1963, it just had to be different. Oh boy, it certainly was.

I know I have been less than complimentary to the standard of music being produced in this year but I do recommend the following in no particular order:-

1. Love Me Do - The Beatles

2. Do You Love Me - The Contours

3. Green Onions - Booker T & The MG's

4. He's a rebel - The Crystals

5. Up on the roof - The Drifters

6. Crying in the rain - Roy Orbison

7. Sherry - The Four Seasons

8. Telstar - The Tornados

9. Breaking up is hard to do - Neil Sedaka

10. The Locomotion - Little Eva

Oh and the notable films released this year which have proved to be popular throughout the following years included:-

Dr. No - The first James Bond film starring Sean Connery, who is still the best James Bond for me.

Lawrence of Arabia - the David Lean classic, with Peter O'Toole and Omar Sharif, a film I could watch again and again.

How the West Was Won - Epic John Ford western starring James Stewart, Debbie Reynolds, John Wayne and others.

The Longest Day - Grandiose war film based on the D-Day landings featuring a tremendous cast including John Wayne, Kenneth More, Sean Connery and Henry Fonda, amongst others.

Mutiny on the Bounty - historical drama with Marlon Brando, Richard Harris and Trevor Howard

Whatever Happened to Baby Jane? - psychological thriller with Bette Davis and Joan Crawford

The Day of the Triffids - science fiction thriller based on the John Wyndham novel

A Kind of Loving - gritty northern drama of Stan Barstow's book starring Alan Bates and June Ritchie

CHAPTER FOUR
1963

"Well, we could be big headed and say we could last 10 years but then again, we may not last 3 months" - August 1963 response from John Lennon when asked how long he thought the group might last.

The start of this new year was heralded by freezing cold weather. Not unusual, you might say, for the depths of winter. You are, of course, right in that sentiment but what we did not know, waking up on that distant New Year's day, was not only the magnitude of the low temperatures we would have to endure, but also how long this particular spell of freezing weather would last. This was in the days, remember, when central heating was only available to the more affluent members of society and so was not a luxury enjoyed in my home. In fact, government statistics reveal that in 1962, 80% of households did not have any central heating so we were hardly unusual. At my age, (13 if you can recall), you went to bed in your unheated bedroom with a hot water bottle to keep your feet warm underneath a variety of sheets, blankets and an eiderdown. You didn't hang about before diving into bed I can tell you. I can remember that my bedroom window was not particularly well insulated so it was not unusual to find ice actually on the inside of the window. Good training if you wanted to go on an Arctic expedition, but not very welcome as a day to day experience.

Getting up in a morning was a challenge too. I, for one, was generally most reluctant to leave my warm bed to step out into near sub-zero temperatures to brave a quick wash in the chilly bathroom but being a teenager I didn't linger too long over those activities. You then hoped that when you went downstairs you found that the coal fire had been lit in the lounge, not that this was an activity that engaged my own attention at all. What me, light a coal fire? Those who know me will know that this was not something anyone in their right mind would ask me to do too often given my proficiency in the do-it-yourself department. I make Frank Spencer look like an expert micro-surgeon. You get the idea. No, if I had had to light a coal fire, which was not as easy as it sounds by the way, the local fire brigade would have been on permanent stand by. We did, however, have the luxury of a three bar electric fire in the dining area so provided you could persuade our dog (didn't I mention the fact that we had a Dalmatian bitch before?) to move from in front of it, again not an easy task, then you could have your breakfast in relative comfort. I am sure most families endured similar conditions throughout this winter.

How bad could it have been, I hear you ask, as we have had bad winters in some years haven't we? Not as bad as this one, believe me. Look it up on Google or You tube if you don't believe me. Brass monkeys were about in abundance. Blackpool, being a seaside resort, does not generally suffer too badly in winter, unlike some inland areas such as Yorkshire and the Peak District, but this particular year saw parts of the sea actually freeze. That is how cold it got. I remember this from the times I used to take our dog for a walk on the beach and saw this for myself. Well, have you actually seen the sea freeze in this area since then? Didn't think so.

I also seem to recall Blackpool's football pitch at Bloomfield Road freezing over solid and some of the players ice skating on it. Not during a match obviously. Sliding tackles with that footwear would have been lethal. No, this was a winter that everyone who lived through it can still recall with a shiver and is still known as the Big Freeze. It lasted for most people until well into March of that year. Now that is some cold spell. Just think about that when you next go to your nice warm bathroom and centrally heated bedroom to sleep under your winter duvet and set your heating to come on well before you arise next morning. Would you swap? No, I didn't think so. Ah, the good old days!

Whilst I was shivering in Blackpool my heroes were embarking upon the start of the year when, for them, everything would go berserk and a year when I, and millions of other youngsters like me, would be excited and enthralled by the music they would produce. It all started with the release of the single "Please Please Me" on the 11th of January and their first appearance on "Thank Your Lucky Stars" on the 19th of January. I missed all of this, however, as I had not yet discovered the joys of popular music for myself. My introduction to it came gradually. As the song climbed up the charts I overheard some boys at school talking about this new group and the new sound they were producing. I was a little intrigued but not enough to pay too much attention at the time. I have, of course, heard the record many times over the years since then but even now the sheer vibrancy and freshness of the sound for that time was truly incredible. Incidentally, there is still a debate as to whether this was their first number one record. It made the top of some music paper charts such as the New Musical Express but not on Record Retailer and if you look in the Guinness Book of Hit Singles it is shown as only reaching number 2.

As the group were proving to be a bit of a success George Martin was anxious to produce an LP (long player for those of you who only inhabit the digital age and are sadly deprived of the joys of buying a 12" vinyl record each with it's own iconic sleeve work which were often works of art in themselves (see Chapter 8), now that is something I am glad my generation had the benefit of) so they booked into the studio at Abbey Road on the 11th of February to record their first album. They had already recorded four songs, namely their two singles with their "B" sides, (again for our younger readers the "B" side was the other side of the 7" record and was generally of an inferior standard to the "A" side though The Beatles would eventually give the lie to this idea with the quality of their later records) so George Martin needed 10 more songs, LP's generally having about 7 songs a side in those days. He asked what they had and what they had was basically their live show from Hamburg and The Cavern. They duly recorded those 10 songs in just that one day but for me it is the last song they recorded which is my particular favourite.

Apparently the clock on the studio wall was fast approaching 11pm and the end of the day's session when they were still one song short of the quota needed. George Harrison suggested that they should do an old Isley Brothers song, "Twist and Shout", which was a staple part of their show but John was struggling with his voice owing to a heavy cold which he had and he didn't know how long his voice would last. Anyway they decided to give it a try and what you hear today is effectively a live version of that song. No overdubs or other studio trickery. Just one take by the greatest group of all time powering their way through this song. For sheer excitement it is hard to match and nothing remotely existing at the time could come anywhere near it. Lennon had given his all and if you listen closely to the end of the song you can just hear him gasp as the track ends. The first marker had been laid down. This was what my generation had been waiting for. We had our new heroes. The LP would be released on the 22nd of March and would be the start of the domination of the music charts by The Beatles for the rest of the decade. It would be number 1 in the LP charts for 30 weeks and in 2012 would be listed as 39th in the list of all time 500 top LP'S by Rolling Stone magazine, almost 50 years since it was recorded. Might last for 10 years eh John?

However, at this time I was still to discover the joys of this type of music and, for now, my life seemed to revolve around my school work and playing rugby for the school team. I had settled well into my new school and, apart from the voluminous homework we used to be given (up to 2 or 3 hours a night during the week), I was enjoying my new surroundings and the company of my schoolmates. I found that Blackpool Grammar School was far more academic than my previous school and I tried hard to keep up with the standards being set by the other pupils.

I have already mentioned the strict discipline enforced by most teachers and my form master at this time, a Mr. H Lander who taught History, had his own particular way of keeping us in line. If anyone transgressed he would approach you and with a few fingers of his right hand he would grasp your hair at the side of your head and slowly twist it round causing your eyes to water quite a bit as you writhed in more than a little discomfort, much to the mirth of the other boys who were just glad it wasn't happening to them. A very effective method of teaching you to pay attention I can tell you, having been on the receiving end of this punishment myself on the odd occasion or two! I wonder if there may be a teacher or two today who would still like to use this tactic at times on some of their unruly pupils but then again this would probably be classed as common assault nowadays and the teacher would undoubtedly be in trouble for employing this punishment. We are, after all, more civilised now aren't we? Yeah right, as you might say.

Academically, I was doing well in the language subjects, Latin and French, and fairly average in the remainder, even the science subjects at this time, but that would soon change and not in a good way. The ones I did struggle with and had no interest in whatsoever were art, woodwork and metalwork. Stop laughing at the back. As far as art was concerned I struggled to draw a stick man let alone anything remotely approaching a drawing which you could decipher. Metalwork just baffled me as my hands would not do what my brain told them to do. They have always had a mind of their own as my wife can verify. As for woodwork, that was a complete disaster. I remember that in class we had been shown how to make a pretty basic broom holder out of balsa wood to screw on to a wall and you could then hang a broom upside down on it. Very useful, I'm sure. Every home should have one. There was just one problem with my effort. I had made the holder with the retaining wood sloping the wrong way so that if it had been screwed to the wall the broom would just have kept sliding off. My father thought that this was hilarious when he examined it and pointed out the error of my ways. I wonder why no member of my family has ever asked me to make anything for them? Do they know something I don't? Anyway, at the end of the summer term my hard work in the "normal" subjects had paid off and I found that I had achieved a lofty position of 10th in the form out of 32. An improvement on my previous year's showing.

With the amount of homework I was receiving I soon lost interest in children's TV but that was to be expected given that I was now 13. The only exception was for a new puppet adventure show called "Fireball XL5". Yes I know the word puppet conjures up images of wooden characters jumping up and down on strings but this show was different. It featured what was known as supermarionation, a souped up version of puppetry if you like, and was set in the space age, something that was very topical at this time with the race to reach the moon in full flow, and was produced by Gerry and Sylvia Anderson later of "Thunderbirds" fame, so it was very well done for the time. "Fireball XL5" was a spaceship commanded by Colonel Steve Zodiac who had, as part of his crew, Robbie the robot and whose mission was to patrol interstellar space and featured all their exciting adventures. No, really, it did. Well it entertained me, but save for a certain programme that started later in the year (of which more later), it was probably the last children's programme to do so. I was growing up at last and children's programmes were no longer for me.

Adult TV shows which I enjoyed this year included "Perry Mason", which was an American legal drama series starring Raymond Burr as Perry Mason, a defence lawyer who always seemed to get his client off no matter how black the case against his client looked. I think O J Simpson must have employed him some years later by the sounds of it. "The Avengers" was a must see programme for me and whilst it will probably seem very tame now, back then it was very exciting and entertaining and I think I was beginning to see the attraction of Cathy Gale but still had no idea why!

The other adventure series which I enjoyed was "The Saint" featuring the suave Roger Moore who seemed to be able to disarm villains without ruffling his suit. Comedy was provided by such shows as "My Favourite Martian" starring Ray Walston as a martian who had crash landed on earth and had unusual powers including, when he raised two antennae in his head, the power of invisibility. He could also read minds and levitate items as well as communicating with animals so this made for some hilarious episodes. There was also a British programme called "It's a square world" featuring Michael Bentine and this programme involved some bizarre sketches which were very much hit and miss and could best be classed, in my view, as a forerunner of some of the surreal comedy which would later be found in "Monty Python" but not in any way in that league. When the sketches worked they were quite funny though.

My favourite, however, was an American import called "The Beverly Hillbillies" featuring a poor backwoods family who lived in a wooden shack and had oil on their land which they sold to an oil company for 25 million dollars and moved to Beverly Hills. Totally out of their depth, their antics were hilarious and the show can still be caught on some of the Sky channels today. Examples of how naive they were are that they thought the swimming pool at their house was a cement pond and they used the pool table as a dining table with the cues used as pot passers. It was immensely popular both here and in the USA and in my opinion was one of the best American comedy shows ever made.

On the other hand, programmes which I did my best to avoid included "The Billy Cotton Band Show" and "The Good Old Days" which were still going strong and also "The Andy Stewart Show" which had taken over, I think, from that other riveting show, "The White Heather Club", but his Scottish singers were certainly not for my generation. One programme which was apparently on at the time, though I can't say I recall it at all, was one hosted by Rolf Harris called "A Swinging time"! I'll bet it was, but I don't think we'll go there. No, on the whole, apart from the odd exception, I was finding TV viewing boring as I am sure most teenagers were. I wanted something different and, for me, in early April of this year I finally found it.

Most of my evenings were spent in our back room at home which effectively was a small dining area with the previously mentioned 3 bar electric fire. I would do my homework on the dining table or, if reading was involved, sat on a small two seater settee. We had an oldish Bush radio set which took ages to warm up once switched on and it was this which was to prove my saviour. One of the lads at school had told me to listen to Radio Luxembourg on 208 on the medium wave in the evening as they broadcast the latest songs and so it was that on one particular night, a Sunday I think it was, I tuned in whilst doing some reading homework and caught a programme which played the new record releases.

I had not been listening long when the presenter said that he was now going to play the latest release by The Beatles due out later that week called "From me to you". My ears pricked up as I had heard their previous release on the odd occasion and quite liked it. After about 10 seconds of the intro I was hooked. A light switch seemed to have been flicked in my head just on hearing this particular song and I had found my new obsession. Life would now change for me forever. I spent the remainder of the evening tuned in to Radio Luxembourg to see if they played it again, which they did, once or twice more. My love of popular music was born that night and has stayed with me ever since.

Why this particular record you might say? After all, looking back now, it does not seem quite as good as "Please Please Me" and I would have to agree, but at that time I had not paid too much heed to the previous record. You have to remember that we had no record player in our house. My parents were not into music in any big way, and pop music shows on the TV were few and far between. Furthermore, the only real pop music station was Radio Luxembourg so this was effectively my initiation into this scene and bang "From me to you" was the bolt which hit me right between the eyes. It did also have a really infectious and catchy hook. Something that The Beatles were brilliant at. I wanted more. From now on, I was only vaguely interested in TV and my evenings were spent listening to the radio.

As money was still tight in our household there was no immediate prospect of my having a record player so I was not able to start buying records until, after incessant pleading, I was finally bought a second hand record player some two years later, but that is for another chapter. Whatever homework I was doing would now be accompanied by the fading in and out transmission signal of fabulous 208. Those of you around back then will remember how distorted the music could become because of this signal problem but you just had to persevere. It could be quite maddening though, particularly if your favourite record was being played. For those of you who weren't there, just put a song on your cd player/mp3 whatever and keep twisting the volume control to near silence and back while imagining phasing occurring occasionally as you do so, (a sound similar to the whooshing sound at the start of Doctor Who) being meshed with it and you get the picture. If you can! You really had to be there to hear it. Anyway, it was all we had so we made the best of it. (How many channels playing pop music do you have today? We had one and a half, if you add in BBC's Light programme).

Talking of which, as my interest in music had now started in a big way, I also became an avid listener to "Saturday Club" which was a two hour programme starting at 10am on Saturday mornings on the BBC Light Programme hosted by Brian Matthews. The only downside to this programme was that you had to put up with some naff live music, for example on the weekend mentioned in my previous paragraph there were featured such luminaries as Russ Sainty and The Nu-Notes (what do you mean who?), The Lorne Gibson Trio (I know, me too) and The Trebletones (I give up on that one) who would generally murder the latest songs by singing their own versions (imagine a very poor X Factor show, no on second thoughts, just imagine a normal X Factor show and you will get the picture) but you stuck with it in the hope that somebody you liked would be on or that a record by one of your favourites would be played. You may not know, but in those far off days the BBC was not allowed to play too many records as the Musicians' Union jealously guarded their right to be employed on music programmes so had an agreement with the BBC which restricted "needle time" i.e. playing recorded music, to a total of 5 hours in any 24 hour period. This was not a restriction which applied to Radio Luxembourg which was transmitted from guess where? Oh come on, you know. Nor would it apply to the pirate radio stations which were to spring up in 1964, of which more later, naturally.

Anyway, just as "From me to you" was about to be released, on the 14th of April the Fab Four paid a visit to the Crawdaddy Club at the Station Hotel in Richmond upon Thames to see an upcoming group by the name of The Rolling Stones, who some of you may have heard of, and so impressed were they with them that George Harrison actually recommended to Mike Smith of Decca that he signed them up. Fortunately for all concerned, he did. Now imagine, turning down the Beatles was bad enough for this guy, but if he had also turned down the Stones...! There would be a lot made by the music papers over the coming years about the "rivalry" between the two groups but it was all a paper fuelled nonsense as both groups liked each other and got on well together, but that hardly sells papers does it?

In fact, The Beatles even gave the Stones a song which would be their second hit, "I wanna be your man" and they would hardly have done that if they had hated each other's guts, would they? But the paper fuelled rivalry would also mean that some teenagers were either in one camp or the other. Personally, while I much prefer The Beatles music, I enjoyed most of the Stones music as well and indeed still do. The two groups never were mutually exclusive so far as I was concerned. Talking of the music papers, my interest in pop music was such that I now started to buy the New Musical Express each Friday to read the latest news and interviews, not only involving my favourite group but other artists as well and also the latest music news generally. The NME also featured the latest weekly music chart as well as news of tours being undertaken. Not that I could afford going to them either, say ah! Eh by gum, times were hard up north tha' knows. Well, they were in this family.

Meanwhile, back in the sober adult world, there was one news item which was unfolding in June of this year and which subsequently became known to all as The Profumo Affair.

Obviously, not being totally oblivious to major news stories (I did watch the news on TV and glanced at our daily and Sunday papers, respectively the Daily Express in the week and on Sundays, the Sunday Express and that bastion of truth and good taste, The News of the World) I was aware of something going on involving a cabinet minister and something known as call girls, which I somewhat naively thought must be female telephone operators (don't laugh, innocent days) although why this was causing such an uproar did puzzle me at the time, I have to say.

Sex education was, I'm afraid, somewhat non-existent for such as me at the start of the swinging sixties and you eventually learned on the job, so to speak. But that would come later. For now, any rudimentary knowledge I had in this department came from anecdotal tales from other boys at school (generally incorrect and unreliable, I later found out) or from the well-thumbed biology textbook section detailing the mating habits of rabbits (not totally helpful given the physical differences between a girl and female rabbit, as I also later found out. Not that I actually dated any rabbits you understand, a few dogs maybe, but certainly no rabbits.). No, most parents were certainly shy when it came to explaining the facts of life and mine were no different. Not that I would have dreamed of asking any such questions. Awkward! No, for now, I was totally ignorant in this department, something I am sure most 13 year olds today would find hard to believe.

So, whilst I was yet to discover the joys of female company and although I had by now discovered pop music, I was still keen on trainspotting. Ah, bless! Before you criticise, just remember that back then there was no internet, facebooking, mobile phones and play stations. No, in those days the only stations which interested me were the ones at which trains passed through or stopped at. Anyway, now we had moved to Blackpool I had a host of new engines to spot (hooray I hear you exclaim, yeah right) as we were near to the West Coast main line and also Blackpool itself had, in summer, all the excursion trains from around the country paying a visit carrying their trainload of holidaymakers.

What's the difference between the East Coast main line engines and those of the West Coast main line I hear you ask (well I do if you have not fallen asleep already during this paragraph and I listen to you very closely). The answer, as any trainspotter worth his salt would tell you, is that each line had it's own unique set of engines and you would rarely see an East Coast engine on the West Coast and vice versa. Now isn't that enlightening? Don't answer. My venue for this wildly exciting pastime was either down near the football ground in Blackpool or at a place just outside Preston called Skew Bridge, which had a nice steep grassy embankment you could laze on in summer with your picnic. A perfectly innocent way to while away your time whist hoping for a Coronation Scot (a "semi" to those of us in the trade, and no I'm not going to explain it for fear of losing readers) or some other express engine to pass by, especially if we hadn't seen that engine before. Sadly, the days of steam were drawing to a close and diesel engines (which I found to be boring - stop laughing) were now coming to the fore and little did I know that I would only have one more year of my hobby left. I was growing up and soon there would be other distractions, but not just yet. You see in those days, hard though it may be for some of you to imagine, we didn't feel we had to be adults at 13 years of age and we could enjoy a natural gradual progression from childhood to adolescence and then to adulthood. Something I feel to be totally lacking for today's youngsters. I know which I prefer.

Enough of this pontificating, let's get back to the music. Friday the 9th of August saw the start of what was, in my humble opinion, one of the most exciting pop music programmes ever made, namely a programme called "Ready Steady Go". This was always transmitted live in the early evening on a Friday with it's inimitable slogan "The weekend starts here" and it most certainly did. It would only run for just over 3 years and would feature all the leading artists over these years, not only singing their own hits, but also being interviewed by the hosts Keith Fordyce and, the epitome of a swinging sixties "dolly bird", Cathy McGowan. No teenage music fan ever wanted to miss this show as it was totally oriented towards the teenage market.

For the first time my age group had it's very own show. There was also the chance for the fashion conscious amongst us (which surprisingly did not include me!) to see what clothes and hairstyles had come into fashion as the programme always had features on this type of thing as well as the latest dances. It really was a groundbreaking programme for the time and was the start of TV noticing that there was a teenage audience to be catered for. At long last me and my generation were being noticed.

Over in the USA, although the population of that country were still oblivious to The Beatles all throughout this year, there was one record label producing a new type of music, the majority of which would soon become well known and loved by me and very many others in the years to come, and run by a man called Berry Gordy. He named his label Motown (eventually known over here as Tamla Motown) as it was situated in Detroit, the motor city of the United States. These were early days for him and his label but the artists he signed up, including those such as The Four Tops, Marvin Gaye, Gladys Knight, Martha and the Vandellas, The Marvelettes, The Miracles, The Supremes, The Temptations, Stevie Wonder and at the end of the decade a group called The Jackson Five featuring a certain Michael Jackson, all of whom would, over the coming decade, produce some of the most memorable music in history.

This particular year saw The Miracles record "You've really got a hold on me" (later to be covered by The Beatles on their second LP), Little Stevie Wonder with "Fingertips Part 2", Martha and the Vandellas with "Heatwave" and also Marvin Gaye with "Can I get a witness". I defy you not to want to get up and dance if ever you hear those last two played. The music produced on this label would be the only music in the USA which would subsequently give The Beatles a run for their money and I, for one, could listen to this type of music endlessly. It still has a vibrancy and excitement to it today. Forget about the atrocious rap music and what today's youngsters call R and B (this was known as rhythm and blues in my day and not at all like the R and B of today), it cannot hold a candle to the magic of Motown or am I being an old curmudgeon? I think we know the answer. Let me just say that I am glad I lived in the golden era of Motown and leave it at that.

This summer had it's fair share of local excitement in Blackpool when The Beatles performed at the Queen's Theatre on the 4th of August and, according to Mark Lewisohn in his book "The Complete Beatles Chronicle", there were so many fans blocking the access roads to the theatre that day that the group had to go through a builder's yard, up across some scaffolding and across the roof of the theatre to get in to the Queen's Theatre to perform. "Beatlemania", as the press would soon label it, had already started in earnest. Not that this youngster was in attendance at either this show or at the following week's show held at the new, luxurious ABC Theatre as for one thing I couldn't afford the ticket, relatively cheap though they were when you compare them to the prices of today's shows, but also because I feared I would not be able to hear the group given the amount of screaming that ensued at each concert.

No, I was sensible, my plan was that I would wait for the screaming to die down and by then I would hopefully be able to afford a ticket to both see and hear them. Surely the screaming could not go on forever? Hmm, some game plan eh? Particularly given that my wife actually saw them twice in Blackpool and never ceases to remind me of this fact.(As an aside, I did eventually get to see Paul McCartney perform at a small venue in Liverpool in 2010 when he performed many of The Beatles numbers for which many thanks to my daughter for obtaining the tickets, second best I know but nevertheless a very good second best). They also released on the 23rd of August, to much excited anticipation, their new record "She loves you". If "Please Please Me" knocked down the dusty walls of the pop industry, this record stamped all over the remains. This record just leapt off the turntable and out of your radio. Enormously successful, it stormed to the top of the charts and was a truly fantastic record and totally original for the times. Heaven knows how the other groups must have felt at the time trying to follow that. However, for me, my only hope of hearing this song was either on one of the TV shows or the sparse radio programmes. Thankfully it got plenty of air play at the time. It is still one of my all time favourites to this day.

Whilst Blackpool hosted weekly Sunday shows featuring the up and coming pop groups, the main summer entertainment was still provided by the summer season shows which this year included Morecambe and Wise at the North Pier and Central Pier had "On with the Modley" featuring Albert Modley. Now I really have no idea who he was but my voluminous research (well, one press of a button on Google anyway) tells me that he was a fading variety performer and comedian whose catchphrase, apparently, was "Eeeeeh, isn't it grand when you're daft." What can I say? I don't think the catchphrase caught on. If Sundays in Blackpool saw the visit of the new artists, South Pier was definitely catering for those who were about to say goodbye, as it featured the likes of Karl Denver, Marty Wilde and Eden Kane. The Opera House wasn't much better with The Billy Cotton Band Show sharing the season with Max Bygraves. Ooh, which to choose? Talk about spoilt for choice on that one. Finally, the ABC Theatre had "Holiday Carnival" starring Cliff Richard, who was no doubt on his summer holiday. I thank you.

Elsewhere, on the 8th of August, a group of robbers had stopped the overnight Royal Mail train from Glasgow to London in Hertfordshire (no I hadn't spotted this engine! It was a diesel, anyway.) and stole £2.6 million pounds, the equivalent of £50 million pounds today. Their antics made national and world wide news as the Police desperately sought to track them down. They were regarded initially as some sort of folk heroes although I have never exactly understood why. What they did do, in fact, was brutally attack the train driver, effectively ending his career as a driver and this assault may have contributed to his early death a few years later. I can only think that some of the public must have had some sort of misguided admiration for the gang because of the audacious way they had conducted the robbery and the vast amount of money they stole. But Robin Hood and his Merry Men they definitely weren't.

When they were finally arrested, they were given severely lengthy sentences, the ringleaders received 30 years, and one named Ronnie Biggs achieved considerable notoriety when he subsequently escaped from prison in 1965 and eventually settled in Brazil from where he would only return voluntarily in 2001. Very little of the money was actually recovered, approximately £400,000 in total, although because of the huge publicity the robbery generated it proved difficult for the robbers to enjoy their haul fully. Still, it generated plenty of news back then and still remains a major event of the time being the subject of numerous books and also a number of films including "Buster" starring Phil Collins.

Anyway, a fairly uneventful summer had drawn to a close for me and following it there was ushered in the start of the autumn term and my new form was now 3A, still hosted by the inimitable Mr. Lander to keep us in line. This would be the final year during which I would be taught all the general subjects as at the end of it a choice would have to be made between the arts subjects, such as the languages, and the science subjects but all that is for the next chapter. After all, I wouldn't want to overload you with too much excitement at once, would I?

Formal school sport for me still revolved around the rugby team. It was now the under 14 team for this year, but a new additional sport which I enjoyed was basketball and I was chosen for my year's school team (no it was not a team specially for kids of a vertically challenged nature. I told you, I was average height back then, it's only over the years that I have shrunk a little). So, plenty of time to avoid lessons when I was away on school sports team fixtures. One sport I didn't bother with too much, however, was swimming, even though I was reasonable at it. I thought I had enough to do with my existing sports. This meant that I would attend the annual school swimming gala as a spectator rather than as a participant and it was to prove a little intriguing for me. Why? The reason was that the gala was held jointly with our sister school, Collegiate Grammar School for girls, and was the first occasion on which I started to take an interest in the opposite sex.

I had been at a grave disadvantage in this aspect as when I came to live in Blackpool in 1962 I had left behind all my junior school classmates in Derbyshire including any girls I knew there and when I started at Blackpool Grammar School for boys this meant that the sum total of girls I knew in Blackpool was zero. Going to an all boys school would not improve this ratio, as I soon found out. Well it's hardly rocket science is it? I can't say that this bothered me until now, quite the reverse. I mean, what self respecting 13 year old would be interested in boring girls? How could they possibly match the excitement of trainspotting or football eh?

Well, soon after I had reached the age of 14 in October of this year my school had it's annual swimming gala which was held one evening at the old magnificent Derby Baths, just a short walk from my house. For those who cannot now remember it, Derby Baths was a fantastic yellow brick building constructed in Art Deco style with an Olympic size swimming pool, diving boards and a sun roof at the top of the building and it was situated at North Shore near to where the Pembroke Hotel is located now. It used to host major swimming events and is a sad loss to the town. The imposing entrance to the baths was on Warley Road and you had to ascend a flight of steps leading to the Baths' main entrance foyer. If you wanted to swim, you paid your admission fee and entered the male changing rooms which were located to the right of the foyer. When you handed your ticket over to the attendant there, you would be given a strong wire coathanger type contraption in which to place your clothes and shoes. You would then be given a rubber ring with the hanger's number on it to wear round your wrist in the pool. Whenever I think of the Baths, I can still smell the aroma of the drinks machine in the changing rooms which dispensed coffee and, my favourite after a swim, hot chocolate.

So far as our gala was concerned, the Baths, with it's 1800 seats, could easily accommodate the two sets of school pupils together and on this evening I was sat with my mates in front of some Collegiate girls of our age who were seated right behind us. One of my mates knew one of these girls from his Junior School days so we started a bit of banter with them and one of the girls passed round the latest Beatles Monthly book (this was a monthly magazine for members of The Beatles fan club devoted solely to the group and their exploits) for us all to glance at. Was this an early form of courtship perhaps, the passing round of The Beatles monthly magazine? Swimming gala duly forgotten, this activity was far more interesting, I thought. Ice duly broken, to my amazement, I started trying to chat one particular girl up and was getting on famously, or so I thought, but my offer of a stroll on the prom after the gala ended was sadly rebuked. Not that I would have had a clue what to do apart from talk but it would have been fun learning. But no, alas for me she was going home with her mates. Nowadays we would no doubt have exchanged mobile phone numbers, texts, emails, facebook etc., but as there was none of this at the time (we didn't even have a phone in my home anyway) that was the last I saw of her. For the first time, at age 14, my interest had been piqued by a girl. Something strange was happening to me. The testosterone had started to flow! Suddenly trainspotting didn't seem quite as exciting anymore.

Back in the music world, whilst myself and everyone I knew had been enjoying The Beatles and their music for the best part of this year, the National press only finally woke up to their existence when mayhem ensued at their performance on Sunday Night at the London Palladium on the 13th of October when their fans stopped traffic all around the theatre. This was a familiar sight at all Beatles concerts by now but the first time it had happened in London at a major event. All of a sudden the press were asking "Who are these guys?" and coined the term "Beatlemania" to describe the fans adoration.

There had been popular artists before of course and there had even been some female hysteria before, but nothing approaching the scale now seen. This was different. You have to understand that the show "Sunday Night at the London Palladium" back then was a big deal. It may not seem so now but at that time this show was THE show for an artist to be seen appearing on and was a mark of an artist finally achieving national major stardom. The show was required

Sunday night viewing for most of the nation and was probably the first time my parents and others of their generation had had a chance to see and hear the group. Even now I can well remember my father's reaction to them appearing on the show which was that they must be miming as he couldn't believe that a group of long haired louts could actually play their instruments. He was somewhat taken aback when I told him that they were not only singing and playing live, but that they also wrote their own songs as well. If he thought the group were long haired louts, I hate to think what he must have thought of The Rolling Stones when they broke big the following year. They made The Beatles look like choirboys!

Within a few weeks of the group's appearance on the Sunday Night show they were appearing at the annual "Royal Variety Show" in front of The Queen Mother and Princess Margaret, exactly one year after they had been appearing at the Star Club in Hamburg as an unknown rock n' roll band. A phenomenal rise for the band in just 12 short months. Even my parents were mellowing a little in their attitude to them, grudgingly. What had been the success of their mercurial rise? As John Lennon was famously to remark when asked that question in the States a year later "If we knew that, we'd all become managers and form our own groups".

My own take on it is that a combination of factors were involved. The music was so exciting, fresh and original; they were four good looking boys for the girls to choose from (well three and Ringo anyway) and they all had the typical Liverpudlian humour which was liberally laced with irreverance on most topics. The girls could choose the one they liked who most appealed to them visually and who they could dote on (mainly Paul) and the boys could choose the one whose personality most appealed to them (mainly John) and John was always my favourite. I loved his voice (still one of the best in rock history) and his witty and sarcastic remarks which appealed to my sense of humour. They had everything my generation needed. I just hoped it would all last for a few years and I could then get to see them live.

Meanwhile two major events shook Great Britain around this time. The first was the resignation of the then Prime Minister, Harold MacMillan, on the 18th of October. The Profumo Affair had taken it's toll on him and he was succeeded by Sir Anthony Douglas Home who was very much part of the existing establishment but I hadn't a clue who he was and frankly, couldn't care less. He was an irrelevance to me and my life. He wasn't really, how could he be as Prime Minister, but you get what I mean.

The other major event occurred on the 22nd of November when President Kennedy was assassinated in Dallas by Lee Harvey Oswald. This news was of seismic importance and caused mayhem with that Friday night's TV schedules. It is one of those events where people say you can always remember where you were when you heard the news, such was its importance. Well, as far as I can recall, when I heard the news I was sat in my back room avidly listening to Radio Luxembourg to see if they would play any songs from "With the Beatles", the group's latest LP which had been newly released on that very day. I think one of my parents came through to give me the news and even I gave up my listening vigil with Radio Luxembourg to see the latest news on the TV. I had never before heard of a top politician being assassinated and particularly one with the charisma of John F. Kennedy. The western world was in total shock and the news would be dominated by this story for some time to come. In fact, with all the conspiracy theories that have abounded since then, it has never really gone away. Will the truth ever come out or was the truth in fact that it was just simply a case of a lone gunman with a grievance? A pretty phenomenal sharpshooter if the latter was the case, if you ask me.

The Beatles ended their musical output for the year with the release of "With the Beatles" LP as mentioned above and also one week later with their new single "I want to hold your hand" which would eventually break the American market for them the following year in no small measure. The new LP was somewhat similar in style to the first LP but seemed to me somehow more considered and assured. It had some great tracks on it such as "All my loving", "It won't be long", "Please Mr. Postman" (their first nod to Motown as this had previously been recorded by The Marvelettes) and the stomping album closer "Money" (another Motown cover, but nothing like the Barrett Strong original version, far better though). It also had the iconic album cover showing the four of them in black and white in half shadow. Oh if only I could have bought these records at the time but I would just have to wait quite a while before I could actually do so.

Whilst on the subject of the new LP, it should be noted (Madonna for one, are you listening!) that not one of the 14 tracks was released as a single even though any number of tracks would easily have shot to the top of the charts. No, as fans, we were not ripped off by this group. You got your money's worth from them, no question. Even the "B" side of their new single, "This Boy", was good enough to have reached number 1 on it's own such was the quality of the music they were now producing. They were truly head and shoulders above any of their rivals.

One TV programme which I have not mentioned until now and which started on BBC on the 23rd of November was "Doctor Who". I can still remember vividly the eerie opening music and title sequence which was to become extremely well known over the coming years and which heralded the start of this show. The programme was, of course, transmitted in black and white but even from the first programme it seemed to have something special about it and from the very first viewing I was hooked. The premise of a time lord travelling the universe in a police box masquerading as a time ship was mind boggling and made for some exciting and, at times, slightly scary viewing. None more so than on the 21st of December with the introduction of the infamous Daleks. They might look quite tame now but believe me, back then, the first viewing of them was something else. They just had an air of menace about them which kept you glued to the screen and there was always the obligatory cliff hanger at the end of each episode to make you want to watch next week's episode. This was gripping stuff and as there was no home recording equipment in those days then you had to make sure you were in front of the TV by screening time. This was generally around 5.30pm each Saturday I think and for this boy and most others of my generation it was totally unmissable and the subject of school time conversation come Monday morning. My favourite programme at this time, without question.

As my autumn term was now nearing it's end and Christmas was fast approaching, tiny Tim was no doubt polishing his crutch and Scrooge was preparing to meet his ghostly visitors (atmospheric eh?) for me the final school social activity was the annual Christmas Fair held one Friday evening at the school in December and featuring stalls, games, raffles and also one room set aside to be used solely as a "coffee bar" with a record player. One of the boys had bought in the new Beatles LP so this was played to the rapt attention of some 40 or so boys and girls. I had not heard it all the way through yet so it had my undivided attention.

Well, it mostly had. I was slightly diverted by another exposure to the fairer sex, mostly the aforementioned Collegiate girls but not the one I had met at the gala, sad to say, but this time I could not pluck up enough courage to chat any of them up. I was far too shy to indulge in that activity. That would change considerably in later years as you will have to wait to find out. For now, I was just a gauche 14 year old schoolboy yearning for a girlfriend. Any girlfriend, I wasn't particular at that time. As long as she had the requisite numbers of limbs and preferably most of her faculties, but that last bit was not totally essential, then it would have been fine but, alas, it was not to be, not just yet. I can see you now with your eyes filling up as you read this. Poor boy. What a shame for me, wasn't it? Stop laughing again. Well, what could a boy do when his only companions were other boys? Don't answer that thank you. It was a rhetorical question.

So, the year of 1963 draws to a close for me. However, I cannot leave this chapter without commenting on this year's Christmas Special of the "Thank Your Lucky Stars Show". You will remember the naff line up on the show from last year. Well you will if you have been paying attention. If you haven't, I will send Mr.Lander round to inflict pain. Anyway, this Christmas Special featured The Beatles, Gerry and the Pacemakers, Billy J. Kramer and the Dakotas, The Searchers and Cilla Black. You can see how things had changed following the mercurial rise of The Beatles and Liverpool acts now dominated the show. It was quite a line up for the time and one that was well received by myself and my fellow teenagers. What would the new year bring and what exciting music would my heroes produce for all their fans, I wondered? Read on for the next exciting instalment. Go on, you know you want to.

As ever, I close this chapter with a list of my favourite records from this year which, unsurprisingly, is dominated by The Beatles. I have chosen 18 from this year as the standard of songs was improving considerably compared to previous years. I am sure you will disagree with some choices but am I bothered, no. It's my book. Anyway here goes and in no particular order:-

1. Please Please Me - The Beatles

2. From me to you - The Beatles

3. Surfin' USA - The Beach Boys

4. Little Deuce Coupe - The Beach Boys

5. Da doo ron ron - The Crystals

6. I only want to be with you - Dusty Springfield

7. It's all right - The Impressions

8. Twist and shout - The Beatles

9. Heatwave - Martha and the Vandellas

10. Can I get a witness - Marvin Gaye

11. She loves you - The Beatles

12. Be my baby - The Ronettes

13. Sweets for my sweet - The Searchers

14. I want to hold your hand - The Beatles

15. You'll never walk alone - Gerry and the Pacemakers

16. All my loving - The Beatles

17. In dreams - Roy Orbison

18. On Broadway - The Drifters

PS. As LP's were now coming to the fore I would mention that, in addition to the two Beatles LP's already mentioned above, there were two other ground breaking LP's released this year which deserve a mention namely "Freewheelin'" by a certain Bob Dylan. Not to everyone's taste I know, but this was in fact a very influential album for the time. The other album, whose tracks still receive considerable airplay each Christmas, was the magnificent "Phil Spector's Christmas Album" featuring Christmas (really?) songs by the groups he controlled and my word he certainly did. Control them that is. You didn't mess with old Phil, as one unfortunate lady would later find out. Anyway, damn fine album in my opinion.

Films released this year included;-

The Birds - Hitchcock thriller with Tippi Hedren and Rod Taylor facing some very nasty seagulls

Cleopatra - overblown epic with Elizabeth Taylor and Richard Burton which almost bankrupted 20th Century Fox

The Great Escape - brilliant prisoner of war film and mainstay of Christmas TV with a terrific cast including, amongst others, Steve McQueen, James Garner, Richard Attenborough, Charles Bronson and James Coburn

The Pink Panther - great comedy with Peter Sellers in his first outing as the bungling Inspector Clouseau

From Russia With Love – the second Bond film and one of the best. It was also the first one I saw in the Cinema

Summer Holiday - a "musical" vehicle of the "Let's do the show right here" variety for Cliff Richard (not to my taste I have to say, but I believe some people quite like it)

CHAPTER FIVE
1964

"Why are you wasting your time listening to that rubbish? No one will remember The Beatles in five years time." Question posed by the father of the author to him in the spring of 1964.

Whilst the comment made by my father to me when he heard me listening to Radio Luxembourg as I was doing my school homework one evening, some time around May 1964, might cause considerable mirth looking back now from a distance of over 50 years (the remark actually became a bit of a family joke between us as I never stopped reminding him of what he'd said over the intervening years), it was not an unreasonable remark for him to have made at that time. You have to remember that pop music was still in it's infancy in 1964 and the stars of the fifties, save for an anaemic Elvis, had mostly drifted away or died and had been largely forgotten as the new stars of the sixties took their place.

Each generation of youngsters would have their own stars to worship so it was certainly not unreasonable for an adult to think that what happened to the stars of the fifties would also happen to our idols and that they would, in five years or so, be replaced by the next set of stars and so themselves drift into obscurity. We, of course, fervently hoped that this would not be the case. We all thought that our idols would last indefinitely and that no doubt we would all stay forever young. After all, as teenagers we were never going to reach thirty years of age and grow old, were we?

The powers that be that ran television must have thought, however, that there was something special about the new music which teenagers were listening to as they decided that, as the new year was ushered in, there would be a new weekly programme on BBC devoted solely to that week's music charts and called "Top of the Pops". It was first shown on New Year's day, which was a Wednesday, and continued on Wednesdays for most of the year before changing to what would become it's regular Thursday evening slot.

The first ever show was hosted by every teenager's "friend" (hmm! not sure about that one now) one Jimmy Saville and featured a girl seeming to play what would be the next record up by placing a needle on the disc on the record player at which point the camera would immediately cut to the artist who would start miming to the record being played in the studio. After the first few episodes of the show the original girl doing this was replaced and in came a luscious blonde (well I thought so, I was certainly growing up!) called Samantha Juste who took over these duties. She was very attractive and would later go on to marry Micky Dolenz of Circus Boy and Monkees fame. Lucky for him. The show always ended with that week's number one so that honour for the first show fell to The Beatles with "I want to hold your hand" although they were in fact absent from the show being engaged at that time on their Christmas Show in London. Anyway, another must see programme for my generation, and indeed the ones to follow, had started. We teenagers were certainly being noticed now and not before time.

As 1963 had been the year in which the Beatles stormed all before them in this country, so 1964 proved to be the year that America fell for their music in much the same way. That country had been in deep mourning following the assassination of President Kennedy the previous November and it seemed as though the country now needed something to bring them out of their torpor. They found this in the exuberance and freshness of the Fab Four. Indeed, they fell for them in such a big way that after "I want to hold your hand" had shot to the top of their charts on the 1st of February the group made their first appearance on "The Ed Sullivan Show" on the 7th of February.

"The Ed Sullivan Show" was a hugely popular entertainment show broadcast coast to coast in America and the programme featuring The Beatles was watched by an estimated 73 million viewers, at the time a record for American TV. What would Simon Cowell give for those viewing figures now do you think? Not only that, but on the 9th of April the group's records held all five top spots in the American charts, a feat that will, I think I can say with some certainty, never be equalled let alone bettered.

Prior to this feat, the American charts had been in much the same state of languor as ours had been in 1962. The great Jerry Lee Lewis, when commenting recently on the group and the impact they had at the time, said that he liked them. Before the Beatles, he said, the American charts had been dominated by the likes of Bobby Vee, Bobby Darin, Bobby Rydell and Bobby Vinton then the Beatles hit and bang, that was the end of all the Bobbies! A succinct appraisal. This was the first time a British act had broken big in the USA and it soon lead to more success for other groups in their wake such as the Rolling Stones, Herman's Hermits, The Animals, The Kinks and many others. America had originally given us rock n' roll and we had now paid them back in spades. Not only that, but the group itself influenced others in America to form their own bands like The Byrds, The Eagles and Bruce Springsteen as well as also influencing the direction in music others would take such as the Beach Boys and Bob Dylan. It was surely no coincidence that Dylan decided to forsake acoustic guitar for an electric one after he had heard the records of the Beatles, much to the annoyance of his folk music fans. As Bob would later remark, "It doesn't take a weatherman to know which way the wind blows."

Talking of America, there was one event there which occurred on the 25th of February in which I was very interested and that was the world heavyweight boxing match between a brute of a man and the most intimidating fighter of his day called Sonny Liston and a brash outspoken young boxer then known by the name of Cassius Clay, but who would soon change his name to Muhammed Ali. Clay had let it be known that he would beat Liston in eight rounds and his brashness had upset a lot of white Americans who, although the contest was between two black men, mostly rooted for Liston as they thought that it was time Clay had his mouth shut for him and this fight was therefore eagerly anticipated both in America and here and I, and most of my schoolmates, very much looked forward to seeing the outcome.

Those were the days before pay per view monopolised big sporting events so everyone could watch these type of events on their televisions for free. Well, Clay won, as most of us all now know, and as Muhammed Ali went on to become the greatest sportsman I have ever seen. As a boxer he was, in the sixties and for some time after, without equal in that sport and was always immensely entertaining whenever he was interviewed. I always looked forward to his fights and never missed seeing them. His athleticism and grace as a boxer were a sight to behold.

Whilst we are on the subject of fighting (although not the professional type), 1964 saw the start of what would be numerous altercations between two sets of teenagers. In one corner were the smartly attired, parka wearing, scooter driving, pill popping lovers of Motown and soul music known by all as the Mods. In the other corner were the greasy, black leather clad, motorbike driving, hair slicked back lovers of rock n' roll known as the Rockers. They did not get on. In fact, I think it is fair to say that they could not stand the sight of each other and whenever they clashed, as they did frequently, mayhem ensued. All much to the delight of the national press as well as to the horror of the hang 'em and flog 'em brigade.

The Easter weekend at Clacton saw the first major coming together of the two tribes and more would follow during the year at places such as Margate, Broadstairs and Brighton. All southern resorts you will note. We were much more civilised up north. Actually, we weren't really, it was just that we were a bit behind in our evolution (!) up here. Whilst there were major battles on the south coast, there were only minor skirmishes up here. In fact, I cannot recall one instance of a battle in Blackpool in 1964 so if they did occur, they passed me by. Not something that would befall my younger brother and his scooter gang in the seventies but that is for a different book and not one written by me. The whole genre of this type of clash of cultures (!) would be very well covered in the later film "Quadrophenia" which did, however, tend to overglamourise the conflicts a little. My sympathies, although I could not by any means claim to be a fully paid up member of the Mod group, always lay with the Mods as I liked their clothes and their music. However, I could only view this from afar as I was just a 14 year old schoolboy so much too young to be involved in those types of japes.

No, for me, apart from the school work and playing for the school rugby and basketball teams, my leisure activity in the spring of this year was ten pin bowling at the Savoy Bowl on the Promenade. A bit more refined than rocker bashing and not nearly as hazardous. A group of three or four of us would go to the Bowl on a Saturday morning if I was not playing rugby for the school team and we thought that not only was it good, harmless fun but we also thought that it might be a good place to meet girls. Whilst there certainly were some girls who went to the Bowl, sadly none of my group possessed the requisite chatting up skills so no liaisons were ever achieved. I enjoyed the games though and the Savoy did have a decent juke box so all in all those Saturday mornings are remembered fondly by me. Where would that elusive girlfriend come from, I asked myself? But no reply came. Would I be single all my life? Well I was 14 and thought that time was passing me by. At 14!

With my interest in girls increasing, I think this is now probably the appropriate time to bring down the curtain on tales of my boyhood hobby of trainspotting. I know you will have been waiting for this bit with baited breath so I will ease your anxiety and hold off no longer. Summer term at school usually brought the possibility of some sort of school outing and to my delight I found out that towards the end of term there was an organised trip to Crewe engine sheds. Wow, I can hear you say, bring it on. No, seriously, Crewe engine sheds were a mega attraction to any schoolboy, and indeed adult as well, trainspotter as the sheds housed many of the named engines which plied their trade on the West Coast main line and as such was a place any serious (was there any other sort?) trainspotter would give his eye teeth to visit.

Engine numbers, and possibly rare ones, would be there in abundance. Not only that, it enabled us to have a brief time on Crewe station, a major junction on the West Coast main line, in which to indulge our pastime as normally Crewe station did not actively encourage spotters in their hobby. They cluttered up the platforms with their anoraks, duffel bags, brownie cameras and notebooks. See, I can be self deprecating. Actually we did not dress like that at all. I might have had a jacket instead of an anorak. "It is just a lazy stereotype which defames the genuine hobbyist." (Quote from Ivor Notebook aged 14). Anyway, I was not disappointed by my visit. If I had to relinquish this hobby, Crewe was as good a place as any to lay it down. It had given me many hours of pleasure over the years but now was the time to move on. Well, particularly so as British Railways was vandalising it's own railway by sending practically all it's stock of engines to the scrapyards of Britain. Thankfully, a few far seeing people saved a fair number of different types of engines for posterity and if you ever do see a steam engine in full flow I am sure it will give you a flavour of what me and countless thousands of other kids got to enjoy.

My school year was drawing to a close with this summer term during which I had enjoyed the privilege of representing the school by playing as wicket keeper and opening bat in the school under 14 cricket team and also representing the school in the athletics team at the Town sports, where I came third in the triple jump and no, there were actually more than three schools taking part before you ask. Cheek. I was probably chosen for the triple jump because all the really good athletes in my year thought this was a naff event so couldn't be bothered to participate in it.

Personally, I was not big on athletics in general but found I was reasonably good at this event. I was a bit like a dog really, I needed a ball to chase to attract my full interest, hence my aptitude for football, rugby, cricket etc. or, alternatively, a girl would achieve this, but sadly there were no events featuring that activity. Well, not at the Town sports anyway. As for school work, thankfully I would soon be able to drop Physics (which for the life of me I couldn't understand), Chemistry (any experiments in the lab involving me had the potential to make Chernobyl look like a minor mishap) and Biology (I would only be interested in the practical side of this subject and preferably not involving rabbits). Language subjects would be my choice for the fourth year of school and beyond.

I have got ahead of myself here a little as there were still two football events which occurred at the end of this football season which had a significant impact on me. The first occurred on the 18th of April when what was to become my beloved Liverpool team won their first league title under the great manager that was Bill Shankly. A more charismatic man would be hard to find and he would inspire his players to run through brick walls for both him and the team's supporters, whom he idolised, none more so than those who stood at one end of the ground behind the nets on what was known as the Spion Kop.

For those of you who are unfamiliar with the name, it comes from the name of a hill which was the scene of a famous battle in the Boer War in South Africa and a number of football grounds had embankments at one end which were colloquially named after that hill. The most famous of these, and certainly the most atmospheric as I was later to discover, was the one at Anfield. I first noticed the supporters on the Kop when BBC showed Liverpool winning the league in 1964 and the sight of 26,000 Liverpool supporters singing and swaying on the Kop made me want to share that experience and watch Liverpool from that part of the ground. I would be fortunate to do so many times in the years to come, but that is for a later chapter.

The other football event of this season which impacted on me took place on the 2nd of May and was the Cup Final at Wembley between Preston and West Ham United. As a 14 year old, still mad on football, I would have gone anywhere to watch a decent game of football but every football fan in the country wanted to go to the showpiece finale at the end of the football season which was then (but sadly no more, having been demoted by Sky to a secondary competition and actually once ignored by Manchester United who deigned to take no part one year, unthinkable in 1964) the annual cup final.

To go to that match was the pinnacle of every fan's dreams. Even if it was not your team, it was still something a youngster longed to do and this was the year I got lucky. It was all thanks to my father who worked for what was then BAC Warton, near Preston, and he came home from work one day and announced he had two tickets for the Final courtesy of a workmate. Did I want to go? Is the Pope a catholic? Did Ghandi wear flip flops? You bet I wanted to go. I was not a Preston fan as such, but would willingly be an honorary one for the day. That is something else which would not happen today. Football is too tribal. You support your team and hope all the others lose. That's the view of most modern fans. A nonsense of course, but that is what has happened to my favourite sport. I, as all who know me can attest, am a fervent Liverpool supporter yet even I once paid my money to see Everton against Manchester United just for a chance to see the majestic, mercurial George Best in action. It didn't matter that I didn't support either team. I wanted to see what I now consider the best player I have ever seen in the flesh ply his trade. I wasn't disappointed. He would be worth untold millions in today's overpaid, overhyped game.

Anyway, back to the 1964 Cup Final. I anticipated a nice train journey down to Euston to see the match but unfortunately expenses, or lack of them, meant that we had to take an overnight Standerwick double decker coach from Rigby Road coach depot to London Victoria. Ah well, I thought, it's the Cup Final so I could put up with the discomfort of an overnight bus journey. Remember, these were the days when the motorway network was in it's infancy and the M1 only ran between Watford and Rugby so the majority of the journey took place on the non-motorway roads of England and seemed to go through every small town between Blackpool and Rugby, hence the overnight journey.

As I couldn't sleep on the bus, the journey seemed interminable at the time. We left Blackpool at 9.30pm on the Friday night and arrived at Victoria at about 6.30 am the next morning, I seem to recall. Only 8 hours or so to kill to kick off at 3pm! Well, as I was in the last throes of trainspotting at this time, I thought it would be a good idea to visit Waterloo station to see if there were any engines of the Southern Region to spot. After all, you would not see any of those trundling into Blackpool North. My father was less than enamoured at this suggestion, unsurprisingly, but reluctantly agreed to it. So, after a greasy spoon breakfast at some cafe we headed over to Waterloo by underground and as it was only still about 8.00 on a Saturday morning, much to my disgust, there were no southern region express trains at the station for me to spot. Big anticlimax, as I am sure my father no doubt thought. The result was that we whiled away an hour or two wandering the streets and taking in some of the sights before heading out to Wembley Stadium.

As we arrived there nice and early we were one of the first in once the gates were opened, so we got quite a good view from our vantage spot at the front of the second tier behind the goal where all the Preston fans were massed. There was the usual pre-game entertainment by the massed bands of some regiment or other marching up and down the sacred turf interspersed with some community singing by the fans conducted by a fat bloke in a white suit on a podium on the pitch (we knew how to enjoy ourselves in those days!) and the time flew by to kick off. No, it did, really. The game and the atmosphere generated in Wembley that day were actually very good.

At that time West Ham had an excellent side with the likes of Bobby Moore and Geoff Hurst in the team who would go on to become world cup winners just two years later and West Ham were firm favourites to win the Cup, but lowly Preston, then a division below West Ham, gave the London side quite a game only losing 3-2 in what was a thrilling match. Well, it was for us football followers.

Some of my readers (if I have more than one that is) may prefer something more exciting like ice-skating or souvenir collecting. It's all a matter of taste. Match over, trophy presented, it was time to wend our way back to Victoria for the overnight coach back home. My first Cup Final experience had ended and a thoroughly enjoyable one too. Wembley would provide me with some really magical moments in years to come, following Liverpool FC, but all that was for the future. For now, on leaving the stadium I had no idea when, or if, I would ever return but at least I had had a Cup Final experience to look back on. The journey back was as endless as ever but at least I could now get some sleep on the way home.

A week or so prior to the Cup Final, on the 20th of April in fact, there was launched a new TV channel called BBC2. The old BBC would now be called BBC1 and the nation now had 3, count them, channels to watch. Actually the new channel, although launched on the 20th of April, did not show any programmes until the following day owing to a huge power failure at Battersea Power Station that night, an inauspicious start. The idea was that the new channel would show more upmarket highbrow programmes, although I don't know where the demand for those type of programmes was coming from. Certainly not from this 14 year old for one, nor any of his mates.

In fact, in the schedule for that first night was apparently a performance from a Russian comedian. I kid you not. Now forgive me if I'm wrong, and I know Russia is famous for some things such as the Bolshoi Ballet, Caviare, Vodka, ballistic missiles etc., but I didn't know producing comedians was high up that list. Indeed, name me any Russian comedian known in the west and I will be more than amazed. Thought so. I mean, a Russian joke, what is one of those? (Reply: What occupies the last 6 pages of the Lada's Users Manual? - the bus and train timetables.) Perhaps a Russian comedian was the controller of BBC2's idea of an ironic joke. I didn't think the new channel would be engaging me much if this was the fare we could look forward to.

The other two TV channels for us common people were not

engaging me much either at this time as I was just so heavily involved in listening to music on the radio in the evenings. Comedy, in addition to the programmes mentioned in the previous chapter, came in the shape of a new BBC1 show called "The Likely Lads" which started at the end of this year featuring the adventures of two working class Newcastle lads and the scrapes they got into. It was a genuinely funny show and would run for 3 years, returning in the seventies as "Whatever happened to the Likely Lads".

Over on ITV, the main fare for me included a new science fiction show called "The Outer Limits" shown late at night and which always started with a sinister voice saying "There is nothing wrong with your television set. Do not attempt to adjust the picture. We are controlling transmission." It was really eerie and some of the episodes were quite scary, combining science fiction and horror quite skilfully with generally a twist at the end of each episode. Right up my street. I thoroughly enjoyed it. I also enjoyed "Danger Man" with Patrick McGoohan as secret agent John Drake and "The Fugitive" starring David Janssen as the falsely accused Dr. Richard Kimble and his quest to find his wife's real killer, a one armed man seen near to his home at the time of the murder. It sounds a bit tame now but it did make for quite an exciting programme and won many awards.

I can't leave the subject of this year's TV programmes without mentioning probably the last children's TV show that entertained me and which I thought was reasonably good, namely "Stingray". This was also produced by Gerry and Sylvia Anderson (of Fireball XL5 fame) with their supermarionation technique and featured Captain Troy Tempest as the commander of a sophisticated combat submarine and his encounters with underwater races (what do you mean you didn't know we had any?) including a mute young woman called "Marina" who could breathe underwater. (Think of a young Brigitte Bardot with gills). Gripping viewing eh? Actually, you would be surprised. It was fairly good back then. You had to be there, believe me.

With the approach of summer, however, there was only one event me and my generation anxiously awaited. The Beatles first film "A Hard Day's Night". It previewed on the 6th of July and was shown in my local cinema, the Odeon on Dickson Road, a short time later. I couldn't wait and went to one of the earliest showings. Now the Odeon cinema in the sixties seated 1800 and I can tell you that it was full for these showings. Not only full, but populated mainly by teenage girls who started screaming when the Beatles first appeared on screen. I was amazed. I thought that that was only something they did at the live shows but no, they couldn't contain themselves could they? Thankfully they didn't scream during the dialogue but they did start up again at the concert showing at the climax of the film. I mean, come on, it was only a film for heaven's sake, not a real live performance!

Actually, it gave me a glimpse of what I had been missing by not being able to see them live. If some girls were screaming at a film then what would the volume be like at one of their shows, I wondered? Anyway, I thought the film was fantastic at the time and it has retained it's humour and originality, as well as the appeal of all those marvellous songs, over the years and is still, in my opinion, the best example of this type of film ever made. Whilst it could not be a totally truthful version of what the group got up to (that would have needed more than an X rating), it did give fans a chance to see how the group lived part of their lives at the height of "Beatlemania" and was undoubtedly the highlight of that summer for me. The LP which followed is still one of my all time favourites and never loses it's appeal.

Contrast this film, which was so entertaining for my generation, with that year's summer shows on offer to the visiting holidaymakers. "Showtime" at the North Pier featured Mike and Bernie Winters (never one of my favourites, I thought they were totally unfunny) and a rising Liverpudlian comedian, Jimmy Tarbuck. Now I thought he was humorous at times. Central Pier had "The Al Read Show", I quite liked Al Read and his dry wit and the Winter Gardens had "The Dick Emery Show". He could be funny but not really to my taste. The Opera House had Ken Dodd who seems to have been playing Blackpool since the Tower was built. In fact I think that he laid one of the foundation stones. Finally, the plush ABC Theatre had "Holiday Startime" with Frank Ifield (no thank you) and Kathy Kirby (yes please! I wished). The ones mentioned above were, however, some of the biggest stars around in 1964 so provided top class entertainment for the visiting hordes.

As we are on the subject of entertainment, you have previously read how deprived me and my generation were when it came to pop music on the radio. Well, this all changed for us up here in the north in July of this year with the start of broadcasting by Radio Caroline North, a pirate (oh arrr!) radio station. The station transmitted from a boat moored off the coast of the Isle of Man which actually played pop music records without any restrictions. It was out of reach of those meddling politicians and unions. Radio Caroline South had actually started broadcasting in March of this year in the south and as we couldn't receive that station here, it's signal being too weak, we had to wait for our own station to start in July. You can't imagine how wonderful this seemed to me. By this time I had obtained my very own portable transistor radio so was not dependent on our old Bush radio any more, thank goodness.

Anyway, after having to listen to the hit and miss signal of Radio Luxembourg in an evening and with precious little on during the weekdays to suddenly have wall to wall hit records was manna from heaven. I was glued to the station and everywhere I went I took my new transistor radio with me. This was the forerunner of ipods and headphones but in this instance everyone you passed could hear what was playing on your radio. (Think of a small ghetto blaster to give you an idea of this type of radio). It would remain my staple listening until the pirates were eventually banned by the idiotic Tony Benn and his cronies in 1967, but more of that later. For now it was "the sound of summer with your favourite listening station, the sound of the nation, Radio Caroline"...or so the jingle went. They literally blew the fusty old BBC Light programmes out of the water, to coin a phrase. Well, they were pirates. Thank you. I'm here all week.

There were two major musical events in Blackpool that summer, neither of which I was able to attend, sadly, but the second of which was to have a lasting impact on my life, eventually. The first event involved those paragons of good behaviour in the sixties and the only serious rivals to the Beatles, namely the Rolling Stones. Let me set the scene for you. July in Blackpool was notorious as being the venue for one particular invasion from north of the border known to all as Glasgow Fortnight, an annual event long looked forward to with interest by the local Police force who would have the Glasgow gangs to deal with. They liked to visit Blackpool en masse and brought their inter gang rivalry with them.

You couldn't move on the Promenade during this particular fortnight without hearing the friendly greeting "See you Jimmy" and if you saw any Scots youths you gave them a wide berth if you knew what was good for you. They were not to be messed with. In fact, you thought twice before venturing down the Promenade at all during this period. Indeed, I well remember one day walking along the Promenade past the old Palatine Hotel near the Tower, which doubled in summer as a type of wild west saloon only more violent, when I noticed a youth of about 18 years of age, leaning against a wall casually cleaning his fingernails with a sheaf knife that must have been nearly 12" long. I soon picked my walking pace up I can tell you. Well, coinciding with Glasgow fortnight this year was a concert by the Rolling Stones held at the Empress Ballroom, venue for top class dancing competitions, on the 24th of July.

Seven thousand people were apparently packed into the venue for this concert including a goodly number of Glasgow's finest youth out for a good time, well what passed as their idea of a good time anyway. It would appear that as soon as the Stones came on stage some outbursts of violence took place between audience members. This may, of course, just have been one of the Scots gangs bidding a fond good evening to one of their rival gangs and wishing them a happy holiday, having earlier partaken of the odd beer or two, but then again perhaps not. It did, however, have the effect of giving the Ballroom a sinister air from the start.

According to the Stones, some of the gang nearest to the stage started spitting at the group. (This was well before the punk era, it must be said, when this activity was to become fairly usual and acceptable at such concerts so the Glasgow youths were well ahead of their time). Keith Richard, never the most shy and retiring member of the group, took exception to this and after "politely" asking the perpetrators to kindly desist from projecting bodily fluids at the performers (I paraphrase) and meeting no response, decided to take matters into his own hands. Not the wisest course of action, you may think, given the composition of the audience as alluded to above. His response to the bout of spitting was to plant his size seven boot into one of the Scot's youth's head as encouragement for them to desist.

Given that this was a Ballroom venue perhaps he thought he was performing a fleckle (ask Len Goodman about this) but it certainly failed to impress certain sections of the crowd. (I can just imagine Craig Revel-Horwood saying, on seeing Mr Richard's high kicking action "That was a disarster darling, the kick should have been much sharper and cleaner"). The rest of the band first looked on with horror at what was unfolding before them and then, when they realised that chairs and other missiles were now heading towards them on the stage, exited with the speed of Olympic athletes. From backstage they could hear the sounds of their equipment being trashed, cymbals being hurled through the air and a grand piano being given the last rites. Police reinforcements, having been requested, duly arrived and a jolly good punch up was had by all. The national press seized on this mayhem with relish and Blackpool Council were so horrified that they banned the Stones from performing in Blackpool for the next 40 years or so. The Council would eventually lift the ban in 2008, not that this would entice the band back here. I mean, you can't envisage the Stones performing at the end of North Pier now, can you?

The second event this summer was the appearance by The Beatles at the Opera House on the 16th of August 1964. An altogether more sedate affair, relatively speaking, than the concert by the Stones.

Nothing special in that, you may say, given that I was not there to see them and that it was not unusual for the group to play Blackpool in the summer season. Well, the importance of this show to me lay in my future. Present that day was my wife, who, of course, I did not then know, and she met a girl of the same age as her outside the venue, which girl would later become a long standing girlfriend of mine and who would, herself, eventually introduce me to my future wife one summer's day on the sunroof of Derby Baths. This is the coincidence to which I alluded in an earlier chapter involving my life and The Beatles, which you have no doubt long forgotten.

Had my future wife not met my future girlfriend at that show then our lives would have taken very different directions. Yes, I have a lot to thank The Beatles for, my wife, on the other hand, is still considering whether this chance meeting was a blessing or a curse! Only joking, I hope. I think it is probably a blessing when I behave myself (not often enough) and a curse when I am in trouble (all too frequently!). It just goes to show how life's little coincidences can lead to major events in your life occurring. Little did we both know that our futures were actually being mapped out that August night. My wife has fortunately retained both her programme and also her seat ticket stub from that fateful night, both of which are framed and have pride of place in my study. An ever present reminder (for us and our daughter as well) of that momentous occasion.

Returning to the subject of TV for one brief moment, I can't leave off mentioning the new BBC2 channel without remarking on one long running programme which started on that channel on Saturday the 22nd of August of this year and which I have enjoyed (mostly!) over the intervening years since then, namely "Match of the Day". This programme enabled football supporters, such as myself, to enjoy recorded highlights of a match from that day's football programme and the very first programme was from Anfield, a venue that was to become very familiar to me in years to come, and featured Liverpool versus Arsenal. Saturday nights would certainly be changed for this viewer from now on.

The start of the new school term in September was the beginning, for me and those of my year, of serious school work involving the build up to the GCE 'O' level exams which would be taken in 1966. This was something which our teachers were keen to emphasise. Slackening from pupils would not be tolerated and we would have end of term marks to show how well, or in my case how badly, we were all doing. Specific science subjects had been dropped by me (huge sigh of relief) in order for me to concentrate on the Arts subjects which were more suited to my mentality, such as it was. As I no longer had to take the science subjects, save for a nominal general science class which engaged my attention for all of zero minutes each week, I had to choose an additional language subject which for me was either German or classical Greek. Why I didn't choose German still puzzles me to this day, given both that I enjoyed French and that it would also have been useful to know what all the Germans were saying about us on the Mediterranean holidays to come, but no, I decided to go with classical Greek. A bit like Latin, not the most useful of languages when you are abroad, there being a positive dearth of ancient Romans and Greeks with whom to converse.

I can only think that I chose it because I was reasonable at Latin and no doubt thought that the same would apply to Greek. Absolutely no logic in that thought process whatsoever, so far as I can now see. So, for me and my other three fellow classmates (yes, three only, as all the other boys faced with this choice exercised common sense and opted for German) taking this subject we now embarked on a fairly intensive two years of studying this subject but what we did not know at the time, was that in the highly competitive world that was then the GCE exams, we would be facing pupils from other Grammar Schools and Public Schools who had been studying this subject for a damn sight more than two years. Consequently, although we didn't know it, we were at some disadvantage when the exams finally arrived, but that is for later.

School sport was, however, something which I continued to enjoy immensely possibly to the detriment of my academic work. At the start of the Autumn term I was appointed captain of the under 15 rugby team which I felt to be quite an honour. Now my daughter Anna, who has seen my escapades on the five a side football pitches for herself, can testify that I became a different person once any competitive game commenced. On entering any sports pitch I would become vociferous, bossy and a particularly sore loser (in fact on this last point I even had to beat Anna every time we played at "Hungry Hippos" when she was about five years old (bully) and even once disabled the battery in the game of "Operation", you know, the one where you need a steady hand to remove bits of a person's body with a small set of tweezers (cunning), to give me a strategic advantage!). Ideal attributes for any team captain, as I am sure you would agree. That was probably why the sports master made me team captain. He must have seen that streak in me!

The added bonus for me was that, as captain, I could also pull rank and take all the place kicks and penalties awarded to my team, something which, given my footballing background, I was fairly proficient at even though I do say so myself. Oh yes, the other attribute needed was probably immodesty! We were by now becoming quite a good team and won far more games than we lost. The annual fixture against Fleetwood Grammar School was always one I particularly looked forward to as firstly Fleetwood Grammar School was then a smallish mixed grammar school which meant that, sadly for them, they could not produce a very good team and were generally soundly beaten but the other, and more important reason, was that the after-game refreshment was always served by the girls of the school (very sexist I know) and very attractive some of them were too. Not that it got me anywhere in my long standing quest for female company, I have to say.

During the course of this year there was an end of an era of sorts for me as my maternal grandparents sold their fish and chip shop in Egerton Square in North Shore, just round the corner from our house, and bought a smaller one down South Shore. I think they were finding the Egerton Square shop too much work given that they were getting on in years and needed somewhere a bit quieter. I well remember that on Saturday lunchtimes in the summer (Saturday was changeover day at the nearby hotels and boardinghouses when existing guests would leave and new ones arrived and so no lunch was available for either set of guests that day) that queues for the shop would stretch round the corner down Pleasant Street for some thirty or forty yards. Totally unthinkable today in Blackpool. No longer would I be able to enjoy their delicious fish and chips every Saturday lunch if I was not involved in an away rugby fixture. I know I am biased but believe me, their fish and chips were extremely good and although the new owners, a Mr and Mrs Green, were reasonably good fryers, in my eyes they were not in the same league. I would, however, have cause to be grateful to Mr and Mrs Green in 1965 and you will find out why when you read the next chapter. Well. I have to keep giving you an incentive to read on, don't I?

October of this year saw a general election and the removal of the Tory government, after some thirteen unbroken years in power, it being replaced by a Labour administration under the leadership of that wily politician, Harold Wilson. I can't say that it engaged my attention much apart from my thinking that Wilson seemed somehow more in touch with normal, working class families than Sir Alec Douglas Home ever did, but that may just be perception. Wilson seemed to appear to have the common touch, whilst the outgoing Prime Minister seemed very much a part of the old, seemingly out of touch, aristocratic order. Well, that is how this soon to be 15 year old saw things at the time.

The other major political topic in November was the debate over, and subsequent abolition of, the death penalty for the crime of murder. Something which still divides people's opinions today. Back then, I was all in favour of it's abolition, but nowadays I am not so sure. In 1964, we didn't have lunatic religious fanatics wanting to assassinate innocent ordinary people and miscarriages of justice in other murder cases could also sometimes happen. The advance in technology has meant that today, forensically, the prosecution can mount a fairly conclusive case against a murderer, something they could not do in those far off days. I, personally, would impose the death penalty for all terrorist offences and I have no sympathy whatsoever for any perpetrators of such crimes. No, in 1964, regardless of the cold war then brewing, we as ordinary people going about our usual business, could do so without fear of any idiotic, brain washed, religious fanatics trying to impose their warped, illogical views on people. It was a much safer world for us all.

Back to something more jollier for the concluding section of this chapter. December saw the release of a new Beatles album as well as a single both, needless to say, eagerly anticipated by this now 15 year old, and probably more than a few others too. Still without a record player, I was relying mainly on the radio for my musical entertainment and a chance to hear the records and was not disappointed. The single, "I feel fine", was mainly a Lennon composition with an infuriatingly catchy hook and needless to say was soon occupying the number one chart position.

The LP "Beatles for sale" had the usual iconic sleeve cover and whilst not being among my all time favourite albums by the group, indeed some critics would argue that this would be their weakest album, if there could be such a thing as a weak Beatles album, at the time it was still considered a fine album with it's fair quota of great songs such as "No reply","I'm a loser", "Baby's in black" and "Eight days a week". It is only in hindsight that it perhaps fails to match the exacting standards of some of their other albums. The sleeve notes by the group's then publicist, Derek Taylor, do however contain one of my favourite lines written about the group and was very prescient for the time, when he said, on musing whether kids of the future would enjoy the album in years to come, "The kids of AD2000 will draw from the music much the same sense of well being and warmth as we do today. For the magic of The Beatles is, I suspect, timeless and ageless." Quite a different perspective than the one offered by my father at the start of this chapter and we all now know who was right, don't we!

This was the year when sixties music really blossomed and started coming into it's own with a wealth of terrific records of which my favourites were:-

1. The house of the rising sun - The Animals

2. Don't worry baby - The Beach Boys

3. A hard day's night - The Beatles

4. Can't buy me love - The Beatles

5. Walk on by - Dionne Warwick

6. I just don't know what to do with myself - Dusty Springfield

7. And I love her - The Beatles

8. Long tall Sally - The Beatles

9. Rag doll - The Four Seasons

10. Baby I need your loving - The Four Tops

11. You really got me - The Kinks

12. Do wah diddy diddy - Manfred Mann

13. My guy - Mary Wells

14. It's all over now - The Rolling Stones

15. Oh pretty woman - Roy Orbison

16. Baby love - The Supremes

17. Always something there to remind me - Sandie Shaw

18. I feel fine - The Beatles

19. Louie Louie - The Kingsmen.

20. I get around – The Beach Boys

1964 also saw some fantastic films released including:-

Goldfinger - the third of the Bond films with Honor Blackman and Sean Connery and definitely one of the best, if not the best.

My Fair Lady - George Bernard Shaw's Pygmalion brought to the big screen with Audrey Hepburn, Rex Harrison and Stanley Holloway.

A Shot In The Dark - the second of the hilarious "Pink Panther" films with Peter Sellers and Elke Sommer.

A Hard Day's Night - just the best pop music film, full stop.

Dr. Strangelove - Peter Sellers in terrific form playing a multiple of roles in this cold war comedy.

Mary Poppins - syrupy Disney musical definitely not to my taste although Dick Van Dyke as a Cockney was somewhat bizarre.

Zulu - Michael Caine and Stanley Baxter take on the entire Zulu nation in epic tale of the Battle of Rorke's Drift

CHAPTER SIX
1965

"People try to put us down, talking 'bout my generation" - The Who - "My Generation"

Whilst at the start of 1965, youth culture in the form of our music, fashion and ideas was now reaching full bloom and we began to think that society was changing thanks to the growing influence of my generation, to coin a phrase, for the older generation there was one event in January of this year which really did signify the end of an era for them, namely the sad news of the death of Winston Churchill on the 24th of January. This was, naturally, a major news event and even I, a callow youth of 15 at the time, could not fail to understand the importance of his passing. I was by now becoming increasingly interested in history at this time, thanks to the fact that it was one of the school subjects which engaged my attention and my passion for this subject has never left me.

I realised how significant an event this was simply by the amount of news coverage it generated at the time and whilst I was not, back then, fully acquainted with just how important a part Churchill had played, not only in the history of this country, but in the history of Europe itself, I was certainly to learn of this in years to come. He had, of course, been one of the greatest war leaders of the twentieth century and it is little wonder that those who had lived through the terrible years of the second world war were greatly affected by his death and wished to show their respect and thanks for what he had achieved. He had galvanised this country into, for a time, single handedly opposing the might of Hitler's formidable war machine which had swept through other European countries like a knife through butter. I wonder how he would deal with the terrorists and their supporters of today. Quite firmly, I would hazard to guess.

Such was the respect in which he was held that he was granted a state funeral by the Queen which was held on Saturday the 30th of January and, although I seem to think I was playing rugby that morning, I do distinctly remember seeing the news coverage of the funeral later that day and being immensely impressed at the organisation and spectacle of it. It must be said, however, that Churchill, whilst being revered quite rightly as a great war leader, was viewed by some members of the working class, my father amongst them, in quite a different light as a peacetime politician. The reason for this was the part he had played in breaking the miner's strike in 1926.

The mining community always regarded him with suspicion after that time and as I was from a mining family, indeed my father, my grandfather and my great grandfather had all been miners, I could understand why there was a certain reservation in how my father viewed him. It is not my purpose in this book to go into all the details of the miner's strike in 1926. Suffice to say that it involved the mine owners, both individuals and companies then, not the government as this was before the nationalisation of the mines occurred, wanting not only to reduce the miner's wages which had already dropped from £6.00 to £3.90 per week over the space of seven years, but also to increase their working hours as well, owing to a drop in demand for coal. The mine owners did not want to see their profits fall, but didn't bother themselves overmuch as to how the miners and their families would fare with this wage reduction. Churchill was a member of the cabinet which broke the strike forcing the miners back to work owing to the severe hardship they were then enduring. This would never be forgotten by the mining communities and impacted on their opinion of him. Nevertheless, they understood, as did all of the older generation, what a huge debt was owed to Churchill by the country at large and accorded him the appropriate respect. I can't imagine this happening to any other politician I have known since that time.

On a personal note, the early part of this year was to prove painful to me owing to two sporting injuries inflicted on me, one of which I suffered whilst playing rugby and the other, somewhat bizarrely, whilst playing basketball. As I have previously mentioned, school rugby fixtures took us far and wide in the north west and on one such occasion we travelled to Millom Grammar School just a little further north than Barrow, so quite a trek. Normally this was just an ordinary fixture, they generally had a decent team but one we could normally beat and so it proved on this occasion. We were winning the game when I received the ball and set off for the opposition try line when all of a sudden I saw stars and found myself flat on my back. A member of the opposing side had caught me with a stiff arm tackle right on the bridge of my nose! Now for those of you who are not familiar with this type of tackle I can tell you it is similar to someone hitting you with a stiff arm smash at head height while you are running past them. It is quite dangerous and totally illegal. Nowadays a player is sent off for this type of offence but it didn't happen in my match.

I slowly started recovering my senses following this assault but was extremely groggy and had blood pouring out of my nose. Game over for me. I watched the rest of the match from the touchline. I think I may have broken my nose as it was somewhat painful and I couldn't breathe out of it for a day or so. I had always had problems with my nose over the years, but this seemed to have exacerbated my condition. It didn't stop me playing rugby though. Injuries like these were just to be expected. Rugby players have never been noted for rolling around on the ground after they have been tackled, unlike certain footballers. You just generally got on with the game if at all possible. Mind you, I wish I knew who had delivered the offending blow. Revenge would have been swift.

The second injury suffered by me this year necessitated another visit to Blackpool Victoria Hospital. Not something you would expect playing a more genteel game like basketball. It all happened one lunchtime whilst playing a basketball house game against one of the other houses in school. These were generally held at the end of term and house teams were supported by other boys from the same house. As the game was in the school gym, the spectators were perched on the wall bars which were on one side of the gym and their vantage points were about six feet high. Unbeknown to me, a heavy cross beam with metal ends had been stood up on end leaning against the wall bars and during the game one kid must have inadvertently, well I hope it was, pushed or dislodged it causing it to topple over and as it fell the metal end caught me flush on the right side of my head. Now that did hurt.

I think I was unconscious for a moment or so and when I came to, I felt the warm trickle of blood slowly running down the side of my face. Needless to say, the game was immediately abandoned and an ambulance summoned to take me to casualty for a check up and stitches. I don't remember any anaesthetic being administered and the doctor just asked me to try and remain still while he went to work with his needle and cat gut. It smarted somewhat, I can tell you, and I still have the lump and scar to this day. No parents were informed of such happenings in those days. In any event, we didn't have a phone and carrier pigeon would have taken too long, so my mother was somewhat taken aback when I was deposited at home by an ambulance, still in my bloodied sports kit clutching my sports bag with my school uniform in it. Can you imagine that happening today? There would be a full inquiry and undoubtedly a compensation claim. As it was, I just considered myself lucky as the doctor who examined me said that if the bar had hit me square on the top of my head then the consequences could have been severe. My wife thinks I am dopey at times so the after effects may still be lingering. Only I could have a head injury playing basketball!

Talking of seeing stars, the space race was now proceeding apace and I followed each American launch with avid interest. On the 23rd of March of this year the first two-manned flight of the Gemini spacecraft was launched from Cape Kennedy and it orbited the earth three times. It was followed in June by the first American spacewalk by astronaut Ed White. The pictures of him outside the spacecraft performing the spacewalk, with the earth pictured below him, were stunning and I found it difficult to grasp the phenomenal speed at which he was travelling whilst actually being outside the space capsule. This certainly captured my imagination as I am sure it did for most boys of my generation.

In December, the Americans managed to achieve the first docking of a space capsule with another space vehicle. A manoeuvre that was essential if man was to travel to the moon. It is difficult, today, to give you a flavour of just how exciting the whole space programme was in those bygone days. We all now know that the moon launches, save for Apollo 13, were successful and the Skylab project, with astronauts spending months at a time in space, has meant that today's youngsters are probably not much engaged by the question of man living and working in space so I count myself fortunate that I was able to enjoy the whole space adventure from it's very start during the sixties culminating in the moon landing in 1969, of which more later, of course.

April of this year was an important date for me as at long last my house acquired a record player. Well, a radiogram to be precise. This was a piece of furniture that combined a radio with a record player and became obsolete towards the end of the seventies with the advent of the hi-fi and music centres. I was not complaining as at long last I would now be able to buy my own records and be able to listen to the music of my choice when I wanted to rather than relying solely on the radio or TV shows. The timing was perfect for me as it was just around the time of The Beatles new single release, "Ticket to ride", which became the first record I ever bought. I can still see it in it's green Parlophone record sleeve. I was in heaven. It was closely followed by my first album purchase, a second hand "Beatles for sale" LP from a kid at school. My record collection was now up and running and over the next few months I was able to buy all The Beatles previous albums to add to my collection.

Over the remainder of the sixties I would be a constant visitor to my local record shop which was Wisemans on Dickson Road, more or less opposite to the Odeon Cinema, as was. The record store had a couple of small booths in those days where you could go in and request a record to be played and it's sound would be piped to the booth you were in. I have to say that I did not use the facility much as I always knew which record I wanted to buy before going into the store but I would occasionally ask for part of an LP to be played if I was unfamiliar with some of it's tracks. This was the only way that you could listen, on demand, to music which you had not heard before.

It is all very different nowadays, of course, as youngsters of today don't even have to visit a record shop to hear or to purchase their music. They can simply listen on-line and either order cd's from such as Amazon or just download the music direct to their computers and phones. As I have commented before, I think my generation got more pleasure from the way we bought our music as it all seemed much more exciting than the way it is done today. I accept that it is more convenient to have music stored on portable devices but there is something a little clinical about the whole process. You can't replicate the thrill we had of going to the record store, handing over our six shillings and eight pence for a single or One pound twelve shillings and sixpence for an album(that's £0.33p and £1.63p respectively in today's currency) and taking your new acquisition home to put on your record player whilst gazing at the album sleeve and reading the liner notes. Not all at the same time, obviously! We weren't that clever.

If Wiseman's didn't have the record you were after, there were always plenty of other shops in Blackpool to try, including Lewis's on Bank Hey Street or Whiteley's on Deansgate, so you were generally able to obtain your record of choice without having to order it. Ex-juke box records could later on in the sixties be obtained from a stall in the old St. John's Market which was at the back of the old Bus Station and to which I became a frequent visitor as they had a new delivery of stock each week. As these were old jukebox records, you had to purchase a small triangular piece of plastic which you then inserted into the middle of the record so that it would play on your home record player as the middle part of the record had previously been removed to allow it to be played on jukeboxes.

Incidentally, I notice that I keep using the word "old" to describe many of the places I used to frequent in Blackpool as most of them no longer exist, for one reason or another, and the adjective "old" probably sums up my feelings in writing most of this book. On the plus side, I don't think the Council have any plans to demolish me just yet, but you never know with them!

Anyway, now that I had Radio Caroline, Saturday Club and Pick of the Pops on the radio as well as my miniscule record collection to listen to, together with the increasingly voluminous homework of anything up to three hours a night to get through, I found that I was spending much less time watching TV but this chapter would not be complete without mentioning some of the TV shows which caught my attention during the year.

One major comedy show had it's pilot episode shown this year, written by Johnny Speight it was called "Till death us do part" starring the late Warren Mitchell as the loud mouth bigot, Alf Garnett, a London docker with more prejudices than the whole of the National Front put together. Some of his rants were so over the top that they were, in fact, hilarious although there were some people who, although they found his attitudes and opinions funny, agreed with what he was saying. Now that was a cause for concern. Sadly the programme cannot be broadcast in today's politically correct environment even though both Johnny Speight and Warren Mitchell have both said that Alf Garnett's opinions were deliberately exaggerated to show how ridiculous those attitudes were. In my opinion, it vies with Hancock and Steptoe as amongst the funniest comedies of the sixties. Dandy Nicholls, as his long suffering wife, was a gem with her own little asides during the show. My favourite line from her was during a Christmas special when Alf was relating the nativity scene and how poor Mary had had to be put up in a stable to give birth as the Inn was full and Dandy Nicholls, deadpan, just said "No wonder the Inn was full. Well it would be, it was Christmas". Priceless.

Another comedy show which I enjoyed was an import from

America, "The Addams Family", featuring a very strange family with some macabre interests and who included a butler who was about seven foot tall called Lurch who said very little and also a dismembered hand which kept appearing, called "Thing". The show was loosely based on the Marx brothers and was very funny. The humour mainly lay in what happened when normal members of the public visited them and how they reacted to the family set up and was a two way thing as the Addams Family regarded normal folk as strange for not having their own weird tastes. Again, I found it extremely funny and the TV series did result in a couple of Hollywood films based on the family which you may have seen.

Adventure came in the form of two new shows. The first was "The man from U.N.C.L.E.", starring secret agents Robert Vaughn as Napoleon Solo and David McCallum as Ilya Kuryakin who worked for U.N.C.L.E. and who were always trying to thwart their adversaries from T.H.R.U.S.H. (nothing to do with any feminine virus I should add) who were trying to take over the world. Ian Fleming, the James Bond creator, had some input in the early part of the series, so you get the picture. It was extremely exciting and well done and I always looked forward to seeing the programme. Indeed, I believe some of the younger viewers, who thought the programme and characters were real (yes, I mean you Ellen Mumby) could write to join the organisation and wait to be called upon to assist our heroes in their perilous adventures! I don't know what they thought they could do if called upon, however, although I am sure my wife would, even at her then tender age, have been more than a match for a foreign agent! So successful was this programme that it was one of the first programmes to have merchandise associated with it, which I believe is extremely collectable these days, and even now the show has it's own website.

The final comment on TV programmes for this year must, however, rest with yet another supermarionation puppet show which, even as a 15 year old, I enjoyed and could be regarded as my guilty pleasure. "Thunderbirds" started on the 30th of September and was actually very watchable. This was a science fiction show again produced by Gerry and Sylvia Anderson and although you knew they were just puppets (no Ellen, they really were - she was in love with one of them, bless) the shows were very well done and ahead of their time for that period. You probably know the characters but if you don't, the series was set in the mid 21st century and followed the exploits of the Tracey family who were headed by multi millionaire Jeff Tracey who had five adult sons who each had their own particular machine and were together known as International Rescue. They were also aided by their all-knowing engineer called "Brains" (who looked like a fugitive from Form 2X at my school. You remember, the form with all the geeks in it except that this puppet was more lively than they were) and together they would rescue people from various dangers. I always thought that the machines were the real stars though. I think that kids of today would probably still enjoy this. Not sure if today's 15 year olds would be that bothered though.

My main interest, however, was not in TV shows, it was in the richly varied music that was being produced this year. Tamla Motown was now reaching what I, and I am sure many others, regard as the start of it's golden period which in my eyes lasted from 1965 to 1967. Such was it's increasing success and importance to the British music scene that there was even one special "Ready Steady Go" show hosted by Dusty Springfield on the 28th of April given over entirely to Tamla Motown and featured the artists who were currently on tour in Britain including the Supremes, Stevie Wonder, The Miracles and Martha and the Vandellas. The reason I say this was the start of the golden era of Motown is demonstrated by some of the releases from that label this year which included "Stop! In the name of love" by the Supremes, "Nowhere to run" by Martha and the Vandellas, "The tracks of my tears" by the Miracles, "It's growing" by the Temptations, "I can't help myself" the Four Tops, "Ain't that peculiar" Marvin Gaye, "I'll keep holding on" The Marvelettes, "I'll always love you" the Detroit Spinners, and "Take me in your arms" by Kim Weston. Each one of these is a timeless classic and many more were released that year, the majority of which were written by either the in-house writing team of Holland Dozier Holland, or the incredibly talented Smokey Robinson. The up tempo numbers will still fill dance floors today as soon as the first bars of any of those songs are heard.

Soul music also started to become popular amongst some music lovers, including myself, this year thanks to the Stax and Atlantic record labels and their first major star, Otis Redding. Broadly speaking, soul was the combination of R&B (not the rubbish that passes for it these days, I mean traditional R&B), gospel and pop. Rock solid rhythm sections, punchy horn arrangements and tight instrumental and vocal arrangements were also the frequent hallmarks of "classic" soul, much favoured by the mods of whom you heard earlier. The standout album which epitomises this sound and was released this year was "Otis blue" by Otis Redding. If you want to know what good soul music is, just give this album a listen. The album was recorded in a 24 hour session featuring the Stax house band of Booker T. & The MG's and the album appears regularly on the all time favourite album lists.

You can understand how fortunate my generation was in music terms when you consider the rich variety of styles we could appreciate in the sixties with not only The Beatles, The Rolling Stones, The Kinks, The Walker Brothers, The Who and The Hollies, to name a few, but also all the other British beat groups, as well as the American groups like the Beach Boys and the Byrds, the Phil Spector produced groups like the Ronettes and the Crystals, the fantastic dance music from Motown and the soul music from the American deep south. There was even the talents of a certain Bob Dylan to enjoy, if such was your taste. Personally, I like most of his music, but I know he has his detractors. We just didn't realise how lucky we were at the time to have access to all the marvellous music produced by these artists but what a soundtrack for us growing up in the sixties.

June, this year, marked a major milestone for me when, for a brief period of a week or so, I finally found myself a girlfriend. Well, I say found, she actually came courtesy of Mr & Mrs Green, the new owners of my grandparents fish and chip shop. She was a petite, blond 15 year old American girl, a relation of theirs, a niece I seem to think, who was staying with them for a short time whilst visiting this country on holiday. I think they had asked my mother, who worked for them in the shop and who knew me (the shop owners of course, my mother already knew me), if I would like to show their visitor the sights and attractions of Blackpool. When my mother first told me of this, I was a bit taken aback but thought hey, a girl, lead me to the water. So I duly went over to meet the young lady who was not only, to my deepest joy, quite attractive but she adored The Beatles too. We had something in common and hit it off straight away.

I was extremely happy to have some female company at last. The few brief days we were together went all too quickly for me as I enjoyed her company very much and the end of her visit culminated in Mr & Mrs Green treating us with tickets to The Bob Monkhouse Show at the Central Pier (don't laugh, he was extremely funny and very enjoyable) as well as paying for us to go to the Odeon cinema to see an American western called "Shenandoah" (quite boring, from what I recall) although I seem to think I spent most of the film trying to pluck up courage to put my arm around my new companion. How innocent I was. (This was all to change a year or so later, but whether all will be revealed you will have to wait and see.) The film finished and so I escorted my date back to her lodgings and was rewarded with my first real kiss. That certainly started my blood racing I can tell you. My first proper encounter with a girl had stirred my interest and how, and had left me wanting more! (Fifty shades of longing, I think it was). I was very sorry to see her go but for me it had been an extremely enjoyable episode. I couldn't wait for more of the same.

Summer term was drawing to it's close but there was some trauma in our house for a time when my father feared for his job. He was working at BAC (British Aerospace now) as an electrician on the Lightning aircraft at Warton aerodrome near Preston. Most of the work there depended on government orders for new military aircraft and the major new aircraft in the pipeline which would secure workers' jobs was a supersonic fighter/bomber by the name of TSR2. Following a change of government in 1964, the whole project had been reviewed and the new Labour government decided that the new aircraft was too expensive to build and it also had doubts as to the true capability of the aircraft. I remember my father coming home one day and telling us that the project had been scrapped and that the men feared for their jobs. Now whilst Blackpool in season was a thriving holiday resort, year round jobs, which were reasonably well paid, were somewhat rare. This period of uncertainty only lasted for a brief period, however, as thankfully new orders began to come in for the Lightning fighter plane so his job was secure for the foreseeable future.

So far as school was concerned, I was enjoying playing in the school cricket team this summer term which meant some Saturday and most Wednesday afternoons were spent either on the cricket field or having a laugh with my teammates on the boundary, if our side was batting. As ever, the bonus was missing some Wednesday lessons even if you had to cover the missed work at night, sometimes. I remember one occasion when my under 15 side had an away fixture at Rossall School. Most of you will know this is a public school situated between Blackpool and Fleetwood with it's own sports grounds attached to the school and the cricket pitch there was immaculate.

I had never been to that type of school before, we only generally played other grammar schools at sport, not public schools, so found the whole set up, including the sporting facilities, eye opening. The boys all seemed very posh to us grammar school kids and they all seemed to talk with a BBC accent which, of course, goaded us into being a bit more coarse than normal. If that was possible. In fact, I remember when tea was taken in a huge dining hall with long tables and benches that some of us, present company included, couldn't resist having a bit of a food fight until our sport's master intervened. I think they beat us at cricket that day but the tea interval more than made up for it. I don't recall there ever being a return fixture though, funnily enough!

As it was my final year before the GCE year at school, the teachers were trying to impress upon us how important it was that we do well in the end of term exams. I must have been deaf to their exhortations as, apart from Latin and Greek, I was well down in class positions in all other subjects culminating in a woeful 27% in the maths exam. The signs were not good and, as I came 20th out of 35 in my class, I wondered how many GCE exams I would eventually pass. You had to achieve at least four subjects, I seem to think, to be admitted to sixth form or, if these were not achieved, you could spend another year in the fifth form resitting exams. What, waste another year? There was no way I was going down that route. I think there was a bit of a discussion (putting it politely) with my father on the standard of my academic work when he saw my end of year report and he definitely thought I was spending too much time listening to the radio and playing my records. I told him that as I was the one doing the academic work then I would decide how I spent my leisure time and he would just have to trust me to improve next year. I was no longer prepared to be told how my life should be lived as I didn't consider that I was a child anymore. There was nothing he could say to that. Would I be able to deliver though? Read the next thrilling chapter for the result! See there is that cliffhanger again.

In those far off days the GCE exams here in the north west were under the auspices of a northern board known as the JMB (Joint Matriculation Board, to be precise) and were known to be quite tough. As an experiment, my school had allowed some of us to take the Oxford version of the GCE exam in English Language a year early, at the end of our fourth school year, as this was regarded as being of an easier standard than the equivalent JMB board exam. I was one of the ones allowed to sit the exam and was delighted when I learned that I had passed. One down, seven to go. I was taking eight subjects in all you see. Anyway, that mollified my father a little. We would have another battle in the coming year when my pursuit of girls began in earnest.

This summer also saw my first period, very briefly I might add, as an employee. One of my Aunties, who lived in Blackpool, had a brother who had started his own scrap metal business and at the time it consisted of just him and his co-worker. I was asked if I would like to work for him for 2 weeks in the summer while the co-worker went on holiday. As it meant earning some money to enable me to buy records I was eager to give it a go. Big mistake. When I turned in for work on the first day, Bill, my aunt's brother, explained we would be going to a scrap yard near Lancaster in his lorry and would have to collect the scrap metal there and put it on the lorry. "How would we do that?" I asked, thinking there would be some sort of machinery that would lift the metal on to the lorry. "You see those two shovels at the back" Bill said to me, "Well, that's our equipment." This didn't look good. We would both have to shovel the scrap metal up on to the lorry. This sounded like hard manual work to me. I was not disappointed. For what must have been a good couple of hours, but seemed like an eternity, we shovelled spadeful after spadeful of thin, twisted, waste metal strands from the ground up on to the back of the lorry. I discovered I had muscles that I never knew existed, each one of which seemed to be crying out in agony for me to stop what I was doing. All of a sudden school work took on a whole new attraction. If this was the real world, roll on September and the start of the new school term. I soon realised I was not cut out for manual labour. Something which those who know me can readily understand. Anyway, we finally completed the Herculean (to my eyes) task and went back to Bill's yard with the load. Come clocking off time he dropped me back home where I promptly deposited myself on our sofa and slept soundly for an hour or so. How I managed to get through the two weeks of work is a mystery to me and, I suspect Bill too. Strangely, he didn't ask me to work for him again and I can't say I blamed him.

Talking of summer, I haven't mentioned much about my activities during this particular period of time in past chapters so let me take you back into the joys of being a 15 year old in the summer season when Blackpool was in it's heyday. I have mentioned previously the attractions such as the Tower, the three piers, the beach and sea, the Pleasure Beach and the Golden Mile and it is the last of these which was to prove a lucrative stamping ground this summer for both myself and three or four of my school mates.

In 1965 the Golden Mile, which broadly runs from just south of the Tower to Central Pier and was neither golden or, in fact, a mile, was nothing like what it is today. In those days, there were numerous small amusement arcades, some of which sported children's rides, but which were mainly given over to slot machines, pinball machines and bingo games. I had already become a little addicted to the pinball machines and got quite good on one or two of them but my group mainly concentrated on the older amusement machines in which you would insert an old penny and have to press a button to try to get a combination of numbers or matching items, depending on which, the machine may then pay out respectively the sums of either three pence, six pence, nine pence or, the jackpot, one whole shilling. Not much nowadays you may say, but in 1965 a shilling was not to be sneezed at.

Anyway, my group had figured out that there was a cast iron way to win on these old machines. Don't ask me how we found the secret, as I can't recall, but the secret was simple. Just before a machine was due to pay out to a punter, if you listened closely to the machine, you could just detect a different sound being made as the penny dropped from the slot into the main part of the machine. I suspect, looking back, that the penny was being channelled into a different part of the machine, hence the different noise. We all knew these machines by our nickname for them which was "Droppers", what ingenuity!

So, we would arrange to meet on the Golden Mile at a certain arcade and then each one of us would casually stand near to one of these old machines and wait for an unsuspecting punter to have a go and we would then listen carefully for the sound the penny made as it was put into the machine. Think of the artful dodger in the pocket handkerchief stealing scene in "Oliver" and you will get the picture. As soon as we heard the machine making it's familiar, well to us anyway, "You will be a winner soon" sound we hoped that the punter would give up on the machine he was playing and move on to another machine before it paid out, sometimes even verbally encouraging them to do so by entreatments such as "This machine's crap, it never pays out, why don't you try that one over there". "Thanks," says gullible tourist, "I will." He, or she, duly exited from the machine and was followed very shortly by the sound of the machine as it spilled out it's pennies to one of my small group. The expressions on the tourists' faces when they saw this was priceless. We could teach Fagin's gang a trick or two and it was all totally legitimate. We were just using our local knowledge. Trouble was, the arcade owner or his security began to get wise to the same four kids keeping on winning on their old machines and although we had a good run for a few weeks, we were eventually barred from all the arcades if we went in together and as the arcade owners got wise to our trick they eventually ditched the old machines and replaced them with shiny new ones which made no discernible noises whatsoever. We were stumped, but we had made a few bob and had had a laugh. Cushty, as a certain wise old boy would one day say.

As we are on the subject of Blackpool's summer season, entertainment for those fortunate enough to holiday in the resort, and no, I am not being ironic here, you were indeed fortunate if you could afford a week or two in Blackpool, was provided on the North Pier by Tommy Trinder's Showtime (one for the older generation, again), Bob Monkhouse (who I have already mentioned) on Central Pier, Gerry and the Pacemakers on South Pier, The Jimmy Clitheroe Show (never understood his appeal) at the Winter Gardens, Thora Hird and Freddie Frinton in a comedy show called "My perfect husband" at the Grand and last, but not least, the very funny Morecambe and Wise at the ABC. Something for everyone in that line up and just one of the reasons why Blackpool was such a big draw for the general public.

In the sixties, most northern towns had their "Wakes Week" where very often the whole town would shut down and most would decamp for their annual holiday to resorts like Blackpool. You could generally tell which Wakes Week was on by the accents you heard in town - for example Glasgow fortnight, mentioned in the last chapter.

However, for me, the major musical entertainment of this summer was provided by The Beatles new film "Help!" at the Odeon cinema. I thoroughly enjoyed the film, needless to say, and also the subsequent LP and single which I bought on the day of their release. The film is perhaps not as good as "A hard day's night" and a bit silly in parts but it did effectively introduce the first music video when "Ticket to ride", filmed on location in the Alps, came on screen. This was the very first taste of what MTV would eventually give later generations. The LP was, in my opinion, a vast improvement on "Beatles for sale" and included, in addition to the title track and the previous single "Ticket to ride", such quality tracks as "You've got to hide your love away" (Lennon's nod to Dylan and his influence), "You're gonna lose that girl", George's "I need you" and, of course, "Yesterday", the most covered song in history, I believe.

Talking of which, the latter song was performed by Paul McCartney for the very first time anywhere at Blackpool's ABC Theatre on Sunday the 1st of August when the group appeared on the weekly summer Sunday show that was "Blackpool's Big Night Out". Whilst I was at home, avidly watching the performance, little did I know that my future wife was sat in the audience, a fact that will always be remembered as she can actually be heard on the live recording of the song which appears on Anthology 2. If you listen carefully to the instrumental break, about half way through the song, you can distinctly hear the anguished cry of "Paul...". That was my wife. Forever preserved for posterity! I have thought of writing to Paul requesting royalties on her behalf or perhaps an acknowledgment on the CD sleeve at least but then again, maybe not. We wouldn't want fans turning up at our door seeking autographs, would we?

Shortly after this performance The Beatles headed off to America for their second American tour, the highlight of which was their appearance at New York's Shea Stadium before about 55,000 fans. A record for the time, as no performer had ever previously appeared in front of such a large crowd. The sound from the concert was primitive, to say the least, as there was no huge sound system or screens in those days. I am convinced that the American fans actually just wanted to be at the concert for a visual experience rather than an aural one especially given that, with the volume of screaming which occurred at each concert, the fans would have struggled to hear any actual music being played. In any event, what cannot be denied is that The Beatles, innovators supreme, had, by their appearance at Shea Stadium, invented stadium rock shows for good or ill, but this writer is certainly no fan of that genre. I think my wife knows how lucky she was to have seen the group at their performing height in a small theatre only two weeks or so prior to their stadium appearance before that huge crowd. I am certainly envious of her in that regard.

As we are on the subject of music, 20th August of this year saw the release of one of the most iconic records, not just of the sixties, but, in my opinion, of all time, when the Rolling Stones' song "(I can't get no) Satisfaction" hit the record stores. It had been released in America a few weeks before this date so, thanks to radio play, I was by this date very familiar with it and bought it as soon as it was issued. The one amazing fact about this record is that both Mick Jagger and Keith Richard, joint composers of it, didn't think it would be a hit single and were only outvoted on releasing it as such by the other band members and their record company. How they could think this was not single material beggars belief. It only goes to show that even the composers of the music are not always the best judge of the commerciality of the fruits of their labours. If you had to choose a top ten of sixties music I'm sure that this record would definitely be high on that list. Nowadays Mick Jagger acknowledges the song's importance by stating that it was this record which turned the Stones from just another band into a huge, monster band. I dare say that the record royalties have not been unwelcome over the years either. This was definitely music for my generation, to coin a phrase, again.

1965 was not all optimism and feel good factor, however, as one of the darkest events of the sixties was now unfolding with the arrest on the 7th of October of a certain Ian Brady. I, like most people at this time, had been fully aware of some youngsters in the north west having been reported as missing and of the Police having mounted searches to try to locate them. What neither I, nor the rest of the country, knew yet was the nature of the horrific crimes committed by Brady and his accomplice Myra Hindley. We were to learn of the depths of their depravity once they both came to trial the following year. As a child growing up in the fifties we were all given seemingly unlimited freedom with the sole warning of never take sweets from a stranger although I don't recall being told why. It was just something your parents impressed upon you.

In that era there never seemed to be any inherent danger involved in playing out either on your own or with your mates. Even as a child of eight or nine you could be left to your own devices, often only turning up back at home at meal times. Brady and Hindley were, I think, the first to take away part of this innocent world from children and following the revelations at their trial, the freedom previously afforded to children had now suffered it's first check. They were, of course, to escape the ultimate punishment following the abolition of the death penalty but if ever there was an argument for it's retention then this case would have provided ample justification.

The 29th of October this year was an important milestone for me when I reached the age of 16 and not only could I legitimately go to see "X" rated films at the cinema (I had in fact been doing this for at least the past 12 months as had most kids my age), but I could now have a drink in bars! No, the age of consent hadn't been lowered especially for me, it was still 18, I had simply now grown up enough to bluff my way into any bar or club with my mates. This was in an era when, if you looked old enough, then the bar staff accepted you and I have to say I was never once asked for my date of birth.

My new adult-type freedom now enabled me to go to the first disco I ever encountered which was held at the newly opened Blackpool Mecca. If, by any chance, anyone reading this has never heard of the Blackpool Mecca then I can tell you it was situated on Central Drive near to the football ground. Once you went into the main entrance and paid your entry fee you went up a long escalator to the first floor on which was situated the huge dancing area with a Hawaiian type bar at the far end of the dance floor and upstairs there were seating areas from which you could look down on the dance floor.

I well remember my first visit to the venue shortly after my sixteenth birthday in the company of some of my mates and some older boys. I fully expected to be challenged in the bar as to my age but no, nothing was said and I had my first drink, a half pint of beer. I was not overly impressed with it's taste and soon drifted on to a drink that was becoming popular, lager. I much preferred it's taste but at this time lager was mainly just sold in bottles, draught lager was still in it's infancy, as I recall. Thursday nights were the nights I, and most of my generation, used to go to the Mecca but at the end of 1965 the music played on the main dance floor was just the standard pop music. The DJ there at that time had not really discovered the joys of Motown. This would come later, in 1967, with the advent of the opening of the Highland Room, of which more later. Sadly, the Mecca building was demolished in 2009, but it will forever be remembered by me as having provided me with my first tenuous steps into adulthood.

Autumn term at school arrived, as usual, at the start of September and ushered in for my class the pivotal GCE year. This was the year that would either see me go into the sixth form in the next school year, with a possible chance of going on to University or, alternatively, either languishing for another year in a class devoted to repeat exam takers and known as 5 Removed or even, more likely, leaving school altogether if the exam results did not go to plan. I realised that this was a major year for me so decided it was time to get my head down, save for Thursday nights at the Mecca and my sporting activities, obviously, and devote myself to studying. My new form was known as 5 Alpha and our form master was our somewhat dour Geography teacher, Mr. Fullelove. He wasn't the one you had to be wary of this year, though, that honour belonged to our Maths teacher, a certain Mr. Ernest Makin, or Ernie, as we called him. Well, at least we did when he was well out of earshot. No, Mr.

Makin was not someone you wanted to get on the wrong side of if you wanted to stay healthy.

If I can describe Ernie for you, I would say, looking back, that he was a more genteel version of "Bluto" from the Popeye cartoons although he was possibly a bit larger than Bluto. He certainly had more stubble. I have no doubt that he shaved everyday, it was just that you could virtually see his beard growing as he taught. He was also deadly with the dreaded wooden blackboard duster should any boy have the temerity to misbehave in class. It didn't matter where you were sat, his aim was so accurate. He would have been marvellous on "Bullseye".

I had a bit of a reputation in class as a joker who could always be relied upon to inject a sharp witticism to enliven any boring lesson but even I paid undivided attention in his lessons. I distinctly remember walking down a corridor in school one day and I passed Ernie, who was holding one boy up in the air by his jacket lapels, the boy's feet dangling about a foot off the ground, whilst Ernie gave him the most severe tongue lashing I had ever heard. I think the boy had dropped a pen, or something. Only joking, but you didn't mess with Ernie. I do, however, have him to thank for eventually passing my maths GCE as he just terrified me into learning the subject. You certainly tried to ensure your homework was correct. His teaching methods, not to say anything about his air of menace, would, of course, be totally forbidden today but it worked for me so thank you Ernie. I also knuckled down in all the other subjects this term and actually received my first reasonable end of term report since I had been at this school. I was still rugby captain but had not let this interfere too much with my studies. I was determined to try to keep this attitude up for the remainder of the academic year and being miserably hopeless at attracting a long term girlfriend certainly helped considerably in this respect. Sadly.

I can't leave this year without remarking on both The Beatles final album and also the single record releases in December. By now, the release of any Beatles music was an important event for me and the impending release of the Rubber Soul LP and the new single was no exception. With the album containing the quality of the songs on it's two sides, the group were again leaving all their contemporaries far behind. Not only were the songs of matchless quality, we were hearing new instruments in pop music, such as the sitar on "Norwegian Wood", for the first time. The album contained classics such as the song already mentioned together with "Drive my car", "Nowhere Man", "Michelle" and the beautiful "In my life". Any one of these could have merited a single release but the group instead issued a double "A" sided single as well, namely "Daytripper" coupled with "We can work it out" on the reverse side. Again, I just had to have these records on the day of release. Waiting for Christmas just wouldn't do.

A trip to Wisemans soon provided me with my latest fix and Rubber Soul still remains one of my favourite albums to this day. The single wasn't too shabby either. As I have already said, we were certainly spoiled by the quality of music produced this year and fittingly, given the title and emphasis of this chapter, one of the last albums to be released this December was "My Generation" by The Who. Another "must have" purchase by me. The lyrics of the title track summed up perfectly what me and others of my age felt at the time.

Although we have all long since "grown old", my generation was one of the first to still feel young at heart when reaching their own sixties milestone. The terrific music of this year still remains fresh to these ears and, to me, will forever remain so. Talking of which, as we are at the end of the chapter, it is "my favourite record" time again. 1965, probably more than any other year in the sixties, provided a wealth of truly brilliant singles so in view of the sheer volume of quality singles released, here is my somewhat lengthened list of favourite singles with the odd album track thrown in :-

1. California Girls - The Beach Boys

2. Help! - The Beatles

3. Ticket to ride - The Beatles

4. Yesterday - The Beatles

5. Like a rolling stone - Bob Dylan

6. Mr. Tambourine Man - The Byrds

7. Some of your lovin' - Dusty Springfield

8. I'm alive - The Hollies

9. People get ready - The Impressions

10. California Dreamin' - The Mamas and the Papas

11. Nowhere to run - Martha and the Vandellas

12. Respect - Otis Redding

13. My girl - Otis Redding

14. You've lost that loving feeling - The Righteous Brothers

15. The last time - The Rolling Stones

16. (I can't get no) Satisfaction - The Rolling Stones

17. The tracks of my tears - The Miracles

18. Stop! In the name of love - The Supremes

19. Make it easy on yourself - The Walker Brothers

20. In the midnight hour - Wilson Pickett

21. Daytripper/We can work it out - The Beatles

22. Norwegian wood - The Beatles

23. In my life - The Beatles

24. Mr. Tambourine Man - Bob Dylan

25. I've been loving you too long - Otis Redding

In addition to the music listed above the notable films released this year included :-

Darling - starring the luscious Julie Christie as a model. What's not to like in that scenario?

Thunderball - the latest Bond epic (passable but not up to "Goldfinger" standard).

What's New Pussycat - a somewhat bizarre comedy but with a very sixties feel to it.

The Sound of Music - but if you think I ever went to see this then you are very much mistaken.

Help! - The Beatles loon about and invent the music video.

The Cincinnati Kid - An American drama featuring poker players and starring Edward G. Robinson, Ann-Margret and the brilliant Steve McQueen

Doctor Zhivago – another epic David Lean drama set in pre-war Russia and starring Omar Sharif and the beautiful Julie Christie, again, with some stunning cinematography.

CHAPTER SEVEN
1966

"There's some people on the pitch, they think it's all over...it is now, it's four." Classic line from commentator Kenneth Wolstenholme on BBC1 as England score their fourth and final goal in the football World Cup Final.

Just as, in my eyes, the nineteen sixties were for my generation, a golden period, then 1966 was, for me, the most memorable year of that astonishing and exciting decade. In fact, if I had to choose one year to relive from my whole period as a teenager then this would be the year I would choose. The music of that year, as I will discuss later, was not only prolific but also quite incredible, producing some of the best songs and albums of all time. As if this was not enough, the year did, of course, have the World Cup, held in England and which culminated, as we all know, in that never to be forgotten day at Wembley when England were crowned World Cup Winners. When will that happen again eh? Not in my lifetime, I venture to suggest. I dare say that the sun also shone all summer as well, it certainly seemed that way. England, both culturally and from a sporting perspective, appeared to be at the centre of the western world and as a sixteen year old, enjoying this to the full, I was in my element. Looking back from this distance I am probably viewing this particular year through "rose tinted spectacles" of course, but leave me with my memories. I only have to hear some of those songs from that year and I am instantly transported back to the epicentre of the "swinging sixties".

It probably wasn't sunny on Saturday the 1st of January, however, when the new year was ushered in. Being 16 years old I probably woke up mid morning to catch the remainder of Brian Matthew's Saturday Club on the radio which that day featured the Merseybeats,

Hedgehoppers Anonymous (What, you've never heard of them?) and Acker Bilk and his jazzmen (Groovy baby, I don't think) and no doubt I decided that I would have been better off staying in bed. I was no longer totally reliant on the radio for my music fix so would no doubt have switched this programme off and put "Rubber Soul" on the turntable for some quality listening, whilst pondering what this year would hold for me. This was the year that would have a considerable bearing on my future. It was my GCE year and the last year I would spend as part of the Lower School. I was determined not to slacken in my academic studies this year and as part of that ethos I decided that after school, instead of being subjected to any distractions at home, I would go to the Reference Library, above the main Library on Abingdon Street, and do my school homework there. It would be nice and quiet, or so I thought.

The Reference Library, as was, has now gone. In those days you would go up the stone staircase leading from the main entrance and on the top floor of the building enter the hushed tones of that part of the Library where there was generally one, possibly two, librarians presiding over a long room of double sided desks which had space for five or six seats together on each side of the desks. You would have a fair amount of room to spread your work out on the desk and, should you need it, reference books for use located on the shelves all around the room. This was very useful in those pre-internet days. Imagine, we actually had to do our own research for our studies instead of copying down some basic information from Wikipedia and then pinching someone else's ideas. A bit like a Labour leader's speech, if you know what I mean. I don't know how we managed. (Ironic pause).

I thought that this would be an ideal working environment for me, and it was, until one or two of my mates started showing up. Once that happened, we generally started messing about much to the annoyance, and quite rightly, of the other people using the Library. What made it even worse was that on some occasions one or two of the local tramps decided to seek warmth and shelter in the Library, it was winter after all, and there was no way you could carry on working if they sat down near to you as the smell emanating from them was something to behold. There was also one old boy who had a habit of banging the desk in time to him reading aloud from whatever book he had picked up and this just made us collapse laughing at his antics in this hallowed room. All good fun but not entirely conducive to serious study. Nor was serious study helped by the fact that there were generally one or two attractive girls also using this part of the Library for their own studies. It improved the surroundings though, I must say. In spite of all this, and especially as we had no central heating at home which meant that I couldn't use my bedroom easily for study purposes without contracting hypothermia, then for the next few winters the Reference Library became my second home.

My conscientious attitude should have impressed my parents but I was not altogether a 100% committed student as I did have, shall we say, outside interests and on one occasion these were to prove a matter of "debate" with my father. Now whilst the sixties were in general exciting and interesting, the one major exception to this was Sundays. My god Sundays could be boring. There was little on the three TV channels for teenagers and the pubs would shut at 10.30pm. Not that I inhabited them on a Sunday night you understand, well I was still only sixteen and not into pub culture at all, such as it was then. I did want some relief, however, from the tedium of a Sunday even if it was the end of the weekend and school beckoned the following morning.

On this particular Sunday myself and a mate of mine had been to a coffee bar in town and had got chatting to a couple of passable girls with whom we then spent the rest of the evening. As the coffee bar turfed us all out at about 10.30pm we decided to prolong the evening with the two girls in that most romantic of sixties venues, a recessed shop doorway. This one was, I seem to recall, on Dickson Road near to it's junction with Talbot Road. Things had just started to get a little bit interesting with my female companion, and I was trying to remember what I had learned from the Biology textbook, when, to my horror, I heard a more than familiar voice shout "Alan, what are you doing? It's time you were home, you have school tomorrow." Great line that, guaranteed to impress any female! Can you believe it though, my father had actually gone looking for me as I hadn't come home and as ill luck would have it he had actually located me in that shop doorway and that is no lie. My female companion consequently made a speedy exit and I was left with steam coming out of my ears.

To say I was livid would be the understatement of the decade. As if it wasn't bad enough that my practical Biology lesson had been so rudely interrupted, just as excitement had been mounting, I had also suffered the humiliation of being called back home like a naughty schoolboy. Oh, I forgot, I was! The upshot of all this was that when I got back home a heated discussion ensued between myself and my father on the proprieties of keeping reasonable hours during school term time. Speaking now, as both a parent and also as someone with more than a few years behind him, my father was, of course, totally right in his viewpoint. Speaking as a then excitable sixteen year old who had been on the verge of finding out what those rabbits actually did get up to in the Biology textbook, I could have murdered him. On which side do your sympathies lie, I wonder? Before you answer, remember you too were sixteen once.

My night time activities did not, however, have any detrimental effect on my studies. My hard work was beginning to bear fruit and at the end of the spring term, apart from Greek, I was achieving reasonable marks in all my other subjects which boded well for the forthcoming exams. Ernie, the maths teacher, had commented that my 51% mark was a satisfactory result but went on to say in his end of term report that "he cannot afford to relax his efforts". A superfluous comment in my eyes as I could have assured him that the only thing that I could have relaxed in his lessons was my bowels when he picked up the wooden blackboard duster and looked for his next target. He always had my undivided attention. In fact he had the whole class' undivided attention.

In addition to my conscientious attitude to school work, I was still rugby captain but this would be the last term I would enjoy this position as my old passion, no not girls, football, came to the fore. All that is for the next chapter though. For now, as spring term drew to a close, my rugby year ended when I was chosen to play for the school first team in April, a team which mainly consisted of 18 year old boys, so two years older than me on the whole, in the school's annual fixture against a team of Manchester University first year students who were, in turn, one year older than our first team. I was honoured, especially when we won and I scored one of the tries. The first team rugby master was suitably impressed and I knew that next year, if I made the sixth form, then I would undoubtedly be playing for the school first team.

What of my favourite group, I hear you ask. What were they up to this year? Well, little did we know it at the time, but 1966 was to be the last year that The Beatles would perform properly to a live audience. That event would occur in San Francisco on the 29th of August. I was still waiting for the ridiculous screaming to die down so that I could possibly go and see them and be able to hear what they were playing. Sadly this would remain an unfulfilled ambition and, of course, if I had known this at the time I would have done all in my power to have obtained a ticket for one of their numerous Blackpool shows and just put up with my wife's and her female compatriots' impersonation of a 747 jet airliner taking off.

Although during this spring, while the group were between records, so to speak, John Lennon gave what would prove to be a fateful interview to a journalist, Maureen Cleave, on the 4th of March during which interview he commented about Christianity and said that he believed, at this time, that the group were more popular than Jesus was. Well, in fairness, Jesus had been dead for some time and had not had any hit records of late. (Come on, it's only a joke. Monty Python got away with more). This comment was, of course, totally unremarked upon in this country but in the bible belt of that most hypocritical of countries, the good 'ole US of A, it was akin to someone having poked a wasp's nest with a stick.

When someone eventually noticed his comment, some months

later, and took it out of context, it created quite a furore. The Beatles were due to tour America in the summer and actually feared for their lives, such was the furore they had created. There have been many contradictory stances taken by Americans over the years, for example the paradox of the commendable sentiment embodied in the line from their constitution which states that "All men are created equal" yet in 1966 a black American citizen was still being subjected to racial discrimination on so many levels. Some men were obviously more equal than others. Indeed, a black man called James Meredith had been shot dead this year in Mississippi by a white man for having had the temerity to hold a one man march to try to encourage blacks to vote. Yet the white southerners were outraged by a throwaway remark made by a musician about Christianity. The mind truly boggles.

Incidentally, even as a sixteen year old I could not understand what difference the colour of someone's skin made. I still can't, some 50 or so years later. Take my love of music, some of the best musicians ever were black. In fact, we probably have the black Americans to thank for our music today, and no I don't mean the deranged mutterings that pass for rap, thank you. I mean the likes of Robert Johnson, Elmore James and their contemporaries. Bluesmen par excellence. The blues music they started in the deep south ultimately led to the creation of rock 'n roll and the blossoming of the various types of music in the sixties. They ultimately influenced musicians such as the Rolling Stones, Eric Clapton, Jimi Hendrix and countless others, to say nothing of the artists who appeared on the Atlantic and Stax labels, as well as Motown.

Talking of music, there was one singer who came to prominence this year and who had, in my opinion, one of the best voices to grace modern music, namely the incomparable Scott Walker. You will remember, if you were paying attention and hadn't fallen asleep, that I did include a Walker Brothers' record in my list of 1965 records in the previous chapter but 1966 was when this singer and his other two group members really reached the peak of their popularity. Indeed, such was their success that, for a time, the members of their fan club actually exceeded those of the Beatles, hard though it may be for you to now imagine.

I had first heard Scott's unique voice the previous year and liked it so much that I had bought both their number 1 single "Make it easy on yourself" as well as their 1965 album "Take it easy with the Walker Brothers" but there is no way I would have braved a Walker Brothers' concert to see them live. Although I was a rugby player, I would not have dared experience one of those concerts. No, I valued my health and my hearing. The Beatles' concerts were apparently like a tea party compared to the frenzied female behaviour which occurred at a Walker Brothers' concert and my wife was, with her friends, one of the chief protagonists and fully paid up member of that particular fan base. If Scott Walker sneezed, she knew about it. I was just happy to hear the music and this year the group gave us an all time classic with their record "The sun ain't gonna shine anymore". It shot up the charts and was followed by their second album "Portrait" which I can still enjoy today. Scott's voice, coupled with his brooding good looks, ensured total female adoration. To put it mildly. I just enjoyed the music but I also wished I resembled his looks a little, given how girls were falling over themselves to see him. A girl did once remark to me that she thought I looked a bit like him, honestly. Her guide dog made no comment.

Back in the serious adult world 31st March saw another general election. The Labour Party had not had a very large majority following the last election, in fact their working majority was only four, so ever the opportunist, Mr. Wilson chose this date to try to win a more substantial majority and succeeded, obtaining a majority of 98. I was more interested in this election than any previous one but was still not old enough, of course, to vote. I can't say that the election result had any immediate impact on me personally at that time but it did the following year when that major buffoon, Tony Benn, abolished our much valued pirate radio stations. That was all for the future though, for now and happily in complete ignorance of what Labour intended, I could enjoy the wonderful sounds of Radio Caroline. You will find it hard to appreciate how much the pirate stations meant to my generation given the plethora of music channels that are around today. You have an incredible choice of what type of music you want to listen to but back then, during the week, we effectively had one commercial station during the day but were joined by Radio Luxembourg at night.

There was one slight exception to this, however, as at night, if the atmospherics were favourable, you could pick up a broadcast from Radio Caroline South and many's the night I took my transistor radio to bed and listened surreptitiously to Johnnie Walker on his late evening show, under the bed covers. The reason was simple. Johnnie had a great taste in music and on his show you were guaranteed quality listening to the latest soul and Motown records amongst others. He was not one of those disc jockeys who were obsessed with the sound of their own voice, an all too frequent occurrence these days I'm afraid, and from what I recall he played plenty of records in his show. Ideal relaxation for me as I settled down in readiness for the next school day and the impending GCE exams. Johnnie would later be employed on the new BBC music station Radio 1 which launched in 1967, but all that is for the next chapter, for now it is sufficient for me to acknowledge Johnnie as having played a major part in nurturing my love of soul music thanks to his show.

Talking of which, I think now is an opportune time to remind ourselves of the classic soul records which were released during this year. These included Carla Thomas singing "B-A-B-Y", Don Covay with "See saw", James and Bobby Purify with "I'm your puppet", James Brown's "I got you", Eddie Floyd with "Knock on wood", Lee Dorsey with "Working in a coalmine" and "Holy cow", Percy Sledge with two all time favourites "When a man loves a woman" and "Warm and tender love", the dynamic Sam and Dave with "Hold on, I'm coming" and "You don't know like I know" and last, but not least, the wicked Wilson Pickett with "Mustang Sally" and "Land of 1000 dances". Truly a golden period for this type of music.

Tamla Motown was also in it's heyday and treated us this year to the release of amazing records such as Edwin Starr with "Headline news" and "Stop her on sight", the Four Tops featuring Levi Stubbs' amazing voice on "Shake me, wake me" and, one of my all time favourites, "Reach out, I'll be there", Jimmy Ruffin with "What becomes of the brokenhearted", Junior Walker with "I'm a roadrunner", Marvin Gaye singing "Little Darlin' I need you", "One more heartache" and duetting with Kim Weston on "It takes two", the Supremes featuring the voice of Diana Ross on "You can't hurry love" and "You keep me hanging on", the Miracles with "Come round here, I'm the one you need" and the Temptations with four classics "Get ready", "Ain't too proud to beg", "Beauty is only skin deep" and "I know I'm losing you". Wonderful stuff, well it was to my ears.

But schoolboys did not live by music alone. No, they had exams to take, well this one did. June saw the start of the quite important GCE 'O' level exams and I was taking a total of eight subjects namely English Language, English Literature, French, Latin, Greek, Maths, Geography and History. The exams were generally each about two hours in length and apart from your book of Log tables for Maths, no other aides were allowed into the exam room. Furthermore, as far as I can recall, there were no multiple choice answers. You either knew your subject or you didn't. No course work either was taken into account. This was the ultimate test of what you knew, or didn't know. Marks, as the teachers were keen to impress upon us, would be deducted for bad grammar, poor punctuation and spelling mistakes. Thankfully bad handwriting was not punished otherwise I would have been struggling badly. That is unless they sent my answers to China for marking as my squiggles would probably have been understood there! It is, in fact, a mystery to me how the examiners ever deciphered my papers anyway. Perhaps they just guessed my answers!

I have to say that I was not overly bothered about the exams and had a philosophical attitude of que sera, sera as Doris Day might have sung. (Not in my record collection I hasten to add). Stress was never on my agenda when it came to exams but I was glad when they were all over. I remember that I always had a slight frisson of anticipation when the invigilator told you to turn your paper over at the start of each exam and you wondered what would be on the other side. My technique was generally to read the paper through first and then choose the questions to answer starting with the easiest first. Why waste time on the ones you would struggle with when you could start garnering marks immediately with the questions to which you thought you knew the answers? I would employ this technique on all my exams from this time on. Once the exams were over I had to wait until August for the results so a reprieve for a couple of months, at least, until my school fate was decided.

Thankfully there would be no chance of boredom this summer as on 11th of July the World Cup in England got under way. Non football lovers have my permission to skip the next few paragraphs. The tournament started with the opening match, England against Uruguay which was a complete anticlimax ending in a scoreless draw. The most anticipated group games, save for England of course, lay with those played here in the North West which included Brazil, then the reigning world champions with the peerless Pele the star of their team, and Portugal who were at that time probably the best European team going into the tournament, with their own mercurial star, Eusebio. The initial group games had not sold out and were not all ticket either, unthinkable today but not uncommon for matches in the sixties and beyond. After all, there was no Sky to overhype the matches and only true football fans actually wanted to go to the games. The prawn sandwich brigade had yet to be invented and corporate hospitality just meant a better class of pie and toilets that actually flushed. Brazil had, somewhat surprisingly, lost their opening match 3-1 to an enterprising Hungarian side which meant they then had a titanic clash with Portugal which they could not afford to lose. This would be at Everton's ground, Goodison Park, on the 19th of July and I decided to try to see this match live.

Although exams had finished, summer term was still ongoing so I had to rush home from school to catch a Standerwick coach from the small coach stand at the end of Pleasant Street, round the corner from where I lived and which was running a coach to the game. I thought there would be no problem getting into the ground as the other games had been played out to about three quarter full capacity crowds. How wrong was I on this occasion as when the coach pulled up near to the ground I noticed that the crowds milling around the ground seemed immense. I dashed off the coach and raced to the ground just to find the gates admitting non-ticket holders closing. Panic stations. Were there any tickets being sold at all I wondered?

I circled the ground and heard one chap offering a ticket at face value but before I could get to him some other fan had got there first. Ticketless, I walked slowly back to the coach only to be joined by a number of others who had also failed to get in. The Merseyside fans had decided, like me, that a showdown between Brazil's Pele and Portugal's Eusebio (think these days of Messi and Ronaldo and you may get an idea of how good those two were) was too good to miss and had turned up in their thousands. It is hard to convey accurately the disappointment of having travelled so far to see the best two players in the world on the same pitch and to be thwarted in your goal. Pubs in those days did not have TV's and there was no coach radio. I hadn't taken my transistor radio with me either so I was well and truly stuffed. I was only slightly mollified when the game finished and those that had actually got in reported that Pele had been kicked by the Portuguese defenders so badly that he only lasted twenty minutes before being carried off so some small consolation that I had not missed seeing him play the full match. More than fifty years later I still regard him as the best footballer I ever saw, but only on the TV and not live. That honour would belong to Manchester United's G. Best and for a Liverpool supporter to admit to that is saying something indeed.

That was my only attempt to see one of the World Cup matches live. I decided that for the future, sat in front of the TV was now the best bet and I didn't miss a game from then on. Although football wasn't the global phenomenon it is today, the 1966 tournament generated great excitement in this country, particularly when England started playing well and started winning. As the tournament wore on the unthinkable suddenly occurred to the nation. We could actually win this thing. What, England winning a world cup! Alf Ramsey, the England manager, had actually fashioned a skilful side who were extremely hard to beat with a world class goalkeeper in Gordon Banks, a world class defender in Bobby Moore and a world class forward in Bobby Charlton. The other players weren't bad either and included in their ranks a young Alan Ball and every Liverpool fan's favourite player at that time, Roger Hunt. After England won a bad tempered quarter final match against Argentina and defeated the talented Portuguese side, Eusebio and all, thanks to two Bobby Charlton goals, England reached the final to face an equally skilful and resilient West Germany who had strode imperiously (did Germans ever do anything else?) to the final held on the 30th of July. A date forever etched in all England football fans' memories.

We all, of course, know now that England won but let me take you back to that long ago summer Saturday afternoon. Most of the nation were avidly sat before TV screens watching either BBC1 or ITV and fervently hoping for an England win. I had rushed home after my summer lunchtime job (see later paragraph) to be in front of the TV with my father, uncle and a cousin who were over from Lancaster where they lived. The game was a rollercoaster and having initially conceded the opening goal to West Germany we were thankfully leading 2-1 going into the final minute of the game when the referee awarded the Germans a somewhat fortuitous free kick on the edge of the England penalty area. Surely they wouldn't equalise with the last kick of the match. They couldn't, could they?

I could barely look at the screen. It was the Germans, so of course they equalised. Extra time now beckoned. We were devastated in my house and now feared the worst. The Germans would not let us off now having got so near to lifting the cup. Enter a Russian linesman who now commanded centre stage. Geoff Hurst volleyed a ball against the German's cross bar and the ball appeared to cross the line as it came down before bouncing back into play. Cue pandemonium in our house as we all shouted goal in unison. No, the referee had decided to consult his Russian linesman to see if the ball had actually crossed the line and if a goal could be given. Now I don't know if the Russian linesman had had any relatives who had fought the Germans in the second world war and he was now considering revenge or, more likely I hope, he just genuinely believed the ball had crossed the line and the goal could stand. We will never know. Suffice to say he signalled a goal. We were back in front. The match was in any event won when Kenneth Wolstenholme uttered those immortal words at the start of this chapter as Geoff Hurst lashed in the fourth England goal to complete his hat trick and give England the World Cup. As a young football fan this was as good as it gets. As an England fan it would actually never get any better but we didn't know that back then on that sunny summer Saturday afternoon. England were World Cup holders. When will we hear that phrase again I wonder?

Oh to have been young and in England in the summer of 1966. The swinging sixties were in full flow at this time with London at it's epicentre. The mini motor car was the epitome of cool, even The Beatles drove one (forget Blair's tepid version of Cool Britannia in the nineties, this was the real thing). British music was at it's height and Mary Quant invented my favourite fashion item, the mini skirt. Girls in the sixties mostly tended to be on the slim side (junk food not having yet entered the nation's diet) and to my eyes there was no finer sight than a pretty girl dressed in a mini skirt walking down the road. Living in Blackpool that summer there were plenty of such sights to gladden this boy's heart particularly given the amount of holidaymakers who visited the resort. I was soon to find an ideal venue at which to engage such girls in conversation so read on if you want to find out more. Oh and welcome back all you non-football lovers.

As school had finished I needed some summer employment to provide me with money for such essentials as records and also to fund my leisure activities. Mr and Mrs Green, the owners of my grandparents' old chip shop, asked my mother if I would like to wash the dishes of those customers who ate in the small dining area at the rear of the shop. I can't say that I was totally over the moon at the prospect of washing dirty plates (not something I did at home, but come to think of it, I didn't actually do anything at home) but the work did have the benefit of limited hours, namely 12 noon until about 2pm, so not only could I lie in each morning but I would also have the rest of the day to myself once I had finished work. Not too taxing then and on that basis totally suitable for this somewhat lazy 16 year old. Actually, there weren't too many alternatives for summer work for a school boy of my age. There was no way I was ever going to get up at stupid o'clock to do a paper round in all weathers and the scrap metal business was already off the menu on account of it involving actual hard manual work. I was a bit stuck because I was hopefully going into the sixth form, exam results permitting, so I could not look for a permanent job. No, dishwashing, glamorous though it seemed (lol as you youngsters might say) was the summer job for me. It would also give me some much needed funds with which to enjoy the summer.

What were my leisure activities that I needed these funds for, you might ask? The answer, my friends, was to be found at the Pleasure Beach and was called The Fun House. Sadly no longer with us owing to a fire in 1991, the Fun House was built in 1934 and in the sixties you paid your entrance fee which I think was two shillings and sixpence (13p in new money) and gained entrance to a large building which comprised of various attractions including, amongst others, a row of huge slides, a fast spinning wheel which you tried to cling on to as it revolved and my particular favourite, "The Barrel" which was a large cylindrical contraption shaped like a barrel which you could walk through as it turned, well you could if you were a local and knew the trick of being able to stand upright as it revolved. It took a few goes of falling head over heels before I mastered the correct technique of walking upright as the Barrel revolved but, once mastered, the Barrel proved a lucrative pursuit for me on two levels.

The first level involved money. Practically every tourist that went into the Barrel fell over as soon as they set foot in it. Walking upright, believe it or not, was quite a difficult proposition in that rolling Barrel. The trick was not to look at the floor as it disoriented you immediately if you did and over you went. To master this particular attraction you had to look outside the other end of the Barrel to see the horizontal and then imagine you were just walking in a straight line at the same speed as the rotation of the barrel. Simple.

Well, as I said, the tourists failed to grasp this concept so went head over heels and ended up either on their back or on their stomach within seconds of setting foot in it and more often than not this led to loose change being scattered all over the Barrel, particularly when anyone rolled upside down. Well, what could a poor boy do (as the song goes) but collect as much loose change as he could and this boy was adept at picking it up surreptitiously at lightning speed. I would, of course, have handed back the change to the tourist who lost the money but the problem was that there were often so many going into the Barrel that you couldn't tell who had dropped what. Well that's my defence your honour and I'm sticking to it. Sunday afternoons were always the best time to visit the Fun House as not only were the weekly holidaymakers in there but day trippers could also be found in abundance and they had mostly all had a lunchtime session in the pub, which hardly helped their vertical stability. It was like taking candy from a baby and greatly supplemented my dishwashing income. I wasn't greedy though and often handed back money to the ones who looked like they needed it. Just call me Robin Hood, or Jeremy Corbyn. Well, I was redistributing wealth after all.

The second, and for me an equally important level, was girls. They hadn't a clue when it came to successfully negotiating the barrel so my particular ploy was to help the most attractive one to her feet after she had fallen over and then show her how it was done. At the very worst it would lead to us both rolling around helplessly on the floor of the barrel if she couldn't keep her feet, a not unpleasurable experience generally, or, if she could actually keep her feet then it often led to her being grateful for my assistance and allowed me to start chatting her up. Every one's a winner, as a certain Del Boy might have said.

I recall some very pleasant and lucrative Sunday afternoons in the Fun House, followed perhaps by a stroll on the beach afterwards if I had been lucky in meeting a visiting young lady and I was sorry when it burned down. It certainly helped me hone my conversational skills with the opposite sex which would prove a boon to me when I moved on to my next, and what was to be my favourite, venue when it came to meeting girls but that is mostly for the next chapter. For now, this particular summer for me will always be indelibly linked with the football and the Fun House. Oh, and the music, of course.

This was the year when LP's really started becoming popular in their own right. In fact, I bought three of the most important albums ever issued this particular year. I can guarantee that they will all feature in most knowledgeable critics top ten list of the all time best albums, namely "Pet Sounds" by the Beach Boys, "Revolver" by The Beatles and "Blonde on blonde" by Bob Dylan. Any one of which would have been a brilliant release for any one year, but to have three released in one year, all in that fantastic summer, was just incredible. "Pet Sounds" was my first purchase and hearing any track from that album evokes memories of that golden summer when all seemed right in the world. So many brilliant tracks masterminded by that wayward and erratic genius that is Brian Wilson. I never tire of listening to it.

The 5th of August saw the release of, in some critics eyes, but not mine, the finest LP produced by The Beatles and some would even say the best LP ever, namely "Revolver". This was the group at it's most creative period to date and included such gems as "Eleanor Rigby", "Here, there and everywhere", "And your bird can sing" and the album closer coup de grace and the pointer to the psychedelic era to come in 1967, "Tomorrow never knows". When I first heard this latter track on playing the LP on the day of it's release, naturally, my jaw just dropped. I had never heard anything remotely approaching the sound on this record before. The group had taken pop music to a whole new level and by doing so found that some of their fans had decided not to continue their journey with them. It was just too far out for some, mainly younger girls, but not for me. Tape loops, guitar seagull noises, Lennon sounding as though he was singing from a bathroom at the end of the hall and some most un-Beatle like lyrics made this a track to truly boggle the mind in 1966. If this was where the group intended going, music wise, I couldn't wait for more. I'd like to hear the girls scream to this one, I thought with some smug satisfaction. They would not be able to, of course. This sound could not be replicated on stage in 1966 and was one of the reasons why the group decided to quit touring. How could they replicate this sound with the limited equipment then available to them? I could understand their attitude but a part of me was hugely disappointed that I never got to see them in the flesh.

The final album of the trilogy mentioned above was bought by me later in the year. I had enjoyed some of Dylan's previous music but had only previously bought his single "Like a rolling stone", which I thought was brilliant. I still think it's the best single he has ever released and probably his best ever song. The new album tracks I had heard had intrigued me so I decided to buy my first Dylan album and I was not disappointed. I know he is an acquired taste and, to some, his voice can sound like a permanent nasal whine but I have always quite liked his singing. It is certainly unique. This double album had some classic Dylan songs on it and culminated in side four being devoted to just one song, "Sad eyed lady of the lowlands", which was ground breaking for the time. Just don't bother trying to decipher any of his lyrics from this period as they appear mostly unfathomable to me, save for classics like "Just like a woman". Whatever you think of Dylan it can't be denied that he was one of the most influential musicians ever. Dylan fans, who almost to a man, or woman, fail to see how great was The Beatles importance for reasons that are lost on me, consider their man the most influential musician of all time. Not for me. He wrote some great songs and influenced a lot of musicians but when compared to The Beatles and what they achieved in seven short years, in my opinion he falls well short of their incredibly high standards. Great album though.

Whilst this particular summer could not be said to have been a vintage one so far as the seasonal shows were concerned, with the likes of Des O'Connor and Kenneth McKellar appearing on the North Pier (now there's an image for you) and the Central Pier had Winifred Atwell and Eddie Calvert (I was surprised there were still enough people still alive from their heyday to appreciate them), the Opera House did have the perennial Ken Dodd and Cilla Black appeared in the ABC summer show. It was, though, the Sunday pop concerts that really showed how big a draw Blackpool was at this time. Should you be so inclined, and have had the necessary funds, then you could have seen many of the top groups sometime during that summer including Billy J. Kramer, Manfred Mann, The Small Faces, Dave Dee Dozy Beaky Mick & Tich, The Yardbirds, The Troggs and the most popular live act at the time, The Walker Brothers. It may not seem much now but believe me these were the top acts of the day and all were extremely popular.

Summer was drawing to it's close and just before it did, towards the end of August, the results of the GCE O level exams were published. I remember it being a Thursday, as it is still to this day, but of course in my day there was no national coverage, TV cameras inside schools or pupils running about congratulating themselves on opening their result envelopes as if they had won the lottery. We had been told that the results would be put up on a board in the school reception hall for all to view from about 9am onwards so we could go and check how we all had done anytime after that. I think on the day I borrowed my brother's two wheeler bike and cycled the four miles or so to school to find out how well, or badly, I had fared.

My father had promised me £1 for each subject passed so I was hoping for a fiver, with a bit of luck, but to my amazement I found that I had passed in seven of the eight subjects taken, narrowly missing out in Greek. I had obtained a grade 7 in that subject when you needed at least grade 6 or above to pass. I was on cloud nine though, as not only had I achieved enough passes to get me into the sixth form, but I could also look forward to receiving the princely sum of £7 which was a not inconsiderable amount of cash at that time and most welcome to me. There was one immediately pressing problem though, which subjects to take in the sixth form? I had to choose three subjects to study to A level standard. Latin was a no brainer as it was my best subject and I also enjoyed History so that was two subjects ticked off immediately. The third was tricky. I enjoyed French but only got grade 4 which was not totally inspiring and would mean I would have to improve greatly if I studied this subject at A level. I thought about this for some time and eventually decided I would give it a go. Well, the French mistress was quite tasty so she tipped the balance in that subject's favour. I would just have to try not to get too distracted in her class, some hope.

I also received an additional present the week of my O level results namely the then current terrific single by the Small Faces "All or nothing", which was given to me by two visiting girls from Chesterfield. How it came about was that they were both my age and were in Blackpool for a week staying at a boarding house at the top of Lord Street. I happened to be walking along that street one day when they saw me, asked if I was local to the area and when I said that I was, they asked me where they should go to have a good time. Naturally, I couldn't resist offering to be their personal guide for the remainder of their stay and showed them all the delights that sixties Blackpool had to offer. The girls were both typical Mod girls, very fashionably dressed with short hairstyles and one of the girls was very attractive. I did my best to try to separate her from her friend so that we could just be together on our own but she told me she couldn't desert her friend. Very commendable, but a little disappointing to me. We did have a good time that week though and on their last day they presented me with their going away gift, the record mentioned above. I loved that record and was going to buy it but they saved me the money. I ended up writing to the girl I fancied and we corresponded for a few months but it petered out eventually. Either she got bored or, more likely, hadn't a clue what my letters said so just gave up trying to make sense of them. Now if only I had had facebook!

September arrived and with it the start of my final two years at school and my first year in the hallowed sixth form. The first task was to confirm which subjects I would be taking which was easy for me as I had already decided. The only problem was the French mistress. In the first French period she went through all of our individual exam results and she saw that mine was the worst of the group. Everyone else had achieved at least a grade 3 but mine was a lowly 4. She said to me that she wasn't sure that I had showed enough ability to be accepted on the A level course as normally they would only take pupils who had achieved at least a minimum grade 3. I told her that I really wanted to study French under her and that I knew I could improve with her tuition (hello) and I must have been persuasive as she agreed to take me into her class.

In fact, so keen was I to learn from her that I abandoned my lifetime school habit of sitting near the back of the class from where I could interject the appropriate smart arse comment whenever the need arose and when you weren't being taught by a blackboard duster-throwing psycopath, and moved to a desk right in front of the teacher's own desk. Now the fact that the French mistress liked to perch on the said desk whilst crossing and recrossing her legs during lessons (think Sharon Stone in Basic Instinct and you might get an idea of the impact this particular manoeuvre had on us) as she addressed us in her sultry French tones had no bearing whatsoever on my decision to take up my new position of sitting at the front of the class. No sir. I just needed to be near the front so that I would not miss anything. Teaching wise I mean, naturally. I am sure the same went for all my other compatriots who normally sat with me at the back of the class but for French made an exception. We were all keen to learn you see. The nerds who normally sat at the front of the class were most puzzled by our behaviour when they found their normal seats had been taken by the miscreants from the back of class. They were also further puzzled when a few of us did our best Pickford's impersonation by moving the teacher's desk to best vantage point just before she came into class so that we were sure to miss nothing. Again, teaching wise you understand. There was a lot of squirming going on in that lesson I can tell you and it wasn't only because the wooden seats were hard.

With entry into the sixth form came a certain responsibility as well. A few of us, myself included, were chosen to be sub-prefects. This meant we could have our own tie but no blue gown. That only came if you were chosen as a full prefect in the final year, another perk of which, if chosen, would be that you had your own prefect's room, complete with radio. No, as a sub species of prefect, we just got the mundane donkey work like overseeing classes at break time if there was inclement weather and everyone was confined indoors. Still, it meant that as a sub-prefect you were beginning to be given a bit of authority as, if lower school pupils did not obey you, then you could report them to the full prefects who had the power to inflict punishment, not of a capital nature, regrettably, on them for their misbehaviour. The teachers also began treating you differently and suddenly you didn't feel like a schoolboy any longer. The downside was that the work required from you on the A level courses was extremely heavy but at least you now had some free study periods in your timetable to assist you in getting through the sheer volume of work. You were being left to your own devices to a certain extent.

The other main difference in sixth form was that we now had an intake of bright pupils who came from other local secondary schools such as Claremont and Montgomery. These were boys who had originally failed their 11 plus exams but had done so well in their O levels that they now entered our school at sixth form level to study for their A levels. In those days there were some excellent secondary schools locally so if a pupil did fail initially to get into a Grammar school he or she still had a chance to do so in later years as some pupils would inevitably blossom academically as their school years progressed. This gives the lie to the politicians' claim that failing to pass the 11 plus meant that a child was forever consigned to the academic dustbin. A slur on the standards achieved by the secondary schools as well as being totally incorrect, but then again, when have politicians ever been right on most topics.

In my opinion, all the abolition of grammar schools achieved was to decrease social mobility by depriving children from poorer backgrounds of the chance to compete at the highest level with children from privileged backgrounds whose own parents could afford to send them to private schools. Can you guess how many of the top politicians went to public schools or where they have chosen to send their children? Yes, you are correct. It wasn't the local comprehensive or, if that is failing, I believe they can now choose to be called an academy. It sounds so much better. The sheer hypocrisy of those who purport to represent our interests is breathtaking. I am thankful the idiots didn't wreck my education but feel sorry for those who were deprived of the chances I had.

So far as my school sporting activities were concerned, I was chosen for the school rugby first team but given that the team mostly comprised of upper sixth formers with the odd lower sixth boy such as myself included, I could hardly complain that I was no longer captain of the rugby team, given my relatively junior status. It was still an achievement to be in the first team at my age. One young man who had joined us from Montgomery school at the start of term proved to be a useful addition to our team. He was a rather tall individual for his age, called Roger Uttley. You may not have heard of him but he would later captain England and be a member of the undefeated British Lions in their tour to South Africa in 1974. He wasn't a bad addition to our team. I think he was something like six foot four when he was 17 so you can imagine the look of horror on the opposing team's faces when he ran out on to the field. My problem, height wise, was not only that I was not as big as Roger, believe it or not, but that I had actually stopped growing at around the age of 15. All the other boys started shooting past me so that not only ended my fledgling basketball career, it also meant that I was struggling to retain my place as a forward in the rugby team. You had to be at least normal height and ideally somewhat taller. I just about managed to hang on to my place in the team for this year but next year I envisaged problems. The school didn't field an oompah lumpah 15, after all.

Two things happened on the 29th of October this year. Well, so far as I was concerned they did. I reached the age of 17 and William Hartnell bowed out as Doctor Who to be replaced by Patrick Troughton. I thought it was quite clever of the scriptwriter to have the Doctor metamorphose into another version of himself but actually played by another actor in a totally different way and this ruse was no doubt instrumental in keeping this terrific series going over all these years. I thought William Hartnell was ideal as the first Doctor and it was interesting to see how the new Doctor took on the role and his interpretation of it. I have to say that my all time favourite Doctor Who was Tom Baker who I thought was brilliant in the role.

What else was I watching at the grand age of 17? Not much if truth be told. Apart from the programmes previously listed which were still running like "The Avengers", now with the delicious Diana Rigg as Steed's sidekick Emma Peel (now I did like her and I was now beginning to understand the leather clothing attraction), there was a spin off from "Z Cars" called "Softly, Softly" which was quite good, and "The Frost Report" featuring, among others, Ronnie Barker, Ronnie Corbett and the soon to be famous John Cleese. On the whole I found this programme very funny and always watched it. Lastly, a very camp (not that I knew what that word really meant) "Batman" started on our screens this year. A world away from the movie versions of recent years, this Batman was very much played tongue in cheek, but I generally enjoyed it.

I did mention earlier in this chapter that I would tell you about my favourite venue for meeting girls, which I happened on this year. A school mate of mine who lived in Cleveleys introduced me to the venue which was known locally as the Queen's Disco (thank you David) and was situated on the Promenade just south of Victoria Road West. It was a large single storey building with a small disco floor in the right hand corner with the main dance floor in the centre of the room. Behind the main dance floor banks of tables and seats were laid out in tiers, gradually rising up towards the back of the building and they provided a great vantage point to check out any girls on the dance floor as well as those entering the disco through the entrance doors at the front of the building.

The venue was also blessed (?) with ultra violet fluorescent lighting which showed up any one wearing white clothing as the clothing took on an eerie luminous glow under the lights. You could always tell when the Fleetwood deckhands off the trawlers were in as they always wore white socks for some bizarre reason but I have absolutely no idea why. You just saw this pair of glowing socks in the darkened room as they strode to the bar. The venue was also blessed with two of the biggest bouncers I have ever seen anywhere. I swear they were as broad as they were tall and they certainly had no idea what a smile was. They ran a tight ship, so to speak, and if any of the white sock-wearing Deckies (here used as an abbreviation for the Deckhands on the trawlers and not to be confused with a later abbreviation for Deckchair attendants, as will be explained later, honestly.) became overly aggressive after having had one too many beers the bouncers were soon in action. Their favourite ploy, as I recall, was to wield the metal drink trays from the bar and bring them crashing down on the poor unfortunate's head. Whist this had a certain entertainment value, it sometimes threw you off your dancing as the percussion they created could clash with the beat of the record. Very inconsiderate. They were not bothered about keeping in time you see. We decided not to complain, though.

The music was generally provided by a jukebox situated right beside the main dance floor and was the first port of call (see the water theme here) on entering the disco so that you could choose the Motown sounds which were always in evidence. Trouble was that there was also the latest pop records on the jukebox as well, so you had to make sure that you and your mates stacked the jukebox with reasonable dancing tunes. Well, you try dancing to Jim Reeves singing "Distant Drums". Actually, I think I exaggerate. I don't remember hearing that record being on the jukebox but "No milk today" by Hermans Hermits was one I definitely do remember being played and you can't dance to that either. This meant that whenever you asked a girl to dance if a good record was on, you had to do your chatting up fairly quickly in case some dross came on the jukebox and your girl headed quickly back to her seat. It did mean, however, that if she stayed chatting to you when such dross came on then you would generally be in for a good night. Swings and roundabouts you see. I started going to the Queens Disco round about the time of my seventeenth birthday and it would be my regular haunt for the next few years. Happy times. Generally! But more of that in the next chapter, if you haven't died of boredom yet.

December 23rd saw the end of an era with the last ever broadcast of my favourite pop programme "Ready Steady Go". I believe the producers thought that the "beat boom", whatever they thought that was, was fading and they cancelled the show. Heaven knows why they thought this as the programme was still immensely popular with those of my generation. Over the three years or so it had been broadcast it had featured all my favourite groups and singers and Friday evenings would never quite be the same again for me after it finished. Nostalgia fix can be had by looking up the programme on You Tube and it certainly gives you a flavour of what we were enjoying at the height of the swinging sixties.

Well finally it's time for the usual list of my favourite tunes from this year. As I have already mentioned, albums were coming into their own but there were still some great singles released, probably the last time there was such a prolific number of quality releases though. So here goes, with some album tracks thrown in and in no particular order:-

1. Good vibrations - The Beach Boys

2. Sloop John B - The Beach Boys

3. God only knows - The Beach Boys

4. Eleanor Rigby - The Beatles

5. Here, there and everywhere - The Beatles

6. Tomorrow never knows - The Beatles

7. I fought the law - The Bobby Fuller Four

8. Eight miles high - The Byrds

9. Goin' back - Dusty Springfield

10. You don't have to say you love me - Dusty Springfield

11. Reach out, I'll be there - The Four Tops

12. River deep, mountain high - Ike and Tina Turner

13. (I'm a) Roadrunner - Junior Walker and the All Stars

14. When a man loves a woman - Percy Sledge

15. Hold on, I'm coming - Sam and Dave

16. Scarborough fair - Simon and Garfunkel

17. All or nothing - The Small Faces

18. The sun ain't gonna shine anymore - The Walker Brothers

19. Mustang Sally - Wilson Pickett

20. Paint it, black - The Rolling Stones

Major films from this year which I enjoyed were :-

A Man For All Seasons - the great Robert Bolt drama about Sir Thomas More featuring Paul Schofield

Blow Up - a cinematic version of the swinging sixties with David Hemmings and Vanessa Redgrave

Alfie - a romantic comedy with Michael Caine and a certain Jane Asher, at that time dating Paul McCartney, but not in the film

Fantastic Voyage - a somewhat barmy science fiction film about a submarine crew being shrunk to microscopic size and then injected into a scientist's body to repair his brain with Stephen Boyd and Raquel Welsh

Grand Prix - a motor racing drama with James Garner but which included real life race footage with Graham Hill, Fangio and Jim Clark amongst others

Khartoum - historical drama with Charlton Heston and Laurence Olivier

Myself and my little brother, Philip, in front of the Metropole Hotel, Blackpool North Promenade 1960.

Creswell Junior School Football team 1960/61 proudly displaying our trophies. I am second from left in the front row.

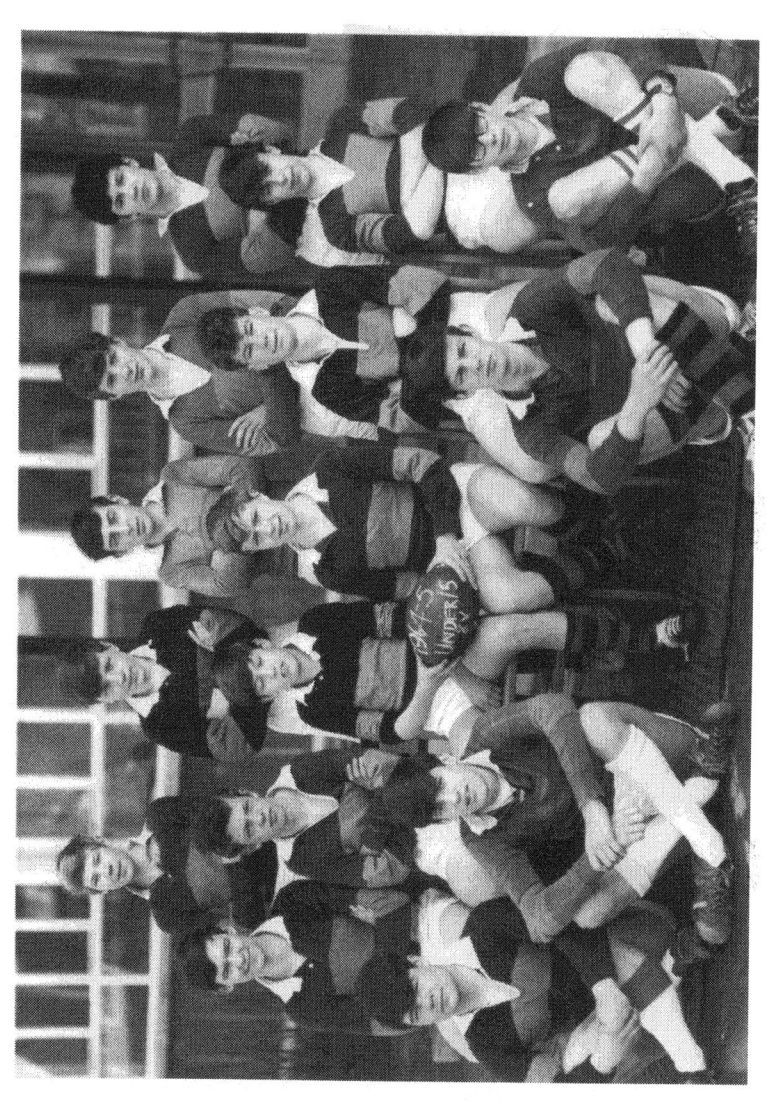

Captain of Blackpool Grammar School Under 15 Rugby Team. I am third from right in the middle row.

163

South Pier deckchair stack - Summer 1968, not in the least bothered about selling my mother a deckchair, but our dog looks as if she wants to buy one.

Same stack as before and I am actually working!

On holiday in Malta September 1969 with the Hilton Casino in the background. Now where did I leave the Aston Martin?

CHAPTER EIGHT
1967

"We're Sergeant Pepper's Lonely Hearts Club Band, we hope you will enjoy the show". The opening line of the first song on the epoch making album by The Beatles.

This remarkable album, issued at the start of summer of this year, marked, in my opinion, the high point of popular music in the sixties. It also ushered in a period known as "the summer of love", when young people actually thought they were capable of changing the world for good and optimism was all pervading. They were wrong, of course. The establishment merely blinked at the brilliant burst of colour which the youth culture produced this year and then ignored it and went on in the same old way. The "Hippie movement" which was fostered by the summer of love didn't know this then. They were somewhat naive and believed that the immediate future was theirs and that a new world order was on the horizon. It was only a matter of time, they thought, before everything would be resolved by peace and love, man, as the Hippies truly believed. I was never wholly persuaded by their simplistic philosophy as even at the relatively tender age of seventeen I could see that wearing a bell round your neck, carrying flowers and chanting a few mantras was not going to solve all the world's problems. If only it could. Still, whilst 1967 was a very enjoyable and interesting year for me for lots of reasons, I was certainly never going to be a hippy.

The year got off to a somewhat sombre start, though, with the tragic death of Donald Campbell whilst he was attempting to break the World water speed record on Lake Coniston in his rocket powered boat called "Bluebird" on the 4th of January. I remember well, seeing the news coverage of his failed attempt and his boat somersaulting spectacularly as it reached a phenomenal 328 miles per hour. Campbell was killed instantly in the crash, but it was many years before his body was eventually located at the bottom of the lake.

The other tragic event early this year occurred on the 27th of January when three astronauts, Gus Grissom, Ed White and Roger Chaffee, died in a burnt out Apollo space capsule at Cape Canaveral. They had been sat in the capsule, which was of the type scheduled to take astronauts to the moon, practising a launch rehearsal for Apollo 1 when a fire broke out in the capsule because of design flaws and the ground crew were unable to rescue the three astronauts before they were overcome with heat and exhaust gases. This was the first major disaster to occur in American's space programme and led to a suspension of manned Apollo flights for some 20 months. Would they still be able to get to the moon before the end of the decade, I wondered? Time appeared to be running out.

Meanwhile, on the record front, I was avidly waiting for the Beatles' new single to be released as it had been somewhat quiet on that front since their last record release way back in August of last year. What could we expect given the direction that was signified by the closing track of "Revolver"? All was revealed on Top of the Pops on the 9th of February when the BBC aired the promotional videos for both "Strawberry Fields Forever" and "Penny Lane". The new single was a double "A" side and in my opinion, not only is this the best single ever released by the group, but the sheer originality and quality of both songs qualify it as probably the best single ever released. I have certainly never heard better over the past 50 years.

I couldn't wait to buy this single when it came out on the 17th of February and it has remained my favourite single since the date of issue. Both sides of the record took inspiration from John and Paul's childhood in suburban Liverpool and as usual with the group, the music was way ahead of anything any of their contemporaries were capable of producing. Given the quality of the single it is astounding that it did not reach number 1 in the pop charts. It was actually kept off the top of the charts by Englelbert Humperdinck singing "Release me". I most certainly would have, if I had been given the chance! I was beginning to wonder if the music buying population were changing as how could anyone, I thought, prefer that middle of the road rubbish to the genius product of my heroes. The answer is that, yes, the record buying public were changing.

My age group no longer had a monopoly in choosing which records should be top of the charts and this, coupled with the fact that The Beatles were no longer performing live and had started to lose some of their young girl fans as a result of that and also with the introduction of their more imaginative and less commercial music, meant that other, shall we say, different types of music were coming to the fore. Nothing wrong in this. Music should always evolve and people should have different tastes. There was just no way I would ever be buying any of Engelbert's, or his compatriots, music. Each to their own.

Whilst The Beatles were still being regarded as pop music royalty, the same could not be said for the press' favourite music villains, the Rolling Stones. They had always been promoted in the press as the complete antithesis of The Beatles, being somewhat "dirty", because of their long hair (!) and "rebellious" owing to various escapades in which they allegedly were involved and the most notorious and latest of such escapades occurred on the evening of the 12th of February when the West Sussex Police decided to pay a visit to Keith Richard's house just on the off chance, you understand, of finding some illegal substances.

The visit, according to popular myth, came shortly after a Beatle, George Harrison, had left the house. You couldn't have a member of pop royalty being linked to anything which may have been tainted with criminality! The biggest myth, however, and still sometimes repeated to this day although being totally untrue, revolved around a certain naked female who, though we didn't know it initially, was Marianne Faithfull and who was allegedly involved having intimate relations with a Mars Bar. Great publicity for Mars Bars but not for poor Marianne who took years to live down this salacious nonsense.

She did admit to being wrapped in a fur rug, and nothing else, on the arrival of Plod but that was not then, nor is it now, any sort of criminal offence. Not that this stopped that paragon of truth and good taste that was The News of the World from running with the story and its consequent myth for all it was worth. They knew what their readers wanted and were determined to give it to them.

The Police apparently found certain substances which were taken away for analysis and, this being Keith Richard's house which, in the sixties, could possibly have doubled as a branch of Boots the Chemist but with more stock, it was not unsurprising that the results showed that any tablets found weren't aspirins and the powder located wasn't talc. It later transpired that the whole search and arrest had been instigated by the aforementioned wretched Sunday newspaper in collusion with a member of the Constabulary (there's a surprise!) and the paper even had a photographer on hand to take photographs of the bust. How convenient.

I, of course, was almost totally ignorant of drugs and what effect they had on people. Of course my curiosity had been piqued by all the publicity drugs had by now been receiving and I had heard rumours of where you could get purple hearts (Dexamyl I believe is the official name and one that inspired a certain denim clad group in later years - Dexy's Midnight Runners anyone?) which would act as a stimulant but I had more than enough natural stimulant racing round in my body in 1967 thank you very much. Bromide might have been more suitable for me then! In any event I was a keen sportsman and thought that drugs and sport would not mix. How wrong was I, eh athletes? I did, however, have total sympathy with the Stones. What harm were they doing even it they were ingesting illegal substances in the privacy of their own home? That was their affair and no one else's, so far as I could see. They were not forcing anyone else to behave like them so I failed to see what all the furore was about. As for the argument that fans like me might want to emulate them because we looked up to them this was arrant nonsense. I liked most of their music but would never have dreamt of acting like them and certainly never considered them, or the Beatles, any sort of role models. We didn't ape our heroes mindlessly back then. They were musicians and, to an extent, fashion leaders and that was all. My generation did, contrary to the press' belief at that time, have minds of our own.

As I was now in the sixth form and not able to earn any money I was given the princely sum of £1 a week pocket money which, although not being a huge sum, did provide me with some very limited funds to go to the Queen's Disco generally once or twice a week. My little group now consisted of about six of us, two of whom were still at school and the rest of the group were all in different jobs. You could generally guarantee that most of us would be in the Disco at the weekend and we would usually grab a table and seats in the elevated section behind the main dance floor from where we could survey the Disco for any attractive girls who appeared. The thorny question would then be which of us would get up and try our luck on the dance floor with any appropriate female. This did cause some friendly disagreements when it happened that we all fancied the same girl and it was very much a case of he who dares wins and a subsequent race to the dance floor quickly occurred.

I seem to remember that if there were ever two girls dancing together then you could guarantee that if one was attractive, her mate would be somewhat lacking in the looks department. Our theory was that a good looking girl had a less attractive friend with her so that she could get the best looking guy with little competition from her mate and the less attractive one always had a good looking friend so that she could profit from her friend being able to attract guys relatively easily. Am I wrong? This resulted in any two of us from my group taking it in turns to have the choice of the most attractive girl to ask to dance but only on the understanding that if you were successful with the good looking girl, your mate could exit the dance floor as soon as possible once he saw that you didn't still need him. I mean, friendship is one thing, but you had to draw the line somewhere. It was each man for himself and it sometimes occurred that I was left on my own dancing with two girls at once as my mate trailed dust in his wake as he headed back to his seat to escape the clutches of the Bride of Wildenstein, or something similar.

The best times though where when there were two reasonably attractive girls and your mate actually fancied the one different to the one you fancied. Better still were the times when a group of girls would be on the dance floor together and we could join them en masse. At least if you weren't successful with the girl of your choice you could still have a dance and a laugh with a group of you all together. Picture the scene, a ring of about 12 or so guys and girls all in a circle dancing round a pile of handbags on the floor. Very sixties. Sounds a bit naff now but they were happy times and on the whole those nights led to some very pleasant, but generally brief, encounters. I am sure there must have been some boring nights with little action but I don't remember too many. I was not too bothered about trying to have a steady girlfriend at this stage as I was enjoying myself too much and didn't want any restrictions. Occasionally a relationship might last a week or so but it was then back to the normal routine. Summer at the Disco was to be even better, I discovered, as the numbers of girls going to the venue increased substantially when the holidaymakers were in town but I will tell you more about that a little later on in this chapter.

In the music world a sensation was caused by the late Jimi Hendrix on the 31st of March when he deliberately set fire to his guitar on stage at the opening night of the tour he was involved in at London's Finsbury Park Astoria. Pete Townshend of The Who had already become notorious for trashing his guitar when on stage with his group but Jimi had to go one better. Jimi was later that same night treated for burns to his arms. Not that this would ever stop him performing his party piece. Purple Haze indeed. But what I find more astonishing than his antics was the actual composition of that tour. The line up was the Jimi Hendrix Experience, Cat Stevens, Engelbert Humperdinck and the Walker Brothers. A more eclectic mix you couldn't imagine. These days it would be like having Daniel O'Donnell appearing with Ed Sheeran and One Direction all on the same bill. I wonder if anyone has considered that possibility? The make up of the audience would be interesting too, wouldn't it!

This tour would actually reach Blackpool a few weeks later when hosted by the Odeon and my wife was in the audience for this show. She actually had the tour poster from that night which has now sadly gone. Now that was what you would call a memento. The diverse nature of the artists appearing on that bill was a good example of how many top acts visited the resort. You didn't have to travel to London or to any of the cities to see the top acts perform but sadly those days have long gone. The equivalent now of those acts which appeared in Blackpool in the sixties would be something like seeing Madonna or Adele appearing on Central Pier. Wouldn't that be a sight to see!

Meanwhile, back at school I had a "slight" run in with the master responsible for rugby at the school. The cause of the run in was the conflict I now had between playing football out of school or rugby for the school. I can't now quite remember the exact circumstances but in spring of this year I had started playing the odd game of football for Wren Rovers second team. This team played in the local Blackpool amateur league on Saturday afternoons so I think I must have first played for them when there was no school rugby match. I had begun to lose a bit of interest in rugby and wanted to play football for a local team. I hadn't played proper team football for about four years and was keen to give it a go. I think I had only played a couple of matches for Wren Rovers' second team before I was involved in a game which my team won 7-2 and I scored four of those goals. Well, as a seventeen year old playing in the adult league, this feat made the people in charge of Wren Rovers' first team sit up and take notice. The upshot was that I was picked to play for the first team the following Saturday. This was more like it, I thought. The first team at that time played in the North West Counties league which was of a good amateur standard. I was thrilled, but the only problem was that the game clashed with a school first team rugby match. What to do? I could hardly play in both.

The only solution I could come up with was to skive off school on the Friday prior to the rugby match, feigning illness, so that I was not picked for the rugby team for the Saturday game. Trouble was, that I had not factored the brain of Britain that was my mother into this equation. What had she to do with all this? Well the answer should have been nothing, but my cunning plan went awry when the rugby master, who whilst not quite being as terrifying as the maths master (you remember Ernie) was only one spot below him in the psycopath league, showed up at my house on the Friday afternoon to see if I would be well enough to play the following day. I was horrified when I saw his car pull up outside our window and heard the knock on our front door. I frantically gestured to my mother to answer the door and tell him I was in bed but no, adopting her best Baldric impersonation she had to answer the door and shout "Alan, there's a teacher from school here to see you". Wonderful!

I went to the door and coughing and spluttering as best I could, I explained I wasn't feeling well so couldn't play for the rugby team. He had his suspicions, I know, as he beheld a healthy looking seventeen year old and I could tell from the look on his face that he didn't quite believe my story. I was less than grateful for my mother's intervention but hoped I would get away with it. I would have done too, I think, except that on my debut for the first team I played reasonably well with my team winning 1-0 and I scored the only goal. What was worse was that the Saturday evening sports paper, the "Green 'Un" as it was then known because it was printed on green paper, clever eh, printed not only all the football league results but also those from the top amateur leagues and my name duly appeared as goalscorer for my team. I just had to hope the rugby master wasn't an avid reader of the paper.

Well, it was with some trepidation that I returned to school on the Monday morning hoping I had escaped the notice of the rugby master but luck had not been on my side. Whether he had seen my name in the paper or had just been told about my exploits by someone else, I haven't a clue, but he tracked me down at first break time that Monday morning and asked me directly if I had been playing football on the Saturday just past and if so, why had I lied about being ill. I came clean and admitted it, as I had to, as the evidence was there for all to see in black and white, well green and black to be precise.

I explained that I had been chosen to make my debut for Wren Rovers first team and I was keen to see if I could play at that level. He then lectured me about having a duty to play for the school team and I disagreed with him as this had been an opportunity I didn't want to miss and that I no longer wanted to be considered for the rugby team. I then awaited the explosion from him but was surprised when he just said how disappointed he was with my attitude and away he went. It was important for me to play for Wren Rovers first team as I still harboured faint hopes that I might become a footballer, something I had always wanted to be since I was very young, and this was my chance to see whether I would be good enough.

So began my short football career with Wren Rovers. Why was it short? The answer came after only a few weeks playing for the first team. I had been doing reasonably well for the team and after one particular home game I was approached by an old chap who said he had been watching me for a few games and had been impressed with me. He told me that he was a part time scout for Blackburn Rovers (then in the second division of the football league) and would I like to sign for them on associate schoolboy terms. Basically this meant as a triallist while they assessed if I would be good enough to make the grade to becoming a professional footballer. I didn't need asking twice and without hesitation signed the forms for him then and there. He told me he would let me know as soon as I was chosen for the junior Blackburn Rovers side.

Imagine my delight at this, which was jolted a few days later when there was a knock on our front door and a scout from Blackpool Football Club (then also in the second division of the football league) had arrived to see if I would sign for Blackpool. I couldn't believe my bad luck as I would have much preferred to have signed for them. I would have been able to train at Squires Gate with Blackpool whereas at Blackburn I just travelled to play for the junior side with no training involved at all and also with me not knowing any of my team mates. There was nothing I could do about this though as I had already committed myself to Blackburn Rovers.

I soon heard from the Blackburn representative who told me I would be playing for the junior side that forthcoming Saturday morning and I should meet him at the old North Station where we would get the train to Blackburn early that morning. I couldn't wait. Once at Blackburn we got off the train and caught the bus to Ewood Park (Blackburn's ground) which in those days was quite an old traditional football stadium, nothing like it is now, and went in at the Player's entrance and into the wood panelled first team dressing room where all that Saturday's teams, consisting of the first team, reserve team, "A" and "B" teams and junior side were posted up on a board on one of the walls. We were playing at home against another local side and the venue was at a playing field somewhere on the outskirts of Blackburn, but I have no idea where. All the Blackburn teams wore the same strip, blue and white shirts, white shorts and blue and white stockings. I can't remember the game now after all these years but I am sure I enjoyed it and after the game I was given my expenses by the club to cover the fares to and from Blackburn plus money for meals. After paying for bus and train journeys I still had a bit left over so had actually earned some money (not much it must be said) for playing the game I loved.

This routine carried on for a few weeks until I was elevated to the "B" team for an evening game against Rochdale "A" team at their first team ground, "Spotlands", in Rochdale. I went to Blackburn's ground straight from school as we had to catch the team coach from the ground. I thought I did ok but found that I couldn't keep up with the stamina side of things and also with all the instructions the coaches were issuing from the touchline. I had always been used to just going out and playing and couldn't take to all the detailed instructions I was being given of who I should mark and where, on the pitch, I should be playing but clearly that was the route any player had to undergo if they wanted to be a professional footballer. I wasn't impressed with that side of things, I have to say.

My fitness, or relative lack of it, was the biggest problem, however, as this game involved playing against other players who had all been used to full time training during the week and it showed. They were far fitter than me. After about 70 minutes I was substituted and the coach in charge of the side explained that whilst he could see that I had ability he did not think I would make a professional footballer. I was disappointed but I could see what he meant. I liked playing the game but I didn't have the mentality and application needed for the professional game. Football to me was just a game to enjoy. It was only some years later that I found out that some professional footballers actually hated the game and dreaded Saturdays coming round in case they didn't play well. This was their career and one bad game could lead to it all ending. Would things have been different for me had I signed for Blackpool and been able to train each week? Who can say. I have my doubts given that I had always hated training for any sport but at least I had given it a go and can say that I have played for Blackburn Rovers, if only in a very junior capacity!

Following my few weeks at Blackburn I drifted back to Wren Rovers for the remainder of the season and whilst playing for the reserve side we reached a Cup Final for the Saturday league which was played on Blackpool's ground, Bloomfield Road, one evening at the end of the season. I had always wondered what it would be like to play on that pitch which, at that time, was one of the biggest in the football league. I soon found out. The pitch seemed immense and certainly provided you with plenty of space in which to play. The game was drawn 0-0 and the replay was scheduled for the following week on the old Blackpool Mechanics ground at Squires Gate. However, when my team showed up for the game we were told that the people who ran the club had decided to play the whole of the first team instead of the reserve team which meant that none of us was getting a game. A very poor trick in my eyes and as far as I was concerned that was me finished so far as the club was concerned. They lost the match anyway so Instant Karma certainly played it's part there!

One thing my Blackburn experience did teach me was that I

would have to ensure that I carried on improving at school with GCE "A" levels now only just over a year away. I would not become a professional footballer but at this stage I still hadn't a clue what I wanted to do so just decided to get my head down academically and do the best that I could. It paid dividends as I attained a heady class position of 3rd out of 32, my highest school position to date and the teachers appeared to be optimistic that I might actually pass my "A" levels. The only blot on the horizon was French. I was avidly paying as much attention as I could to what the French mistress was teaching us but sometimes found things hard in lessons. I was 12th out of a set of 14 so would have to improve greatly if I was to pass and reach a level acceptable to a University because now, I was beginning to think of trying to extend my education and going on to University although at this stage I had no idea as to what subject to read. That was something I would have to decide early on in the next academic year, my final school year.

Friday the 26th of May this year was a somewhat unique day for me as it was the day that I went to my first live music concert. The concert was held at the Empress Ballroom in Blackpool and topping the bill was a new group fast becoming known for their psychedelic sound and unique light show. They were the Pink Floyd who would become quite popular in later years! I had been impressed by their first single, "Arnold Layne", which had just crept into the pop charts at number twenty but their sound intrigued me and as the admission price of the concert was fairly low I decided to go and see them play. They were amazing and performed to their own light show which featured a multi coloured backdrop of light which appeared to have been projected through a lava lamp on to a screen behind them and when coupled with the incredibly way out, for the time, music they played produced an atmospheric evening not to forget.

The audience seemed to comprise mainly students and was certainly not your usual pop music concert. No screaming whatsoever! The audience was actually interested in what was being played. So impressed was I with the group that I went out and bought their first album later in the year, "Piper at the gates of dawn", which was totally outside the type of music I generally bought but I thought it was fantastic. My ethos has always been that if you liked a particular record, regardless of it's type, then buy it and enjoy it.

Talking of buying music, the event I had been eagerly awaiting for some time had now arrived. The new Beatles' album, "Sergeant Pepper's Lonely Hearts Club Band", was due for release on the 1st of June but I had located, on Church Street, a small record shop which was set in what appeared to be an old man's front room, I kid you not. The LP's were all displayed in small square wooden racks secured by what appeared to be one of his leather trouser belts which he had to undo if you wanted to look at any of them. The belt I mean, not his trousers, obviously. This was because, unlike the proper record stores which just had record sleeves on display, he had the actual vinyl in the record sleeves so didn't want anyone "borrowing" them without paying, if you see what I mean. Anyway, I had been in his shop the week before just browsing and had asked him if he was getting the Beatles new album in and when it would be on sale. He told me to come on the 31st of May, the day before official release date, and I could buy it. Well, needless to say I couldn't resist that. Being able to buy the album before anyone else, I'll have that, I thought.

I had only heard about one track before I bought the album and the reviews in the pop press were intriguing to say the least as most reviewers didn't know what to make of it initially. This sounded interesting, I thought. What did we have in store from my heroes? I was not to be disappointed. You know how you can remember with clarity certain events which have stuck in your mind even after many years have passed, well, 31st of May was one of those days for me. It was a gloriously sunny early summer day and I couldn't wait to get home to hear the album for the first time. The radiogram we had in our house was now situated in our back room so I put the album on the turntable and sat in the sunshine on our back door step and listened to the glorious sounds which emanated from the speaker. I was hoping the music would be similar to Strawberry Fields Forever and Penny Lane and I was right. I was absolutely stunned by the inventiveness, originality and musical content of the album on first listening. I just couldn't get over how good this album was and must have played it about three times in succession. Each time hearing something new.

It is, of course, difficult to portray just how great an impact this album had at the time. For those of us privileged to hear it fresh for the first time was some experience. Over the years since then it has had some detractors, generally people who were either not born in 1967 or who were very young at the time, who have labelled it overblown and overproduced, but for me it is simply the best album any artist has ever done for a number of reasons. It took music, at that time going through a very experimental stage with the psychedelic movement in full flow, to a totally different and higher plane but more importantly it achieved what no other music could, as aurally, it literally portrayed a snapshot of that unique summer of 1967 and always will.

It encapsulated in one LP the colour, spirit and feel of the time like no other album has ever achieved. Music can often evoke particular memories when hearing a song played which is associated forever with a particular event in your life but this album actually evokes a whole period of time, not just one event. It is no exaggeration to say that this LP was the sound of summer of 1967. For those reasons it will always be the top of my all time list of albums and I firmly believe that it has never been bettered. Indeed, it often appears on the all time best album lists at number one, even after nearly fifty years, and is widely regarded as the most important album ever made. I certainly considered myself fortunate to be one of the first to own this album. My only complaint was that Strawberry Fields and Penny Lane should also have been included on it, as was originally intended, but EMI wanted those tracks released as a single and Brian Epstein, apparently, didn't want the two tracks included on the album so he overruled George Martin on this point.

The album was followed by the group's next single, "All you need is love", which was an anthem quickly taken up by the hippies during that summer of love. Peace and love was the all pervasive mantra and in Blackpool it was not unusual to see middle aged holidaymakers wearing what appeared to be cow bells round their necks, like so many cattle having escaped winter pasturing (and possibly Julie Andrews too) in the Swiss Alps, the cow bells being an emblem of that woolly hippy philosophy and no doubt freshly purchased from the stalls on the Golden Mile. It was certainly a bizarre sight I can tell you. The single itself was premiered by The Beatles live on a world wide TV programme called "Our world", broadcast to some 400 million people on the 25th of June. I can't remember too much about the programme though so I probably must have stopped watching as soon as I had seen the Beatles' segment. The other record which was released at this time and which also encapsulated the summer feel and the vogue for psychedelic music, was Procol Harum's haunting song "A whiter shade of pale", which seemed to be number one in the charts for the whole of that summer.

My only concession to the hippy style was a somewhat colourful combination of clothes I chose to wear (it's called fashion, dear) comprising black and white checked hipster jeans with obligatory wide leather belt, a pink patterned shirt, yellow neckerchief scarf (yes, really) and a darkish striped Edwardian style jacket. Very Carnaby Street, or so I thought. All worn with a splash of Brut, naturally! How I had the nerve to wear this crazy ensemble as I walked down Lord Street to the Bus Station to catch the evening Bus to the Disco I have no idea. Now, if I had to wear a similar outfit to this and walk down the Lord Street of today, it would probably be seen as quite normal and not out of the ordinary at all! See how ahead of the times I was. The striped jacket did look very cool under the ultra violet lights, honestly.

Although this was the summer of love in Britain, there was not much love going on in the middle east when the six day war between Israel and Egypt broke out on the 5th of June. The Jews and the Arabs did, of course, get on with each other as much as the Mods and the Rockers here did but the difference was that they had bigger weapons and didn't need to go to Margate for their conflict. The

Arabs badly miscalculated the fire power available to Israel and the conflict was soon over, in Israel's favour, but it was a portent of conflicts to come in that volatile part of the world and the consequences of that conflict still affect the Middle Eastern nations to this day.

Distinctly lacking in any element of love, also, was the Judge who presided in the trial of Mick Jagger and Keith Richards which began on the 27th of June following the "Redlands" drug bust earlier in the year. Both men were found guilty and Mick Jagger, for possessing four amphetamine tablets, received a sentence of three months imprisonment, and Keith Richards, for allowing his home to be used for smoking cannabis, was handed a one year jail term. Unbelievable. It seemed that the establishment had decided that the Stones, and all their ilk, had to be taught a lesson. Times were certainly different back in, for a brief moment, the "not so swinging" sixties.

Now whilst I do not in any way condone drug taking, if any adult wishes to partake of that "activity" and it doesn't impinge on me then I have no problem with it at all. I might think that they are idiots, but that is their choice. The Stones were in their own home, harming no one, but this was not good enough for the establishment. A lesson had to be handed out. Thankfully the general outrage the sentences caused at the time led to the Appeal Court overturning Keith's sentence and reducing Mick's to a conditional discharge. The Stones, however, showed no gratitude as they then proceeded to inflict their woeful Sergeant Pepper copy album "Their Satanic Majesties request" on their undeserving public. I really like the Stones and most of their music but psychedelia and trying to emulate the Beatles was not their bag. They would rectify this error of judgment the following year to the relief of most Stones fans, including me.

Talking of love, one aspect of an expression of this which had previously been illegal was decriminalised on the 4th of July with the passing of the Sexual Offences Act which meant that consenting adults of the same sex could now have their own open relationship without fear of prosecution. In any civilised society this has to be totally correct and was a good example of how the sixties brought a certain enlightenment to this country. This would be followed by the Abortion Act in October which decriminalised abortions and at last gave women power to make their own decisions over matters affecting their own bodies. I know that both these pieces of legislation were not approved of unanimously but for me it showed that society was becoming more tolerant and less dogmatic and that could only be a good thing.

There was not, however, much for me to enthuse about so far as new TV programmes were concerned save for one iconic series and a first showing of a hilarious and much loved cartoon show. The iconic programme was "The Prisoner". A very sixties influenced spy fiction series starring Patrick McGoohan as an unnamed British agent who found himself held captive in a mysterious seaside "village" patrolled by heavy security and spy cameras with some bizarre large "balloon" type objects which captured anyone who tried to escape. Now it may sound like the product of an imagination which had come in too close a contact with hallucinatory stimulae but it was actually a very good programme and has achieved cult status over the years. I certainly enjoyed it. The cartoon show was the always amusing "Tom and Jerry" which is probably totally politically incorrect in these straightened times but back then it was hilarious with ""Tom" always on the receiving end of his attempts to catch and eat "Jerry" the mouse. I always thought that the best episodes were those involving "Spike", the American bulldog, and the cartoon violence was always ramped up a notch when "Spike" was featured. "Tom" did, however, always manage to survive the violence meted out to him, somehow.

Summer entertainment in Blackpool this year, which I know you are just desperate to hear about, was provided at the North Pier by Dickie Henderson, Andy Stewart and Hope and Keen. Bet you're sorry you missed that one. Yes, I was too! Central Pier had Jack Storey (no, I've no idea who he was either) and an upcoming ventriloquist by the name of Keith Harris. The Opera House featured

Bruce Forsyth and a singer called Millicent Martin while the ABC Theatre had Frank Ifield and Jimmy Tarbuck. My much valued pocket money was not wasted on any of that fare, I can tell you. Still, it must have pleased the holidaymakers. Well, the older ones didn't get out much I expect.

As for me, I was now finishing my final term in the lower sixth form this summer and having to take the annual end of year exams. Next year there would be the mock "A" levels followed by the real thing so I was keen to do as well as I could. Although my class position dropped slightly to 7th out of 31, the marks in my "A" level subjects had improved so there was now a real possibility that I might actually achieve sufficient grades in the exams to be accepted at University. I would now have to give some real thought as to what subject I would read as I would have to make my choice of both this and my favoured University early in the Autumn term. That was for the future though. At this stage there was still a summer for me to enjoy.

The summer job that I, and a lot of my mates, would have liked was to be taken on by the Council as a Deckchair attendant. I had often wandered down the Promenade in summer and seen the student Deckchair attendants having a laugh, chatting up the holidaymakers and getting a nice tan without seeming to do too much work. That's a job for me, I thought, but on applying to the Council I was told that they only took school leavers and College or University students as well, so while they wouldn't employ me they did ask me to apply the following year. As I had been unsuccessful in that quest I decided to have one last summer of idleness (now there's a surprise!) sponging on parents and a great time I had as well. One of my Queen's Disco group had his own car as he had a job so he could ferry us all about on our jaunts which sometimes comprised of us heading down to the beach for a game of football and also of seeing if there were any attractive holidaymakers wandering around. That was the life. Cruising around on the Promenade in his car with the radio playing the latest songs. No worries and not a care in the world. You didn't need a fortune to enjoy yourselves back then. You had a laugh with your mates and there were always girls to pursue. What more could a healthy seventeen year old wish for?

The pursuit of girls was still mainly carried on, by me, at the Queen's Disco which now had the added bonus of the numerous holidaymakers who came from all around the country. You have to remember that at this time foreign holidays were exotic and generally only for the rich, so if you wanted a holiday in the sixties, Blackpool was number one on your agenda. This meant lots, and I mean lots, of young, often attractive, girls who were really after having a good time. Not a falling down drunk good time, that didn't go on in the sixties. No, it meant enjoying yourself and having a good time mostly in the company of the opposite sex. The girls on holiday who came to the Disco wanted some fun and we were just the group to give it to them. What was most appealing for us was the thought that they would only be here for a week or so and they would then be replaced by the next influx of holidaymakers. I generally exchanged addresses with those girls I met and fancied most as it was always possible they would make a return journey to the resort and this led to a fair bit of correspondence as the summer progressed. Yes, I actually had to write letters. Remember them. No mobile phones, lap tops or i-pads in those days, of course, merely actual letter writing. A lost art I think, these days.

I remember that my system was not infallible though, as I found out later in the year. During this summer I had met one girl at the Disco who hailed from North London and who was visiting relatives in the resort. I quite liked her. She was attractive and had short blonde hair and was very much a mod in the way she dressed. While she was here I took her out one night to the Mecca and a place called the Highland Room, which had just recently opened. This was a smallish disco on the top floor of the Mecca building and if I remember rightly it had a tartan decor with Scottish insignia on the walls, hence the name, but the real joy was the music they played there.

There was no jukebox at this venue but an actual proper disc jockey who played Motown and Soul, so right up our street. We had a very enjoyable few days together before she went back to London. I had exchanged addresses with her and she said she would probably come up later in the year and we could meet up then. The problem was that she never told me exactly when she would be coming up and when she did eventually show up one night at the Queen's Disco she caught me red handed being "friendly" with another girl. That was the end of what could have been a good friendship, if a bit long distance, but what did she expect me to do? After all, I was never going to be a monk was I, and there were just too many temptations (and I don't mean the group) around! It was a fun packed summer though and one I thoroughly enjoyed.

However, all was not completely rosy in my world though, as on the 14th of August there came the death of the pirate stations. The Labour Government, led by Harold Wilson, had passed an Act in Parliament effectively banning these stations from broadcasting. At a stroke, my generation had had our beloved music stations ripped away from us by some middle aged and elderly politicians, who had no affinity with us or the music we enjoyed, and we were left with the BBC and the crackling signal that was Radio Luxembourg...again. We were back to 1964 and the fare we had to endure then. The politicians claimed that they had to ban the pirate stations as they were interfering with foreign radio wavebands which, to me, sounded an unlikely excuse. After all, in the case of Radio Caroline North for example, which was moored off the Isle of Man, it's signal was hardly strong enough to reach the south of the country let alone Europe. No, for me there was only one reason for the ban, and that was control of radio broadcasting, or rather a lack of it, on the government's behalf.

So long as the pirates broadcasted from their ships they were totally independent of control by either civil servants or politicans and that was far too dangerous a situation for the establishment to tolerate. Never mind the pleasure the pirates gave to millions of listeners, that was not something that bothered the politicians. In any event, we listeners were mainly under 21 so too young in those days to vote and therefore without any influential voice at all. What did it matter what we wanted. The sop we were given was Radio 1 which began broadcasting on the 30th of September and, so far as I was concerned, was a very poor substitute to what had gone before. The only consolation was that we did now have a station which played our music during the day but as the likes of the late great Kenny Everett would eventually find out, you had to toe the line if you wanted to stay employed and it would never be a truly independent station like the pirates were. Politicians, they would control every aspect of your life if only they could.

Another sad event occurred on the 27th of August with the death of the Beatles' manager, Brian Epstein, from an overdose of tablets. Although I for one didn't know it at the time, Brian Epstein was a homosexual and had led a troubled life because of this. In addition to his chequered private life, he was also concerned about how his role as the Beatles manager would pan out for him now that the group had given up touring and were no longer so reliable on him. There were rumours at the time that his death was possibly suicide but I think this most unlikely, although he had been prone to bouts of depression in the past. It is interesting to speculate on what might have happened had a certain Raymond Jones not asked him for that record by the Beatles way back in 1961 which prompted him to see them perform live at the Cavern and then become their manager. Would music have taken a different path but for that one event occurring? It is always possible that the group, with their inherent unique talent, would have been discovered by someone else but we cannot be sure of that. I am just glad that he did make that fateful lunchtime visit to the Cavern. My life, for one, has certainly been much the richer for it.

Summer now over, it was back to the Grammar School for the final year of schooling as an upper sixth former. It hadn't seemed five minutes since I had first started at Highfurlong, the site of the old Grammar School (another use of the adjective "old" you see) and I was, for my final year, chosen to be a full prefect. This was the position which brought with it a number of perks. The good ones were that we had our own private room on the ground floor with our own radio and even masters would knock on the door before being admitted. Also we had our own lunchtime dinner setting away from the rest of the school and as this usually occurred after all the rest of the school had eaten, it meant that if there was any surplus food available, then we had the benefit of that surplus. We were growing young men, well most of us were. Some of us still resembled lower members of school in height terms!

Now, school dinners. I have not covered this thorny topic previously but at our school the rear of the main hall was partitioned off from the remainder of the school hall by sliding doors so that, combined, it could be fully used for morning assembly. At lunchtimes there would be square tables laid out in the dining area, each one seating eight boys and the meals came delivered to each table in metal containers. One container for the meat course, one for the potatoes and one for the vegetables. The head of table would then dish out the respective portions. No canteens with self service in those days and I was not overly enamoured of school meals generally. The meat could be either tough or grisly or both and the potatoes were generally of the mashed variety. Chips, sadly, were nowhere to be found at our school. Pudding was not much better either and there was one combination which, if served together, meant the perfect storm of no food for me and that occurred when there was a main course of liver and onions with cabbage (which I hated) followed by dead fly pie (not literally, it was actually a sponge with currants in it but probably still tasted like my first description) and custard. A lethal combination so far as I was concerned. I had actually stopped having school dinners for a brief period while in the lower sixth and instead enjoyed the delights of a meat and potato pie and buttered barmcake from the nearby shop on the corner of Mowbray Drive. Tasty! Don't know what Jamie Oliver would have made of that, though.

Anyway, as I was saying before I rudely interrupted myself, prefects' school dinners were somewhat privileged so far as portions were concerned and on one famous occasion there was myself and three other prefects, all members of the rugby team as it happened, with healthy appetites, having to share three containers, each container meant for eight boys, of cheese and onion pie, mash and baked beans. Well you just had to, didn't you. We polished off the lot but had difficulty moving after we had finished and pudding was certainly not required. The prefects' room was also out of bounds for most people all afternoon! (Think of that scene round the campfire in Blazing Saddles and you will get the picture).

Being a full prefect also meant that you had to wear a blue gown, similar to a master's gown, when on duty at break times or when sat on the stage at school assembly each morning, in front of the whole school. It also meant that you had to take turns reading the morning's lesson at assembly before the whole school and so this was my first attempt at speaking in public. I think the first time I did it I was surprised anyone heard my voice above the sound of my knees knocking together in trepidation. We also had a rota of dinner and break time duties which involved patrolling the school and, in bad weather, supervising classes. I used to enjoy thinking up weird topics for any essay I had to give a junior boy for bad behaviour. I thought lines was far too easy a punishment and that an essay on an obscure subject would exercise the boy's mind more! But by far the best part of being a prefect was the downtime we had in our own room. Free periods were supposedly for study time, but not for us. We profitably used the free period time to invent a card game called "Clag", similar to a whist type game, and there was always someone available to play this game during these free periods. Cards had to be hastily hidden, however, if a master ever showed up.

Autumn term meant, however, having to apply to an organisation known as UCAS and listing six Universities of your choice with your chosen subject which you wished to read at said University. We had been warned by our teachers that the Universities were competitive and did not like being listed much below number three on your list, so we had to choose carefully. I had decided to read Law if I was successful in my "A" levels. I didn't fancy carrying on with any of my "A" level subjects and in the sixties, a professional like a Lawyer,

Doctor or Chemist, was still highly regarded. Sadly, this is no longer the case as far as Lawyers are concerned and if I had my time over again there is not a cat in hell's chance that I would have chosen that particular career for a whole host of reasons which I do not intend to go into here, but, then again, I dare say a lot of us would do things differently with the benefit of hindsight. Which University would I choose though?

In 1967, at the time I had to make my choice, there were about 45 Universities in total but not all of them had a Law Faculty. I think that I had been given a book from my School detailing the various Universities and the courses they ran but there was only one for me, if I could get in, and which had a fine reputation as a Law School, and that was Liverpool University. I had read that a new, purpose built, Law Faculty had recently been completed which looked magnificent in the photographs I saw and Liverpool, for me, had two main advantages over all the rest. The first was the culture of the city, coupled with it being the home of The Beatles, and the second was the football team, Liverpool FC and the Kop. So my number one choice was made and was followed by the other main northern Universities like Manchester, Sheffield, Leeds etc but if truth be told, I was hoping my number one choice would accept me.

I duly submitted my application and waited. I think I must have been given a glowing testimonial by my school as I soon received an offer of a place from Manchester University who required three "C" grades at "A" level. That means nothing nowadays, of course, as the current exams, coupled with marks for course work through the year, bear no resemblance to the exams taken by my generation. In fact, I understand that nowadays the top Universities are reluctant to rely solely on the GCSE exam results, unlike in my day, and have their own exams as a mark of a pupil's ability. In order for me to achieve a "C" grade in 1968 I would have had to have been in the top one third of all candidates who took the exam. Quite a stiff proposition. I heard from Sheffield that they wanted to interview me in December before deciding whether to make me an offer of a place and, to my joy, I also heard from Liverpool that they too wanted to interview me in

January 1968 before making their decision also.

Prior to going to Sheffield for the interview, my school set up a mock interview panel comprised of a couple of my teachers who grilled me on my interests and on why I had chosen that particular University to study Law. I remember that they were not impressed when, on being asked by them what newspapers I read, I said the Daily Express and News of the World! Well, it was the truth. I couldn't help what garbage my parents might want to read and I was certainly not shelling out my own money to buy newspapers. No, my money was for buying the NME (which I didn't tell them about) and was also to be spent on other leisurely pursuits. (Girls and drink, anyone?).

The teachers told me that as I was intending to read Law, the University would be expecting my reply to this question to be that I read the Times as it contained the Law reports. The Times! Oh yes, I'm sure my parents would have been overjoyed to have swapped their Daily Express for the Times! Not much difference is there? Anyway, I'm sure the News of the World had the odd Law report in it from what I can remember as from time to time it appeared to feature tales of what a misbehaving vicar got up to in the vestry, as reported in the latest criminal trial. I think it concentrated more on the intimate details of the crime rather than any legal arguments, though. Still, it was a start I thought, but no, I was told not to mention that learned journal.

So, to Sheffield. I duly set off by train one morning in early December to Sheffield University and my first ever interview. In those days Sheffield Law Faculty was housed in what I think was quite an old building and I have to say that I was not very impressed with the University surroundings. I was interviewed by a senior member of the Faculty who asked me about my interests and why I wanted to study Law at Sheffield. I gave him the prearranged answer about Sheffield's fine reputation both as a Law Faculty and as a University in general. Total hokum, of course, as I really hadn't a clue about how good or bad they were but had been briefed about my response by my teachers. Sheffield was down on my list purely to fill out the required quota of six Universities. I was not originally sure that I even wanted to go there but I was convinced of this once I had had my interview. Sheffield wasn't for me. They must have liked me though because they did subsequently offer me a place and again asked for a minimum of three "C" grades, just like Manchester. The best thing about the day of the interview though, was that I was able to buy from one of the city stores the Beatles new EP (extended play featuring six songs for you non-vinyl people) "Magical Mystery Tour" which had just been released and came with a lavish booklet which I read on the train journey home. So, whenever I hear that song or others from the EP, like "Fool on the hill", I am always reminded of my first interview on a cold December day in Sheffield.

As the year drew to a close, there were two events which put a bit of a dampener on what had been, up to then, a thoroughly enjoyable time. The first occurred on the 10th of December with the sad death in a plane crash of the great Otis Redding, just as had happened to Buddy Holly, and who was surely the finest soul singer of all time. I had bought a couple of his albums previously and always enjoyed the depth of emotion he achieved in his songs and amongst my favourites of his were "Respect", "I've been loving you too long" and "My girl". The second event was the showing on black and white TV of the Beatles' new film, "Magical Mystery Tour", on the evening of the 26th of December and which caused quite a stir at the time.

Boxing day night in the sixties was a night when it was still quite traditional for the family to settle down all together to watch the evening entertainment on the TV. Normally this would involve some naff variety type show. I had been adamant, however, that in our household the must see programme that evening was the new Beatles' film. I really didn't know what to expect, given the direction that the Beatles had taken with their music, but I knew it had to be good. Well, it was the Beatles, after all. I didn't think that it would be another "Help!", but I was totally unprepared for the bizarre fare that was offered up to the nation that festive evening. Now even I, an avid Beatle fan, had to admit that on black and white TV the film left me wondering what on earth had I just witnessed as the film ended. Naturally, the reaction from my parents was to the effect of "well that was a load of rubbish wasn't it" and, of course, I just had to defend the artiness of it all, didn't I?

The press, however, had a field day. They had long been waiting for the first opportunity to have a go at the group and they made the most of it. Universal condemnation was swift and vitriolic. I must admit I was extremely disappointed with the film at the time. The film was certainly way out, but not half as bad as was painted in 1967. It was just too much for a normal evening's viewing in those times and not being shown in colour did the film no favour at all. Colour TV for most people was still a few years away. Was this the beginning of the end for the Fabs? Certainly not, but they were no longer the universally adored mop tops of yore who could do no wrong and they would not be making any more "arty" films for public consumption, that was for sure.

The end of the chapter means it's favourite records of the year time, again. I could just say the album "Sergeant Pepper" and leave it at that but in addition, and in no particular order, those records which stood out this year were :-

1. Respect - Aretha Franklin

2. Strawberry Fields Forever c/w Penny Lane - The Beatles

3. For what it's worth - Buffalo Springfield

4. Light my fire - The Doors

5. Waterloo Sunset - The Kinks

6. A whiter shade of pale - Procol Harum

7. Soul man - Sam and Dave

8. Such a small love - Scott Walker

9. You're my everything - The Temptations

10. I can see for miles - The Who

11. I never loved a man (the way that I loved you) - Aretha Franklin

12. Reflections - Diana Ross & the Supremes

13. The look of love - Dusty Springfield

14. Take me in your arms and love me - Gladys Knight and the Pips

15. (Your love keeps lifting me) Higher and Higher - Jackie Wilson

In addition to the Beatles' album, the other albums I enjoyed this year included "Piper at the gates of Dawn" by Pink Floyd, "Scott" by Scott Walker and "Forever Changes" by Love.

In the film world my personal favourites were :-

A Fistful of Dollars - the first of the Clint Eastwood iconic spaghetti westerns featuring the man with no name. Although it had been made in 1964 it wasn't actually released here until now, but a great film.

The Dirty Dozen - an all action war film with a terrific cast including Lee Marvin, Charles Bronson and many others.

You Only Live Twice - this year's Bond film with Sean Connery and a screenplay written by Roald Dahl.

In the Heat of the Night - a very atmospheric murder mystery tale with Sidney Poitier and Rod Steiger set in the steamy heat of a Mississippi town in summer.

Bonnie & Clyde - the terrific, but very violent, gangster film starring Faye Dunaway and Warren Beatty

To Sir, With Love - a British drama film set in a secondary school and starring Sidney Poitier

Far from the Madding Crowd - the brilliant adaptation of the Thomas Hardy novel starring the delicious Julie Christie, Terence Stamp, Alan Bates and Peter Finch.

For a Few Dollars More - second in the Clint Eastwood spaghetti westerns and even better than the first one (see above). Filmed in 1965 but not released here until now.

CHAPTER NINE
1968

"Eveywhere I hear the sound of marching charging feet boy, 'cos summer's here and the time is right for fighting in the street, boy"- Opening line to "Street fighting man" by the Rolling Stones

From a historical perspective and, indeed, from my own personal perspective, 1968 was a pivotal year in the sixties decade. At the end of the year the Stones released one of their finest albums, "Beggars Banquet", on which was featured the song listed at the start of this chapter and which accurately captured the atmosphere which pervaded a large part of the western world for most of this particular year. It was a year of protest by students in Europe and a year of tragic events in the USA which culminated in the historic manned Apollo 8 mission which orbited the moon for the first time and returned safely to Earth. It was also a year in which I would finally leave home and achieve a (small) level of independence.

As the new year began, I was counting down the days to my interview at Liverpool University which occurred early that January. Having had my interview at Sheffield, a few weeks before, I thought that I was now reasonably well prepared for what I might be asked at the Liverpool interview. The day of the interview I caught a train from the old Blackpool North station direct to Liverpool Exchange station, not something you can do anymore as both of the original stations were demolished some years ago. On arrival in Liverpool city centre for the first time, I thought it wise to take a taxi to the University as I was unsure of how long it might take me to walk to the campus and so I had my first encounter with the wit and wisdom of a native scouser, the taxi driver, who was keen to talk about his football team, the mighty reds of Liverpool. The taxi dropped me off right outside the new Law Faculty and I was greatly impressed with the look of the modernist architecture of the square brick and glass building which housed the faculty. I reported to reception and was told that I would be interviewed by no less than the Dean of the faculty, Professor Seaborne Davies. This was different to Sheffield, I thought, where I had been interviewed by just a senior member of the faculty, but not the Dean.

I had no idea as to how eminent a person the Prof, as he was known to his students, actually was at the time of my interview and only found out some time later that he had not only been a member of Parliament for a brief period of time but that he had also, as a member of the Criminal Law Revision Committee, had a large input in the compilation of what became the Theft Act 1968, which was a major revision of the law of deception at that time. My one good piece of luck, being interviewed by him, was that he was in fact a welsh rugby fanatic. I had gone prepared to be grilled about Law and why I had chosen Liverpool as the first University on my list but he had obviously read my school testimonial and saw that I had previously been a captain of rugby and now played for the school first fifteen so all he wanted to talk about was my sporting prowess. Forget Law, did I enjoy rugby and what position did I play? This was a bonus, I thought, as he was such a humorous and interesting person to talk to and the interview just flew by. He told me that he wanted a wide social mix of students in his faculty, both sportsmen and academic types, so would not ask for equal grades from each student who applied. In my case he told me that while a normal requirement for entry would be two B's and a C he would make an exception for me and he offered me three C grades but only on the basis that if I achieved them I would choose Liverpool rather than Manchester or Sheffield, who had both made the same offer to me.

I was over the moon, in football parlance, and even more so when I encountered a fellow interviewee sat in reception. I had been told to wait there after the interview concluded and would then be given a guided tour of the faculty and so I sat down next to another young man who I can only describe as looking like a refugee from one of my school's X stream, you remember them, the geeks with the bottle bottom glasses who had their noses permanently stuck in a book. I asked him if he had had his interview and he confirmed that he had and that he had been offered two B's and a C for entry and what had I been offered? Well, I wasn't about to tell him about my preferential treatment now, was I? I just confirmed that I had been made a similar offer and left it at that. A member of the faculty then took us on a guided tour of the building including the lecture rooms, Moot room (effectively a mock court room, and very impressive it looked too) and the well stocked Law library which was sometimes used by some members of the Liverpool legal profession, as well as the students. I was amazed and, not that I had, but if I had had any doubts about Liverpool beforehand, then the layout of the faculty and the facilities it had would probably have assuaged any of those doubts. It even had it's own coffee bar.

Following completion of the tour around the faculty I was then asked if I would like to see the University Sports Centre which was situated more or less opposite the Law faculty and I said yes, I would indeed. My fellow interviewee declined, for some reason. The Sports Centre, which had also recently been completed, housed an indoor five a side football pitch, squash courts and a large swimming pool. When can I start, I thought. This was right up my street and the sports centre was the icing on the cake. I would just have to make sure that I achieved the right grades as this was definitely the place where I wanted to be when October rolled round. I returned home and on the journey back I imagined the time I would have in Liverpool, utilising the sporting facilities to their maximum and thinking about all the girls who would be attending the University and who would be available for socialising and other activities. Well, it was the swinging sixties after all.

A few days after my interview I received written confirmation of the University's offer of entry and my studying routine then settled down into it's well worn path involving frequent trips to the Reference Library on Abingdon Street for the odd hour or two of quiet study. Well, sometimes it did. Although I was full of good intentions, I couldn't let the studying interfere with either my social life or my sporting life. More on the social life later. My sporting life involved my playing for the school rugby first fifteen at full back. I was no longer big enough to be picked as a forward for the team but I was spritely enough to play at full back and I had one big advantage which was my footballing ability. If I received the ball in a defensive position it was no difficulty for me at all to find the touchline much further down the pitch. Not only that, I was the place kicker too, which meant that I took virtually all the penalties and conversions awarded to my team.

We had, by now, developed into quite a formidable rugby fifteen and won practically all of our matches in my final year and we were ably led by Roger Uttley who I have mentioned before. Roger (known fondly by his fellow prefects as "Lurch", though not to his face for obvious reasons, the nickname having been chosen because of his likeness to the character of that name from The Addams Family TV programme, although it has to be said that the TV Lurch was slightly better looking than Roger) still towered head and shoulders above most people of my age and on the rugby field he was a colossus. He could generally be found carrying the ball with about three members of the opposing team hanging on to him for grim death trying to bring him down. Quite a sight to see. We were just glad that he was on our side! I would not have fancied trying to stop him in full flow and I was extremely pleased that he went on to be such a star for England and the Lions as he was a genuinely nice guy.

As I have touched on the fact that this particular year saw violence explode on the streets of Europe it is opportune to mention one of the causes of this unrest, namely the Vietnam war. This war had gradually escalated as the sixties progressed and world wide news coverage now meant that for the first time, thanks to this news coverage, the population of this country, Europe and, indeed, the USA, could see in graphic detail on their TV screens the full horrors of this type of conflict. My generation simply could not understand why the USA wanted to fight a war in a far off Asian country and many young Americans tried their best to avoid being drafted into their armed services and being called on to fight in this war. Mohammed Ali had even given up his boxing world title and gone to jail rather than fight in this war and many young Americans fled to Canada to escape the draft. America thought that they had no choice but to fight the communist Viet Cong as, they reasoned, if Vietnam was taken over by communists then all the neighbouring Asian states would follow suit, just like a pack of dominoes falling over, one after another. They would, however, be proved to be hopelessly wrong in this thought process (not for the last time either) and all that ultimately happened was that many young Americans lost either their lives or suffered war injuries needlessly. The politicians suffered neither of these fates, but then again, whenever do they?

In this country, thankfully, Harold Wilson refused to be drawn into this conflict but this did not stop the student protests, the largest of which was the Grosvenor Square riot on the 17th of March. Thousands of students demonstrated in front of the American Embassy in Grosvenor Square resulting in more than 200 arrests and showed exactly how much opposition to the war amongst the younger generation existed in this country. These protests were mirrored elsewhere in Europe, particularly in Paris. I agreed wholeheartedly with their sentiments and, ultimately, the Vietnam War proved a fruitless exercise of armed force by the Americans, who were eventually forced out of South Vietnam in 1973 when they were defeated by the communist forces of the North. A small guerilla armed force had defeated the mighty USA.

Meanwhile, on the 16th of February four young men and their entourage, in search of inner peace and the meaning of life, embarked for India for a stay with the giggling guru known as the Maharishi Mahesh Yoga. I had, of course, seen TV coverage of the Beatles with the guru from last August when they all attended a seminar with him at Bangor, at around the time of the death of Brian Epstein, and I was intrigued as to what they saw in him. Apparently, he had given to each of them their own personal mantra to chant to aid in their own meditation and so they decided to learn more about Transcendental Meditation by attending his meditation centre in India. It was all totally above my head but I thought that as long as it didn't interfere with their creative juices then what they did in their spare time was their own personal affair, bizarre though it seemed to me at the time. It didn't last, however, as first Ringo returned complaining about the food and then John began to have his doubts about the Maharishi's real intentions, believing that he had improper designs on Mia Farrow, who was part of the entourage, and also that his financial expectations were, shall we say, more avaricious than would have been expected from a normal holy man. The Maharishi had reputedly asked for 25% of the band's profits from their next album to which John had reputedly replied "Over my dead body". Meditation may have had it's price, but Beatles' royalties were never going to be part of that equation. The Beatles returned home to England with most of the material for their next album having been written during their Indian sojourn and the Maharishi drifted into obscurity, having enjoyed his five minutes of fame.

For me, the only meditation I was involved in at this time was meditating about my A levels and trying to remember all that I had been taught to enable me to obtain my required grades come exam time. In preparation for those exams, it was customary for pupils of my generation to sit what were called mock "A" levels and these were effectively a trial run for the real thing. I think I am right in recollecting that these took the shape of practice exams, with previous A level papers acting as the template for the type of questions we would be asked, and we were subject to this test during the spring term.

The exams were regarded by the school as quite important as they not only provided a proper test of what we would be asked in the real exam but also, more importantly, they gave an indication of how well, or badly, we were expected to do. I therefore worked reasonably hard prior to the mock exams as I now had the incentive of a place at Liverpool dangling before me and I really wanted to achieve the necessary grades to be accepted there. I thought that I was well on course for success as, when the results came in, I had achieved an A in History, a B in Latin and a D in French. If I achieved those grades in the real exams then I was convinced that they would be sufficient to see me admitted to Liverpool University. All that I had to do was to keep up my work schedule and surely everything would fall into place. It was not to prove to be quite so straightforward in practice, however, as will be revealed later.

Just before the Easter holiday, America suffered one of it's worst tragedies when Martin Luther King Junior was assassinated in Memphis by James Earl Ray. King had been at the forefront of the Civil Liberties action movement for many years and a passionate advocate of non-violence in trying to rid America of it's insidious treatment of it's black citizens, particularly in those states located in the deep south. A wonderful orator, he was widely admired by most of the intelligent white Americans and was a revered leader of his own community. America's big problem though, both then and now, was it's obstinate stance that most Americans have the right to bear arms, a proposition enshrined in it's constitution. This, on occasions, has led to some tragic deaths and King's assassination was a prime example of such an event. Over the intervening years since his death there has been some speculation as to whether Ray was innocent of the crime or whether he was involved in a conspiracy with the government and others, to have King killed. After all, Americans love their conspiracy theories. Whatever the truth may be, and some government records on the investigation into the assassination are not due to be made public until 2027 for some reason, the simple fact is that the black community lost it's main spokesperson and leader in 1968 and the world became a much poorer place because of it.

Away from the arena of world events, my social world now included regular trips to the old Derby baths swimming pool which was only about a half a mile from my house. I used to go there frequently on a Sunday afternoon with one of my Queen's Disco group who lived on Derby Road, near to the baths, and as his name was also Alan, and he happened to be over six foot tall, he was known as "big Al" to us all in order to differentiate between the two of us. You can probably guess what I was called. Anyway, we had discovered that Derby Baths had a sunroof on the top floor which faced south and was a perfect place for sunbathing and chatting to any girls who had decided to avail themselves of that facility. As the sunroof was sheltered from the wind, it was the perfect place for relaxing and getting a tan and if you got too hot then you just went down the flight of stairs, which led up to the roof from the pool area, and cooled off in the magnificent seawater swimming pool. The baths had an Olympic size pool with three diving boards of varying heights and also a spring board, all adjacent to the deep end of the pool, which was some fifteen feet in depth at this end of the baths. If anybody was either brave or foolhardy enough to dive off the top board, which was about thirty six feet high, one of the pool attendants would blow a whistle, the deep end would become clear of swimmers and the whole baths seemed to stop and watch the dive being performed.

I ventured up to the second highest diving board, about fifteen feet high, on occasions, and that was plenty high enough for me. From that board you still seemed to hit the water with sufficient force to have you anxiously feeling to see if your swimming trunks had become dislodged during entry into the pool! One of our favourite games was throwing the rubber ring tag you had been given, and which had your clothes hanger number on it, into the deep end and then you had to dive down to retrieve it. Another favourite was seeing how far you could swim under water without surfacing. I managed either two widths or one full length of the pool at a time, which was no mean feat. By far the best game though, was throwing an unsuspecting girl into the pool and then diving in after her. Obviously having first surreptitiously checked to see that she could actually swim! And whilst also avoiding the prying eyes of the pool attendants who, for some reason, weren't too keen on this activity. Sunday afternoons became quite a good laugh for the two of us and even better when, on some occasions, we were joined by a couple of girls we knew.

Evening entertainment was still mainly provided by the Queen's

Disco and was to be our staple for most of this year. I had had one or two brief periods of going out with a girl or two for a few weeks at a time, and one even had her own car, which was a great incentive to me who was usually reliant on public transport, but there was no serious steady girlfriend as such. I just enjoyed the time I spent with the rest of my group and the occasions Big Al and I managed successfully to meet and spend an evening with a couple of likely girls. It helped that we had the use of his own car, although I am not certain he was too enamoured with me and my companion always having the privilege of the back seat while he did all the driving!

Another source of entertainment which rivalled the Disco in importance occurred whenever anyone knew someone who was having a house party. In those days houses would not be trashed during such parties, although the bedrooms were usually popular for some reason. We were always keen to find a party as it normally meant free drink, records to dance to and girls to chat up. It didn't seem to matter if you didn't know the host. As long as you knew someone your host knew, you could always blag your way in by saying so and so had invited you. Indeed, on one notorious occasion I remember that myself and my mate had been told of a girl's birthday party being held somewhere in Blackpool.

We didn't know the girl from Adam but as our informant knew her address we decided to see what the party was like. For some reason, on the night of the party, neither of us could remember the girl's name but we didn't think that this would be a problem as the party would probably be in full swing when we arrived. Wrong. As it happened, we were the first to arrive and were met at the front door by one of the girl's parents. Fortunately he just asked if we had come to the party and showed us into the lounge and then went to fetch his daughter, whom we had never met, and had no idea as to her name. Awkward! I then had the bright idea of reading through the birthday cards which were lined up to see if any of them had her name written on them and I managed to locate one. It did save some embarrassment, but not completely, as when she came into the lounge she saw two young men and she had absolutely no idea who we were, or, in fact, who had invited us. Given the scarcity of any other guests we decided to make our excuses and exit, stage left. In future we vowed to do a bit more research before crashing any other parties.

There may well have been various other parties in East London this May when the Police finally arrested the notorious gangsters Ronnie and Reggie Kray on the 8th of that month. The twins, whilst in the vanguard of organised crime in London, had been involved in armed robberies, arson, protection rackets and violent assaults and their arrests must have come as a welcome relief for much of the East End. Their careers would later be glamorised in 1990 with the film "The Krays" starring the Spandau Ballet members Gary and Martin Kemp. I dare say a good many of their victims found nothing glamorous in the treatment they received from the twins, such as George Cornell, a member of a rival gang, who was shot by Ronnie Kray in the Blind Beggar pub in 1966 whilst "The sun ain't gonna shine anymore" played on the pub jukebox. Ronnie was apparently heard to say to his hapless victim that "it certainly ain't gonna shine for you anymore" before exiting the pub. Probably not something Scott Walker had in mind when he first sang those words.

Manchester United fans were certainly partying at Wembley on the 29th of May when their team became the first English side to win the prestigious European Cup. I have to say that, even as a Liverpool fan, in those days I actually wanted United to win as they were a British side and football fans at that time were quite happy to cheer on a side other than their own in such a competition as this. Can you imagine any United fan nowadays cheering on Liverpool in any competition at all? No, me neither, but in fairness that is something which is prevalent now with all the fans of any team. I think it is quite sad that the enmity which has crept into football nowadays means that a fan will only support his or her own team and no others, but that is just one of the things which has changed since the bygone era of the sixties. I thoroughly enjoyed watching the 1968 final between United and the Portuguese side, Benfica, and was pleased that their brilliant manager, Sir Matt Busby, had overcome adversity to triumph in club football's premier club competition. I'm sure United fans enjoyed equally seeing my team's five victories in that competition in the years following their own triumph. Ironic pause. Again.

The end of May for me saw the start of the A level exams and what would be the ultimate test of my ability to obtain the grades necessary to have me accepted at Liverpool University. Going into the exams I felt reasonably confident, as my mock results had been fair and I had continued to work hard, or so I thought, in the intervening time. Well, allowing for a reasonable social life of sport, visits to the disco, girls and parties that is. Pity there wasn't an A level in those subjects though.

Anyway, the exams finally commenced and I found them to be a good deal harder than the mock exams had been. I thought my History essays had been reasonably good and was fairly confident of a good mark. I knew my subject and believed that I had been able to answer the questions satisfactorily. French was as hard as I thought it would be. We had had to read Albert Camus' novel "La Peste" ("The Plague" to give it it's English title) in French as our set book, which was no mean feat, as well as reading a Moliere play, "Le Misanthrope", also totally in French. That play was set in the seventeenth century and it was supposed to be a comedy of manners but was as funny as Des O'Connor on a bad night. I just hoped that I had done enough to secure the necessary grade. Finally Latin, in which I had previously done reasonably well, proved to be very difficult. In fact, I remember that I struggled badly with the unseen prose which is where you were given some Latin text to translate into English. All in all, I thought that it was going to be tight when the results came out in August, but felt that I probably had done just enough to achieve the required grades. All that I could do now was wait for the middle of August, when all would be revealed.

Meanwhile, the second tragedy to befall America this year occurred during my exam time when Robert Kennedy, John F Kennedy's brother, was fatally shot by Sirhan Sirhan in California on the 5th of June. He had been running for the Presidency and had just won the California primary election when, on addressing some of his supporters in the Ambassador Hotel in Los Angeles, the Palestinian gunman opened fire and shot him three times, resulting in his death. He had suffered the same tragic fate as had befallen his brother some five years earlier. This time there would be no real credible conspiracy theories. It emerged that the gunman had felt betrayed by Kennedy's support for Israel during the six day war in 1967 and had decided to wreak his own revenge. America lost a potential President and a supporter of both civil liberties and also of minority groups, such as America's black population. No wonder the top American politicians travel with such a horde of FBI agents to protect them nowadays. Land of the free, indeed. I think that I prefer some "liberties", such as the right to bear arms, to be curtailed thank you very much. I'm sure John Lennon would have agreed with this sentiment.

Talking of whom, although he did not appear in the film released on the 17th of July, except for a brief cameo at the end of the film, his music and that of the other members of his group played a prominent part in the film which was "Yellow Submarine". This was a British animated musical film inspired by the music of The Beatles and was an incredible animation film for it's time. Indeed, if you watch it today it is still very entertaining and it was widely praised at the time of it's release. I remember seeing the film sometime in late summer in a cinema in Wrexham. Why Wrexham? Well, it happened that Blackpool were playing against Wrexham in a cup match and as a few of us had a spare day we had decided to have a day out. As we had arrived in Wrexham in the early afternoon and found that there did not seem to be much happening in the town, in fact I think it was probably a Wednesday and the town was shut, or so it seemed as the tumbleweed drifted past us when we got out of our car. We wandered about for a bit and saw that the film was showing in the main cinema so we decided to take it in before going on to the match. Ah, the idleness of youth. I thought the film was fantastic, the music brilliant, but I don't remember the football match much. That was to be my one and only visit to Wales until 2001 and Liverpool's successful FA Cup triumph against Arsenal at the magnificent Millenium Stadium in Cardiff.

I am, however, getting slightly ahead of myself in chronology terms as by the time of our Jolly Boys' Outing to sunny Wrexham I had already left school and found myself a summer job. I had applied again to be a deckchair attendant and to my delight I was accepted by Blackpool Council as one of the summer "Deckies", as we were all known (and not to be confused with the earlier abbreviation used to denote Deckhands. See, I said that I would explain. We didn't wear white socks either!). I was told to report to the Deckchair office, which was a glorified subterranean concrete cave near to where the new Tourist Centre now sits, one morning towards the end of June. As I had completed my A levels, I was not required to stay on at school until school finally broke up in mid July. I could leave immediately after the exams, which is what I did. I had had enough of school and as it was left up to a pupil to decide if he wanted to leave, in my particular case I did not need asking twice. I couldn't wait to get down to the Promenade and earn some money.

The first morning of duty I, along with a number of other new starters and some University students who had been on the deckchairs in previous years, gathered at the deckchair office at about 8.30am and were told our duties. In 1968, when Blackpool was still the prime holiday resort in the country, there were over 30,000 deckchairs in total on the Promenade stored in neat stacks at various points along the Promenade from the furthest southern outpost at Harrowside to the most northerly outpost at Little Bispham. Most stacks had two sets of deckchairs and required a two person team, one to take the money and issue tickets, the other to hand out the chairs and stack them when they were brought back. Holidaymakers were given an incentive to return the chairs, as if they produced their tickets when they brought their chairs back then we would give them a small refund. It generally worked well, but occasionally I found out that you had to tramp over the sands at the end of the day, or before the onrushing tide came in, whichever first occurred, and rescue some abandoned chairs.

The "glamour" stacks, if they can be called such, were the ones situated on Central Promenade known as Palatine (just south of the Tower and opposite to where the old Central Station site was), Luna Park (just next to where the old Lifeboat station was and near to Central Pier) and Foxhall (situate opposite the old Foxhall hotel). Whilst most stacks on the Promenade comprised of two sets of deckchairs, each set stored under it's own green canvas cover tied to the Promenade railings, the stacks mentioned above each had three sets of chairs and this meant that the stack would have to be manned by three people as there were so many chairs stored in those stacks. About 1500 or so chairs at each of those three stations, if I remember rightly. What is more, in 1968 the hotels and boardinghouses were generally offering their guests full board which meant that most of the chairs would be returned at lunch and then rehired straight after lunch for the afternoon session. On a hot sunny day you had to work fairly hard and at the end of the day you headed for the nearest watering hole for some well earned refreshments.

I enjoyed the job immensely though, and it gave me my first insight into the vagaries of the "great" British public. It was amazing the things that you were asked while you were working on the Promenade. My particular favourites included a Scottish couple asking me, while I was on the Foxhall stack, if I knew where the Tower was and no, they were not joking, they were deadly serious, believe me. I just told them to turn round and I asked them if they could see that big iron thingy poking up into the sky. Well, surprise, that is the Tower! The second, and somewhat more bizarre request, was from a holidaymaker who wanted to know the best place to meet someone in Morecambe. Hello! Was this Blackpool Promenade we were on, I wondered? As it happened, I did have some knowledge of Morecambe as in the fifties my family would sometimes visit my uncle Cyril and his family at their home in Lancaster during the summer holidays and whilst there we would sometimes take the electric train from Lancaster to Morecambe where we could happily play on the sands. Well I could, anyway. So I didn't need to ask the audience, my fellow deckies, who were both looking on in bemusement at this request, or phone a friend. I just said that the best place to meet someone in Morecambe would be in front of the Pier. Well, unlike Blackpool, Morecambe only had one of those so problem solved. You had to be a smiling deckchair attendant as well as a local mastermind in those days.

We did manage to get our own back, occasionally, on the unsuspecting public however by using the well known deckies trick of sending out the "joke chair". Now those of you familiar with a deckchair may know that it can sometimes be a little problematical to put up, as my daughter Anna was to find out some years later when she appeared on the TV programme Saturday Morning Superstore, aged 5, in the eighties and her challenge was, for herself and her companion participating in the game, to put up a deckchair...wearing boxing gloves. Well, we didn't need those props for our little game. All we did was dislodge and turn round one of the wooden struts on the deckchair making it impossible for it to be put up correctly and hey presto, the "joke chair" was created. Simple if you knew how, but to all intents and purposes the deckchair looked, to any unsuspecting holidaymaker, perfectly normal.

One sunny day on the Foxhall stack myself and my fellow deckies, who just happened to be my old school mates Roger (he of rugby fame) and Brian, who had also been in my rugby team, decided to liven our day up by pulling this stunt. You had to choose your target carefully and we generally aimed for a family as they would normally all get involved in trying to put up the chair and would take any failure in good heart. We didn't have to wait long before our target family arrived and we duly included the "joke chair" in the ones that they hired. We then stood by the Promenade railings and waited for the fun to start. Father of the family tried first, but naturally with no success. His wife seemed to start getting agitated with him for not being able to put it up and so she had a go.

Again, no luck. This was normally the cue for the head scratching and standing back and looking at the chair to start, as they all tried to figure out what they had been doing wrong. By this time the three of us were falling about with laughter at the sight of the "put up a deckchair" competition which was then unfolding on the beach in front of us. Needless to say, other holidaymakers on the beach would generally join in as they had already put up their own chairs fairly easily so they thought they would lend a hand and show the luckless family where they had been going wrong and gradually a crowd scene would be formed, but this chair defeated them all. Who needed Candid Camera when we could play our own pranks? Eventually the holidaymakers realised that this chair just couldn't be conquered and brought it back complaining that it was faulty. We expressed surprise and said we would report it to our bosses and back in the stack it went, waiting for the next unsuspecting victim.

What happened if it rained, I hear you ask? Well, if the day started with wet weather, the practise was to remove several chairs from the middle of the stack that you were on so that you could create a small seating area and then you would pull the canvas covering back over the stack and so you had created your own little den, where you could perch on the bottom of a chair and listen to the rain pelting down on the canvas above you. Rivetting. In all honesty, that could be pretty miserable, but I don't remember too many occasions like that in this particular year. The worst was if it started raining when you had hired out all the chairs from your stack as at the first drop of rain all the holidaymakers, emulating Peter Kay's shout of "It's spitting, everybody in" but some forty years early, legged it back from the beach and made for your stack in unison where they just threw down their chairs anywhere they could and then thrusted their tickets under your nose, clamouring for their refunds. I recall one woman actually berated me for hiring a chair out to her when I knew full well that it was going to rain. Now I may have been a fund of local knowledge but that did not extend to my predicting the timing of rainfall! Myself and my fellow deckie would then get properly soaked stacking all the chairs correctly and getting them covered up as soon as we could because the holidaymakers didn't take too kindly to getting "soggy bottom syndrome" the next day if the chairs had got too wet and hadn't dried out fully in time overnight.

So the summer drifted on and I soaked up the sun in my relatively carefree job. Most weekdays on the deckchairs were the same except that the stack you were on varied from day to day. I preferred the stack at Gynn Square as the holidaymakers staying at North Shore were a little more refined than the ones staying in the middle of Blackpool and you were tucked out of the way on the lower walk with the stack facing the sea. It meant that you missed out on all the Promenade sights and the banter we had with our fellow students who had opted to work as conductors on the trams (more money but longer hours, shift work and not as healthy or as glamorous as us Deckies, well that's what we all thought).

Saturdays were usually less hectic, as this was changeover day, when those holidaymakers who had been in Blackpool for seven or fourteen days would go home after their holiday had ended, to be replaced by the next incoming batch. Sundays could be murder, though, as not only did you have the staying holidaymakers but, if you were on any of the central stacks, you also had the day trippers to contend with too. On a sunny Sunday in July or August you could sell out a whole stack in 45 minutes. Hard work, but it meant that you could then relax for most of the rest of the morning, until the lunch time return started. As there was a mix of girls and boys on the deckchairs your day could also be brightened considerably if you were lucky enough to have one of the attractive girls as your fellow Deckie, as I did on quite a few occasions. There was also the chance that a visiting young female would ask you for the benefit of your local knowledge as to where she and her friends might go to have a good time that evening and then I was only too keen to extol the virtues of my local venue and arrange to catch up with her there.

But all good things had to come to an end. Before I was due to finish my first season on the deckchairs, I had my A level results to contend with, which came out in the middle of August. On the fateful day I had taken a day off from my employment and again cycled to school early in the morning and on arrival in the main entrance hall I cast my eyes down the list of names on the board which held all the results to see how I had fared. No envelope opening or press coverage, naturally, in those days and we could all see how each of us had done at a glance by looking down the list. I looked for my name and then had a bit of a shock, to put it mildly. I had achieved a C grade in Latin, fair enough, a D grade in French, probably to be expected, but, and here was the bolt of lightning, a D grade in History. A D grade, when I had got an A grade in my mock exam. I was dumbfounded. How could that possibly be, I wondered? Realisation that I may not now be off to Liverpool started to set in, coupled with deep disappointment. I spoke to my History teacher who was as puzzled as me at my poor showing and he suggested that I ring the University as soon as possible to see if they would still accept me with my lower grades and, if not, then we should see about an appeal against the grade I had been allocated. He just could not believe the grade I had achieved.

I cycled back home thinking about my poor results and what impact they would now have on my future as a budding lawyer. I decided to follow the teacher's advice so I rang the University from the always somewhat smelly telephone kiosk at the top of our road. (For those of you who never experienced the joys of the old red telephone kiosks they all seemed to smell as though someone had decided to relieve themselves in there the night before.) We still had no telephone in our house at this time so the public telephone was my only source of contact and on speaking to the University I was told that they would now have to consider my results and make a decision. As they could not ring me, they asked me to ring them back in a couple of days. Those couple of days dragged by but when I did ring the University back I was told that the Dean of the Faculty had been impressed with me at interview and that he had decided to offer me a place, even though my grades were below the ones normally required. What a relief it was. I would be off to Liverpool at the start of October. Me, originally a former village boy from a small mining community and in whose family there had been a long line of miners, I was now being given the chance to become a professional, a lawyer. All thanks to our long lost grammar school system which enabled people like me to progress without either myself or my family being landed with any debt whatsoever. Now that was what you called "social mobility".

What else was happening during this summer? Well, the summer shows in Blackpool seemed to be comedy oriented as the North Pier had Mike & Bernie Winters (see previous comments) with Mike Yarwoood. Central Pier featured Solomon King (a one hit wonder with "She wears my ring" and no, it's not worth tracking that down on You tube, believe me), Don Partridge (a two hit wonder, he was formerly a busker before hitting the big time) and Les Dawson. The Winter Gardens was graced by The Tommy Cooper show (now he was funny), and the Opera House had what seemed like Blackpool's resident comedian, so often did he appear in the resort, Ken Dodd, who probably didn't let the audience go home until the Illuminations switch on. Finally, one for people like me to avoid, there was the ABC "Holiday Startime" with Engelbert Humperdinck and Ted Rogers. I think that the last show would probably now be officially classed as torture and would have Amnesty International trying to close it down.

Elsewhere, trainspotters of the country were in despair this summer. No, they hadn't been given complimentary tickets to the ABC "Holiday Startime Summer Show", it was because the last official steam train ran from Carlisle to Liverpool Lime Street station on the 11th of August. The final end of steam on mainline railways and truly the end of an era. Of course, trainspotters could still "spot" the diesel and electric trains, should they so wish, but any old trainspotter will tell you that there was nothing to beat the excitement of a mainline express thundering along at full steam. It truly was a magnificent sight and the preserved steam locomotives still draw crowds whenever they take to the rails. I am certain that the newer, cleaner trains, efficient as they are (?), will not have the same nostalgic pull when they themselves are eventually withdrawn from service. I think that it is a real shame that young boys of today cannot experience the innocent delight which my age group had in this harmless pastime but, then again, it would probably seem very tame when compared to the gameboys and playstations of today and, in any event, what parent of today would be happy to allow his 10 or 11 year old to take himself off to sit near to a railway line or on a station for several hours at a time? We live in different, less gentle, times now, don't we? British Rail would have cheerfully scrapped every single steam locomotive in existence but, thanks to some well meaning individuals and groups, a fair number of steam locomotives have actually been preserved and can be found heading enthusiasts' excursion specials during the summer months. A fine reminder of those bygone days of steam.

Summer having now ended, along with my first stint as a deckchair attendant, University beckoned. I had received all my information from the Law Faculty, including a list of books which they expected me to buy for use in my first year and also confirmation that I would spend my first year in Hall, which was to be Roscoe Hall, and which was situated on the south of the city, near to Sefton Park. This was fortunate for me as a school friend of mine, Brian (he of the "joke chair" jape and fellow member of the rugby team), was also going to Liverpool University to read Chemistry and he had also been given a place in Roscoe Hall. Furthermore, he knew someone with a small van who could take both us and our belongings to Hall so he arranged that we would both go down together, in the van, on the Sunday before the first week of term at the beginning of October. I couldn't wait. I was finally able to leave home and have my own first taste of independence. Also, there would surely be plenty of girls attending the University who, no doubt having had to study hard for so long to achieve their grades, were probably now desperate for some male company and the chance to have a good time away from home, or so I thought. Sport, drinking, girls and parties, with perhaps a few lectures thrown in if possible, this was my idea of what University would be like for the next three years! If only.

As it happened, as far as my parents were concerned, I may well have left home on the Saturday rather than the Sunday for all they saw of me that weekend as I actually spent the whole of the Saturday night on the eve of my departure for Liverpool at an all night party and didn't roll back home until about 9am on the Sunday morning. Not something that I am now particularly proud of, looking back, but when you are 18 years old there is generally only one person who counts in your universe and my only intention was to have as good a time as I could before beginning my academic studies with no thought for anything else. I had met an attractive young lady a few nights before who said she had been invited to this party and would I like to take her. Well, I was hardly going to be ungallant and say no, was I? This was a legitimate party invitation, after all, and a final chance to enjoy myself before all the hard studying started!

Brian, and the man with the van, collected me and my belongings late on the Sunday morning following the party previously mentioned and we headed off to the Hall of residence. I told my parents that I would probably be back sometime during the first term and would write to let them know. How archaic it all seems now but given that we didn't have a home phone, letter writing was the only effective method of communication available. Unthinkable now, of course, but that is how it was for me and my family in 1968. I did make sure that I took with me my record player, a second hand stereo player I had bought a year or so earlier, and some LP records, as I was sure that I would be needing those. Apart from clothes and a few basic supplies, this was all that I took with me. I really had no idea what I would need as this was the first time that I had ever been away from home but as Liverpool was only 50 miles or so away from Blackpool, coming home would not present any great problem if I needed anything further.

On arrival at Roscoe Hall, Brian and I went straight to the Porter's lodge and we were given our respective room keys and some information about the Hall and it's rules. The Hall complex, which comprised Roscoe Hall and it's sister hall, Gladstone Hall, was relatively new back in 1968 and both Halls shared the same communal facilities and both were exclusively male. First big disappointment. I had been allocated a room on the first floor of K block and Brian had a room in a block about 50 yards or so away from my own block. My room was effectively a small bedsit equipped with a single bed, washbasin, french doors leading on to a small balcony overlooking a grassed quadrangle area, a wide fitted desk and chair and a fitted wardrobe area. Each set of six rooms on the same floor in the block had it's own communal kitchen area, toilet and a bathroom area with a bath and shower. I was quite impressed with all of this as it was certainly a step up from what I had been used to in our small terraced family home. The room also had central heating as well so no more getting up briskly on a cold Winter's day. Sheer luxury. As our arrival at Hall was on a Sunday, and term had not yet started, we were one of the first to arrive in Hall so we had chance to have a good look round and found that in the reception block area there was a large dining area, a small shop, two television rooms and a games room with both a snooker table and a table football machine. Excellent. The only thing missing was a bar and a few girls and it would have been just right!

The following day most of the students began to arrive in Hall and they were all very friendly and introduced themselves straight away. One of the students in my little section was a second year Vet and he arranged for all of us to have coffee in his room where we could each get to know one another. I then found out that my next door fellow student was just starting his second year and he was called Peter and hailed from Coulsdon in South London and was reading History. Peter would prove to be a good friend to me whilst he was at Liverpool and showed me the do's and dont's of Hall etiquette. For example, all girls had to be out of rooms by 11pm. This seemed crazy to me. What was going to happen after 11pm which would not happen before that time? Some strange logic was being applied here, I thought. It just meant in practise that if any girls did stay after the witching hour then they would probably stay all night as no one could say anything if they left in the morning. Peter also explained to me that round the corner from Halls was Penny Lane, of Beatles' song fame, but that I would not recognise the road as such because there were no actual road signs there. The reason for this was that the students kept pilfering the signs to put them up on their bedroom walls and the City Council had got fed up with having to keep replacing them. They eventually painted a sign on a wall on the road while I was there, as not even we could pinch a wall! Well, not easily anyway. The Chinese chippy on Penny Lane, Kwok's I think it was then called, was to become a firm favourite over the next year or so.

The start of term was mostly taken up with Fresher's week and being gently led into the University regime. In those days Fresher's Week did not mean an excuse to get legless. It was a period when all the various student society groups had stalls laid out in the main Student building, the Student's Union, opposite the grand Roman Catholic Cathedral, or Paddy's Wigwam as it was known to all the locals, and each group laid on their own exhibition to try and attract you to join. I was particularly taken by the stall for the Apathetic Society but was told that there weren't many members as no one could be bothered to join. Student joke. I won't be troubling Ken Dodd, I think. Des O'Connor perhaps.

However, the only organisation that I was actually interested in was for one of the four University Football teams and I duly put my name down for that. Trials for new players were held at the University Playing Fields on Mather Avenue quite near to the Halls of residence and I, along with three or four others, were driven to the trials one evening by a student who had just graduated and had recently signed for Liverpool FC, namely a young man by the name of Brian Hall. He has sadly died recently but he did go on to have an illustrious career with Liverpool, appearing in the 1974 Cup Final when Liverpool demolished Newcastle United 3-0. On the drive from the University to the playing fields I remember that he regaled us with an anecdote or two about Liverpool's then charismatic manager, the late great Bill Shankly, and he encouraged us to pay a visit to Anfield to take in a match. I didn't need much encouragement at all as this was one of the reasons I had chosen the University in the first place.

At the football trials I scored a goal quite early on in the game and was then pulled to one side and told by one of the University first team side, who were overseeing the trials, that I would be playing for the University Fourth team in the first fixture of the University season. Freshers normally started off in this team and then worked their way up to the first team over the course of their three year stay. Every Wednesday there would be a fixture against another University, either at home at the University playing fields, or away at the other University's home ground, and Saturdays would often involve a fixture against a local Liverpool amateur league side. My friend from Blackpool, Brian, had had trials for the rugby team and had been chosen for that team so our Wednesdays and Saturdays were now spoken for.

So far as my Law course was concerned, I soon found out that there were about 85 or so of us in my year made up mainly of male students with only 8 or 9 girls in that number and similar numbers in the second and third years of the faculty. Second big disappointment. One girl for every ten boys! Not exactly a ratio that I had been hoping for. That has changed considerably since then, however, as now there are more female lawyers than male ones. On being given our timetable for the weekly lectures and seminars I was amazed to find how few lectures we actually had to attend during the week. On a Wednesday, for example, we only had one one hour morning lecture to attend and the rest of the day was free. Very handy for my participation in the football team. This was certainly different to school. After a lecture had finished we were then expected to work on what we had been taught and flesh out our notes by reading up further on the subject. It was totally down to us how much work we did. The only criteria was that we were expected to pass the end of year exams otherwise we may not be invited back for a further year. I had always been used to a structured way of learning so this was totally new to me and I have to say that I thought that I would now do the minimum amount of work to enable me to pass the exams and enjoy myself as much as I could.

Student financial support came in the form of a grant from the local education authority and as I qualified for a maximum grant, because of my parents' earnings, this meant that I received the princely sum of £360 for each term. After taking out Hall fees for full board it meant that I had about £10 a week, I think, for living expenses, though my memory may not be totally accurate on that score. I do remember that it was enough to ensure a reasonable social life though, which included frequent visits to the Brookhouse Pub on Smithdown Road and less frequent visits to the Rose of Mossley Public House in Mossley Hill. Both were well known student haunts back in 1968. As the grant was given to you at the start of term you had to make pretty sure you didn't blow it all in the early weeks, so a certain financial discipline was required on that score. I made sure that I budgeted properly so that the grant lasted me for the full term, as there was no backup funds available to me once the grant had been exhausted.

So far as the University social life was concerned, this revolved around either the student dances and the music concerts, held each Saturday in the Mountford Hall in the Student's Union, or attending a party, if you got to hear of one. The dances involved a trek from Hall to the Student's Union on public transport as none of my fellow students had a car when I first started at the University. I have to say that I was not impressed with the dances. The music played there was rubbish, not the soul and Motown that I had been used to at home, and the University girls were far more reserved, shall we say, than the girls I was used to meeting at the Queen's Disco. Contrary to what I had imagined, they were not desperate for male company, well not mine anyway. The parties were not much better either as in my experience the good looking girls who were at these parties were generally either with someone or were on the lookout for a well heeled student with a car, which left me out. Imagine, they were not all falling over themselves to go out with me! Third big disappointment. After a few weeks of absolutely no female company whatsoever, but plenty of sociable nights at the previously mentioned hostelries, I decided to head back home for a weekend. Well, I needed some clothes washing (launderettes were never high up on my must see places to visit in Liverpool) and a good night out at the Disco was also required.

As I was a student I decided to try the student's then favourite mode of travel, hitch hiking, and save on bus and train fares. In the sixties, quite a few students would hitch hike if they wanted to go anywhere. I borrowed my friend Peter's University scarf, the student's universal badge of honour, although I had never actually bothered buying one myself, as the scarf was a required item of clothing for hitch hiking and signified to any passing driver that you were a poor student and it was virtually a guarantee that a lift would be offered.

I duly set out on the bus from Liverpool City Centre early one Friday afternoon to a roundabout on the outskirts of Liverpool at a place called Old Roan, near Aintree, where the main route into Liverpool met the Ormskirk road. The small roundabout has long since gone and has been replaced by a huge interchange where two motorways now converge and is now known as Switch Island. I was generally quite lucky and normally picked up a lift in a car or lorry within 15 minutes or so of starting to hitch. Sometimes I would get a lift straight to Blackpool but more often than not I would be dropped off at the Dock Road in Preston and a lift from there to Blackpool was often quite easy to obtain. Generally the drivers would be chatty and I used to enjoy those journeys. In all my three years of hitch hiking I can honestly say that I never had one bad encounter. The reverse hitch would be from near to the Premium Bond offices on Preston New Road and would again sometimes be straight through to Liverpool or again being dropped off on the Dock Road, so my thanks to all the kind drivers who helped me out during that time. You would have to be mad to pick up any hitch hikers nowadays though, sad to say. Anyway most sixth formers now seem to have cars, never mind the University students, so I don't think they need to hitch anymore.

It was on one of these weekend visits home that I met up with a girl who I had first spent an evening with at the Queens Disco during the summer. She had long dark hair, a nice figure and I thought she was very attractive. Her name was Susan and she was in the sixth form at Collegiate Girls' School, the sister school of Blackpool Grammar. We spent an enjoyable evening together and I asked her for her address and said I would write to her when I returned to University. I did actually already have two girls with whom I was in correspondence at this time, as I had been out with both once or twice, during the year, but overall I preferred Susan. This was to prove a fortuitous choice for me as unbeknown to me at that time, Susan was actually the girl who my future wife, Ellen, had met several years before at the Beatles' concert and it would be Susan who would eventually introduce me to Ellen. If I had not gone home that particular weekend how different might my life have been. On such chance encounters are lives altered.

Talking of the Beatles, the major event for me and the rest of their fans was the release of their double album, simply known as "The Beatles", but to all their fans known as the "White Album", for obvious reasons, on the 22nd of November. As I was in Liverpool, what better place to buy the album on the day of it's release than from a shop in Liverpool city centre. I duly went down to Lewis's (actually this Lewis's store was the first store opened in the country under that name) situated opposite to the Adelphi Hotel, on the morning of it's release and I had arranged to have a Friday afternoon unveiling of the album in my room in Hall to which I had invited some fellow law students and Beatles fans for our first ever listening. Each album had embossed on it's front cover a unique reference number. I am sorry that I eventually sold my copy as I recall the number on the front of the album was quite a low one and nowadays the lower the number, the more valuable the album is. I believe, in fact, that at the time of writing this, Ringo is just about to auction his own album which was the first one ever printed so has the number 000001 and it is expected to fetch about £40,000!

Anyway, as it had been over a year since the release of Sergeant Pepper, we were all on tenterhooks to hear what new music the Fab Four now had to offer to us fans. The answer, as every Beatles' fan now knows, was an eclectic mix of practically every musical style going. From the pop of "Back in the USSR" and "Ob-la-di, Ob-la-dah", the wistful songs like "Julia" and "I will", the heavy rock of "Helter Skelter" (soon to be tragically taken up as a theme song and pointer by a certain Charles Manson) and "Birthday", to the sheer lunacy and bizarre experience of Lennon's "Revolution number nine". We all had hysterics when we heard that last one and definitely thought that he had lost the plot. Sergeant Pepper this definitely was not. I had my reservations about the album back in 1968 and thought that there was some dross intermingled with the usual brilliance, but George Martin, I believe, was right when he later said that as a double album there was just too much on it and that if certain tracks had been removed (he didn't say which, but I am sure Lennon's track would have been the first one chosen for removal, but don't tell Yoko) it would have made a fine single album. I know some music afficionados still think it was one of their best, but not me. Good, but not great, is my view.

Just before my first term ended, on the 3rd of December, I got to pay my first visit to Anfield to watch the mighty reds play at home. I had not had the chance to go to Anfield before as each Saturday I was either playing for one of the University football teams or had paid a fleeting visit home. This game was an evening match that I was able to attend and was against Southampton, which the reds won 1-0. Although Anfield wasn't full, I did have my first experience of standing on the Kop and joining in with the other fans on the club's anthem, "You"ll never walk alone", before the match started. Only an ordinary league match, but the atmosphere and the humour I encountered that winter's evening were something else. I was hooked and have been ever since.

The ground was, of course, very different to the magnificent stadium it is today. The only seating areas were in the old Kemlyn Road stand, now the expanded Centenary Stand, and also in the old main stand which was demolished some years ago. The ground itself in 1968 held 54,000, when it was full to capacity, with 26,000 of those standing on the old Kop. No wonder visiting teams were intimidated by the sight and sound of 26,000 mad Liverpool fans standing behind one goal. The only downside to standing on the Kop was that when it was full, it was impossible to get to any of the toilets, hence the popular phrase in the ground of "roll up your footy echo" if you felt the need to relieve yourself. With the consequent result of wet trouser leg syndrome occurring nearby! Today's prawn sandwich brigade and club shop souvenir hunters would no doubt be horrified, but that was football in the sixties. A working class game played, not by multi millionaires, but by people from the same background as their supporters and who did not imagine themselves as either style icons or inhabiting a different planet from the rest of us.

It cost five shillings in old money (25p nowadays) to go and stand on the Kop and you didn't need to plan your visit months in advance and also take out a second mortgage for the cost of a ticket, in order to do so. You got there early enough to get in and if you didn't, well, you were locked out. Everyone who wanted to see a league game could do so with minimal expense. Now whilst today's facilities at grounds are fantastic and I wouldn't for one moment advocate going back to the primitive facilities of the sixties, the game has to me lost it's soul which it has sold to it's paymaster, pay TV. How ordinary working people nowadays can afford to go to games with their children beggars belief. That is if they can get tickets to the games in the first place. I make no apologies for saying that I prefer how football was in the sixties, before the advent of Sky and BT, but then is that because I am now an old curmudgeon?

Term having finished, I was now ready to start my next seasonal job as...a postman. I had applied successfully to Royal Mail, as it then was, for the position as a temporary postman for the two week period leading up to Christmas. In those days the Royal Mail needed to take on temporary staff to help with the volume of mail they had to deal with in the run up to Christmas. On arrival at the sorting office behind the main GPO on Abingdon Street I, along with a few other temporary workers, was first shown round the building and saw how the mail was sorted. I was then allocated to the regular postman who I would be assisting and he told me where I would be delivering mail, what he referred to as his "walk". My "walk" happened to be at Highfurlong, near to my old Grammar School, so I was very familiar with that territory. He first arranged the mail in the sack and then gave it to me and told me where to start off and to return once I had completed the "walk". I quite enjoyed it, I have to say. We didn't have any uniform so I just wore my trusty green Parka coat and an armband which I had been given signifying that I was a temporary postman and off I went.

There were two main hazards I encountered in doing this job. The first was the unpredictable nature of the letter boxes at each house. Some were absolutely lethal and would try to take your fingers off, so hard was the spring attached to the letter box opening. The second hazard was the postman's favourite, the dog. Thankfully on my "walk" I never encountered anyone's dog outside their house but I do remember one small yapping dog at one particular house who went berserk when I delivered the mail to the house. I couldn't stand small yapping dogs so I decided to have a little game one day. I went up to the door as though to put the mail through the letter box and I heard the yapping dog bounding towards the door. I listened and ascertained that there was no one at home so I then peeped through the letter box and saw this Yorkshire terrier type dog looking at me and growling. Well, I just pushed the letter through the box, just far enough for the dog to keep trying to leap up and grab the letter, before withdrawing it. Rinse and repeat. The dog must have been well knackered by the time it's owners got home.

Once I had completed my "walk" I caught the bus back to the sorting office but the regular postman was not happy with me the first time I did so as, in his words, "You've come back too early. You'll make me look bad if my boss sees you back so soon. Bugger off round town or somewhere for half an hour or so and then come back." Clearly my regular postman had other activities he indulged in after his "walk" had ended, if this was anything to go by. Well, I did as I was told and combined my official duties with a bit of window shopping. The afternoon activities usually involved pushing a mail collection cart to the various postboxes near to the GPO and emptying them a few times during the afternoon, as well as collecting the mail skips from behind the main GPO counter. I thought the work was quite boring on the whole, but enjoyed the "walk" and, of course, the money. Two weeks wages meant that I would have spending money over the festive period. I needed that because it was during this Christmas break that I began going out regularly with Susan. I had arranged to meet up with her once I had returned from Liverpool and she became my first steady girlfriend from that time onwards for the next four years.

The final, and quite momentous, event of this year was the Apollo 8 mission to send astronauts out of earth's orbit for the very first time and have them orbit the moon. The mighty Saturn Five rocket was launched on the 21st of December and it took the astronauts three days to reach the moon which they eventually orbited a total of ten times. I had been thoroughly fascinated by the American space programme throughout the decade and was avidly glued to the TV whenever there was any news coverage of the astronauts and their mission. Some years later I would actually be fortunate enough to visit Cape Kennedy, as it then was, and see for myself the launch pad and the huge Saturn Five rocket that launched the astronauts into space. I cannot imagine what it must have been like for them to have been sitting on top of a 365 foot rocket as the moments to countdown ticked by and to have felt the rocket's massive engines fired up. I have nothing but admiration for the immense courage of those men. I well remember seeing the stunning pictures of earth taken from the spacecraft as it emerged from behind the moon and you could see for the first time the brilliant blue image of earth set against the dark background of space. It initially looked quite impressive on the TV screen just in black and white but when the colour images were printed in the newspapers it was incredibly dramatic. For me it emphasised how small the earth really is when seen in conjunction with just a tiny fraction of our small section of the Universe. The pictures also poignantly revealed what appeared to be the beautiful fragility of the earth which is effectively our lifeboat in space. This was a spectacular way to end the year and provided some solace for the inhabitants of the USA after the terrible assassinations which had occurred in that country during the year.

Musically, I didn't think that this year had been a particularly vintage year on the whole, so far as the quantity of good record releases went, but there were still some terrific records amongst those that were issued during the year and here are my favourites:-

1. I say a little prayer - Aretha Franklin

2. The weight - The Band

3. Hey Jude - The Beatles

4. Sunshine of your love - Cream

5. Son of a preacher man - Dusty Springfield

6. I close my eyes and count to ten - Dusty Springfield

5. All along the watchtower - Jimi Hendrix

6. Suzanne - Leonard Cohen

7. Alone again or - Love

8. I heard it through the grapevine - Marvin Gaye (with, for me, the coolest intro to a record ever)

9. Street fighting man - The Rolling Stones

10. Jumping Jack Flash - The Rolling Stones

11. America - Simon and Garfunkel

12. Mrs. Robinson - Simon and Garfunkel

13. I get the sweetest feeling - Jackie Wilson

14. You're all I need to get by - Marvin Gaye & Tammi Terrell

15. Joanna - Scott Walker.

16. Wichita Lineman - Glen Campbell

So far as albums were concerned, these were beginning to assume greater importance in the record industry and this year those which appealed to me included "Beggars Banquet" by The Rolling Stones, "The Beatles" (or the "White Album") by The Beatles, "Songs of Leonard Cohen" by Leonard Cohen and "Bookends" by Simon and Garfunkel.

Films I enjoyed which featured this year were:-

The Graduate – an extremely funny film with Dustin Hoffman and Ann Bancroft and that magnificent soundtrack from Simon and Garfunkel

2001 : A space odyssey - Superb, if baffling, science fiction by Stanley Kubrick

Bullitt - with the inimitable Steve McQueen and the killer car chase to end all car chases.

Oliver - probably the only musical I have ever enjoyed. Don't know what Dickens would have made of it though. Oliver Reed was, however, terrific as Bill Sykes, as was Ron Moody as Fagin.

Planet of the Apes - a science fiction film with a great twist at the end.

The Thomas Crown Affair - a great robbery heist film, very sixties in feel, featuring Steve McQueen with the beautiful Faye Dunaway who even managed to make a game of chess erotic.

Barbarella - with Jane Fonda. A bizarre science fiction film that all the chaps at University wanted to see, for some reason.

The Lion in Winter - a great historical drama based, loosely, on

Henry II, played by Peter O'Toole, and his wife, Eleanor of Aquitaine, played by Katherine Hepburn, with some terrific acting from the all the cast.

Where Eagles Dare - an Alistair McLean novel made into a rivetting war film with Richard Burton and Clint Eastwood.

The Good, the Bad and the Ugly - third in the trio of Clint Eastwood spaghetti westerns and one of the best westerns ever. Again, although filmed in 1966, it was not released until now in this country.

CHAPTER TEN
1969

"That's one small step for man, one giant leap for mankind". - First words spoken by Neil Armstrong as he stepped from the Lunar Module and became the first man to walk on the moon.

The final year of the sixties decade was to prove to be the most historic year of this and, indeed, many previous decades, as it eventually saw the realisation of John F. Kennedy's bold statement, uttered way back at the dawn of the sixties, of America sending a man to the moon and returning him safely to earth before the end of the sixties. Though, as 1969 started, it was going to be touch and go as to whether his promise would actually be fulfilled. We all now know, of course, that the first moon landing was successful. Well, all of us apart from a few cranks that is, who still think that the moon landing was just one giant conspiracy and that man didn't actually land on the moon at all. If they hadn't, it would have had to have been a giant conspiracy indeed, given the numbers of people who were involved with the space programme, the people who manned the space tracking programme around the globe, the broadcasters who assisted in transmitting the news and pictures of the event and, not least, the Russians, at that time America's sworn enemy and heavily embroiled in the cold war between the two nations. Don't you think that the Russians would have been the first to cry "fake", given how much they had invested in their own space programme, only to be beaten at the last in the race to the moon by the Americans? Some conspiracy! But the moon landing is for later in the chapter. For now, the start of the year for me meant my returning to Liverpool after the Christmas break for the commencement of the spring term.

I had, by now, been fully integrated into the swing of life as a

University student. A typical week for me would see two or three one hour lectures a day with the odd seminar for a group of six or seven students thrown in. Whilst the lectures would be one hour of fairly intensive note taking, the seminars would be more discussion based. Often these involved a discussion of some set work which you were supposed to have done beforehand. That was the theory anyway. I recall that the criminal law seminar, which was fixed for a 9.30am start, was sometimes swerved on account of it's starting at such an unearthly anti-social hour. Well, it was from this student's perspective as to make a 9.30 start would have meant getting up at about 8am (not an hour most students of my acquaintance saw awake and sober) in order to have first had breakfast in hall, then to walk to Smithdown Road for the bus into the city and then finally arrive at the Law Faculty. Totally unreasonable to have expected a nineteen year old student to do this particularly following a heavy social night. I'm sure you will agree with me on this. I certainly should have appreciated those days more, looking back.

Intermingled with the academic work was the away University football fixtures held on every other Wednesday. These were entertaining days out. Most of the trips were to northern universities and it was a bit of an unwritten rule that all the teams, both rugby and football, would, if at all possible, after their games meet up on Wednesday evenings at a college in Manchester then called UMIST (University of Manchester Institute of Science and Technology, to give it it's full title) which always held a Wednesday dance in the college and which was always well attended. Now I have to say that whilst I did socialise a little with my fellow members of the football team, I was far more interested in socialising with my mate Brian and his fellow members of the rugby team, who always seemed to provide you with a much better laugh, although they often sailed fairly close to the wind with some of their off the field activities, as they did on two memorable occasions at UMIST.

The first occasion was when we had met up and were enjoying a convivial drink or two in one of the bars. Well, this was the rugby team we are talking about and, like all rugby teams, they did enjoy the odd drink now and then. On the actual bar we were drinking in there was a small barrel from which was dispensed sherry and which just rested on the bar itself. The barman would turn the tap on the barrel and out would pour the sherry for the prospective customer, as and when needed. When the barrel became empty, it was simply removed from the bar and replaced by another barrel. Two of the rugby team, on seeing this, suddenly had the bright idea of relieving (this will be an apt choice of words if you read on) the barman of one of his empty barrels when he wasn't looking and decided to refill it themselves, but not with anything you would actually want to drink, unless you were in the desert and dying, literally, of thirst. After absenting themselves for a short while with the barrel they duly returned and surreptitiously placed the said barrel back on the bar, in it's usual resting place. We then waited anxiously for someone to ask for a first drink from this barrel. You can perhaps imagine the tears of laughter which occurred when the barman pulled the first glass of sherry from the replenished barrel only to be greeted with a yellowish liquid emitting steam, not an amontillado or pale cream I can assure you, as it flowed into the sherry glass. As the barman looked in bemusement at the glass of unusual liquid he had drawn we all headed for the bar's exit, fairly swiftly, as you might imagine.

The second, and far more notorious occasion, happened a few weeks later and made the news in the following day's papers. One of the more boisterous members of the rugby team (everything is relative and some members were indeed more boisterous than others, hard though it may be to imagine) was somewhat inebriated on this particular evening, quelle surprise, and for some reason decided that it would be a good idea to sound the fire alarm to see what happened. I know this as I was walking quite near to him when he smashed one of the small glass fire alarm buttons and no, it most certainly was not me. All hell then broke loose. The loudest fire alarm I have ever heard went off and about three thousand students exited the building fairly rapidly where we were all met by what seemed like the entire Manchester Fire Brigade, who were just arriving. Perhaps they had heard how popular this dance was, but probably not. They were not amused when they found out that it was a false alarm and I for one can't blame them. Stupid prank to play. Excitement over, we duly headed back to our coaches for the journey home and it was only next morning, when I was sitting in the hall dining room having my breakfast, that one of my fellow students who knew that I played for the football team asked if I had been at the UMIST dance the night before. He then showed me the article in the daily paper which reported on the mass evacuation from the dance and how the College authorities were anxious to track down the culprits involved in the false alarm. I think the UMIST dances were given a wide berth by our teams for a week or two after that.

There was one notable land mark occasion involving The Beatles this year as, on the 30th of January, they made their last "public" appearance as a group when they performed a brief concert on the roof of their own building in Savile Row in connection with a documentary film they were then making and which would turn out to be "Let it be", which was eventually released in May 1970. They performed a few numbers to a small audience of office workers who had gone on to nearby roofs to hear them play and they also managed to halt the traffic below, resulting in a visit from the Police who asked them to curtail their activities. At the end of the performance John Lennon concluded events by saying, deadpan, "I'd just like to say thanks on behalf of the group and myself and I hope we've passed the audition." I think that even Mike Smith, he of Decca fame in the 1962 chapter, would now concur that the group had indeed long since passed the audition. As I was in Liverpool that day and not London, I naturally missed the last chance to see the greatest band of all time play live. It was fitting in a way that having started playing before twenty or so people in small venues in their early days, they now finished playing before a similar number on that wintry January day. It was not quite the end of the group yet, however, as there would be one final studio album to be completed in September, as we shall see.

My football playing days with the University side came to a sudden end this term though. It came about because I was now going back home every two weeks to spend the weekend with my girlfriend and the captain of the football team told me that unless I was willing to play for the University team every Saturday then I could not expect to be picked just for the Wednesday games. I could see his logic and thought about it for all of two seconds before deciding to stick with the social routine with my girlfriend. Girls or football? I was no George Best, so I couldn't have both and whilst I enjoyed playing football, I enjoyed socialising with my girlfriend more. Funny how my opinions had changed since I was a ten year old, when football was the only thing that mattered, but that's adolescence for you. In addition, my mate from the Queen's Disco, Big Al, was going out with a girl called Anita at this time who was a good friend of my girlfriend so all four of us generally went out together on my weekends home and we always had a good time. It certainly broke up the weekly University routine.

Something else which broke up the University routine were the pranks we indulged in whist in Hall. There was the "water bucket" prank. In the kitchen part of the block was a large waste bin and the trick was to get an empty waste bin, fill it half full with water and then lean it against an unsuspecting student's room door, knock on the door and hide round the corner. Those doors opened inwards so as soon as the student victim opened his door to see who was there, the bin would topple over sending a wave of water into his room. Very funny for the pranksters, as they heard the swearing from the recipient of the prank, not so much for the poor student on mopping up duties. I soon got wise to this prank and always opened my door very gingerly. Another favourite was "hide the milk bottle". Each day, if you wished, you could pick up free from the Porter's lodge several slices of bread, a carton of milk and a quarter of butter as part of your daily food ration. Evening toast and coffee was a staple of many a late night whilst pouring over your books or playing cards, depending on what type of student you were. I must say that I did enjoy a good game of cards. As our rooms had no fridges, in Autumn and Winter we generally left the milk out on the small balcony, to keep it cold. This particular trick involved hiding a carton of milk somewhere in a student's wardrobe, hidden from view, where it would gradually turn rancid with the heat of the central heating and would then emit an evil smelling odour causing a frantic hunt by the student for the offending article. That one was a slow burner.

As pranksters you always had to be able to improvise whenever an opportunity presented itself which was too good to pass up. This occurred one day very late at night when one of us spotted a large stray dog which had somehow gotten into the quadrangle area and was wandering around. We immediately leapt into action and cajoled the dog into following us into one of the blocks where we very carefully tried to open a student's room door. Students at that time sometimes foolishly left their doors unlocked at night if they were in their room. I never did. I knew what my set of friends were capable of. Anyway, we found an unlocked door, gently opened it and ushered the dog into the pitch black room and closed the door. It must have gone nosing around as shortly after it's entry into the room we heard a loud shout and exclamation of fright from the suddenly awoken student, who was no doubt extremely puzzled as to how a large dog had gained entry into his room. We scattered as soon as we heard him opening his door in order to release Rover back onto the corridor whereupon we seized Rover and tried the trick a few more times until the novelty wore off.

One prank which was actually planned well in advance of this Winter term was Roscoe and Gladstone Hall's Brass Monkey night. On the first really cold winter's night of this term the tradition was to grab one of the most irritating members of Hall, voted the Brass Monkey, but not in any election you would recognise, remove all his clothes and throw him into the pond which was in the grounds just outside the two halls. The trick was in getting the unsuspecting victim down to the pond area as you had to go by the Warden's house and he would no doubt have heard the shouts of any unwilling victim being carried past his windows. Well, on this particular night, the victim was told that yours truly would be the recipient of this treatment so that he would go voluntarily down to the pond area, suspecting nothing untoward. I have to say that I was not too happy with this pretense as I feared that one or two of the more boisterous members of Hall, who I knew well, might just decide it would actually be more fun to have me as the actual victim rather than the intended one. It was therefore with some delight that I heard the self declared master of ceremonies announce to all and sundry present that this year's Brass Monkey would be the intended victim and not yours truly. Sigh of relief from me. God it was a cold night as the hapless student was grabbed and parted from his clothes, then thrown into the freezing pond water in just his underpants. It made for hilarious viewing though. Particularly when he trudged back to his room trailing water like some monster from the Black Lagoon. Students, eh? What can I say. Work hard, play hard. I'm not sure about the former, but we did our best to live up to the latter.

Back in the real world, there were two highly important aviation events which occurred within the space of a few weeks at the start of this year. On the 9th of February came the maiden flight of the Boeing 747, soon to be christened "the Jumbo jet", and on the 2nd of March the test flight of that most iconic of aircraft, sadly no longer with us, Concorde. The 747 is, of course, still flying passengers around the world, albeit in a more modified and upgraded version of the original. Concorde's last flight, however, would be on the 26th of November 2003. I would have loved to have flown on Concorde for the experience of the flight. In it's early days I did manage to see it for myself when it did a fly past along Blackpool Promenade sea front at low altitude and the noise of it's engines was just incredible. What a magnificent sight though. I don't think that I have ever seen a more graceful aircraft and I think it a great pity that it is no longer flying.

Someone who most definitely often had his head in the clouds got married on the 20th of March when John Lennon, now divorced from his first, long suffering wife, Cynthia, tied the knot with that bizarre female enigma, Yoko Ono. When The Beatles eventually broke up in 1970 many fans, me included I have to say, thought that she was the main protagonist and had diverted John away from the group. This is, of course, totally incorrect as we have all subsequently found out. The group had actually started falling apart without any input from Yoko. Whether she actually hastened things along is a moot point, but the simple fact is that they had all outgrown one another and there were just too many egos which needed satisfying to enable the group to go on much longer. I was never a fan of Yoko's and thought that she and John were living in cloud cuckoo land with some of the strange antics in which they were involved, never mind the dubious quality of the "music" they produced together. I do, however, wholeheartedly concur with their efforts to promote world peace though. A wonderful Utopia if it could be realised, but one which in reality will never exist. Nations will inevitably clash with other nations and we will always have the religious lunatics to contend with. Now there's a conundrum in itself. These religious idiots purport to follow a god who is supposedly peaceful yet down the ages it has been a case of pity the poor person who does not follow their ancient and medieval beliefs. Why anyone should need to murder another person who chooses to believe in logic and rationality rather than their own strange, illogical faith in any afterlife just dumbfounds me. I don't know what John would make of things now. "Imagine no religion" he sang, if only. Rant over.

Well, nearly over, as I am touching again on one of my favourite pet hates. Politicians. Now don't get me wrong, I fully agreed with their action when they passed The Representation of the People Act 1969 this year on the 17th of April and which had the effect of reducing the voting age from 21 to 18, as from 1970. I fully believed that 21 was much too high an age restriction for voting. After all, in 1969 you could pass your driving test at 17, legally drink alcohol at 18, join the army and learn to kill at the age of 16 but not elect a member of parliament until you were 21. A bit illogical to say the least, and it was high time that the voting age was changed. I think that the age limit is now correct and I have no truck with the politicians who believe it should be lowered to 16 or 17. I'm sure, looking back, that we can all feel that we were somewhat immature even at 18 years of age, let alone 16 or 17, and I don't think, with the passage of nearly fifty years since the voting age was changed, that youngsters have become any more mature than my generation were at that age. Politicians love to tinker though and it wouldn't surprise me to see the age limit lowered in time. I was pleased that I would be able to vote in the next election to be held in 1970 although I have sometimes wondered over the years why I have ever bothered given the inept and corrupt way that politicians have behaved since I was first able to vote.

As the 1968-69 football season began to draw to it's close, there was one very important match at Anfield on the 28th of April when Liverpool played Leeds United in what effectively was a league title decider for that season. Liverpool had to beat Leeds to have any chance of gaining the title but all Leeds needed from Anfield was a draw. The match was on a weekday evening and we believed, given the importance of the game, that it would be a lock-out so me and a few of my friends arrived fairly early at the ground. We were proved right as the gates at the ground were locked an hour or so before kick off, with a few thousand still outside and unable to gain entrance. I have been on the Kop many times over the years when it has been full but it has rarely been as packed as it was on that day. Once you took your place on the Kop you literally couldn't move and had to make sure you didn't stand behind a crush barrier, which was not to be recommended, because every time there was a crowd surge, which occurred every time Liverpool attacked the Kop end, the crowd surged forwards and you found that you had suddenly gone down about twenty steps before you were then carried back to your original position. We never imagined that any harm could come from these crowd surges but the events of Hillsborough in 1989 would, tragically, give the lie to this. The atmosphere in the Kop that April day was incredible and whilst no football grounds these days can replicate those types of atmosphere, mainly due to the all seating rules in the stadiums, from my point of view I think it is a small price we have to pay to ensure the full safety of spectators. What I can say is that, regardless of the somewhat uncomfortable viewing you had to endure on days such as this, it was worth it just to have sampled the sight and sound of the Kop in all it's sixties glory.

Anyway, back to the match. Leeds United were, in those days, a very formidable outfit who were notorious for their win at all costs mentality, instilled in them by their manager at the time, Don Revie.

Liverpool, on the other hand, were a side which had been very successful during the sixties but that team was now beginning to age, and Bill Shankly, Liverpool's manager, would soon have to gradually replace the stars of his first successful side. The game was a titanic struggle which yielded no goals and so gave the league title to the Leeds side at the final whistle. The Leeds team, at the end of the game, all ran to the Anfield Road end of the ground, directly opposite the Kop and where the supporters of opposing teams always stood, to receive their acclaim as champions from their own travelling fans. What happened next was truly remarkable and something I have never encountered in some sixty years of watching football. As the Leeds team turned back to the centre circle to acknowledge the applause of the Liverpool supporters, the Kop began chanting "Leeds, Leeds..." and "champions". You just simply would not have heard that at any other ground, then or since. It would be the equivalent nowadays of Liverpool winning the title at Old Trafford and the United fans chanting "Liverpool", yeah right, when hell freezes over. Different times, but it showed the class of the Liverpool fans then, and even the Leeds manager acknowledged this by sending Bill Shankly a telegram the following day congratulating the supporters on their sportsmanship. I was proud to be a Liverpool supporter on that day and, apart from the horrendous events at the Heysel stadium in 1985 when 39 Juventus supporters tragically lost their lives in a decrepit, poorly stewarded stadium, I have remained proud to be a Liverpool supporter to this day.

Before I draw the curtain on my first academic year at the University I must mention some of the more formal occasions which happened in Hall during the year. Each block in Hall had a resident tutor, a mentor if you will, whose job, in addition to being a lecturer, was to help with any problems you might have with your student life. He would also customarily dispense sherry at Sunday lunchtimes just before Sunday lunch if you stayed in Hall over the weekend. I didn't have any student problems myself, but I did enjoy the sherry! There were also formal dinners held throughout the year which would be attended by some dignitaries or other and on which occasions you had to wear your University gown. The food on these occasions was generally of far better quality than we normally experienced for our regular evening meals and we were allowed to take drinks into the dining hall which naturally led to an enjoyable evening being had. Finally, there was the end of year formal dinner at which you were allowed to take your respective girlfriends and this was generally quite a swanky event with everyone smartly (well for students that is) dressed and the girls all in their posh frocks. I invited my girlfriend down to this dinner and we assured her parents that she would be able to stay overnight in the guest room in Hall. That would have been her and about eighty others that is, though we didn't tell them that, obviously! Must have been very crowded in there, I'm sure.

At the end of May came the year end exams which I successfully negotiated and so ended my first academic year at Liverpool. I had met some good friends, had some good nights out, enjoyed a few silly pranks and in between, studied a bit of law. I was really enjoying my student life and looked forward to October and the start of the second year. Meanwhile I had already reapplied to Blackpool Council for summer work as a deckchair attendant and had been accepted so, shortly after returning home, having first had to manhandle practically all my University belongings single handedly from Hall into Liverpool to catch the bus back to Blackpool, no easy feat that I can tell you, I started back on the deckchairs at the beginning of June. The second year on the Promenade was just as good as the first one, except this time I wasn't too bothered about chasing girls as I now had my steady girlfriend for company and the bonus now was that she had learned to drive so we sometimes had the use of her mother's little Austin A40 car. I had not bothered learning to drive yet, there was no point as there was still no car available in my immediate family. Anyway, I was more than happy to be ferried about either by her or by Big Al if all four of us went out together. We still went to the Queen's Disco and parties but occasionally ventured further afield. Not as far afield, however, as a certain Neil Armstrong was about to venture that summer.

Before that event though there were two departures, of sorts, within the entertainment industry, both occurring within a matter of weeks of each other. The first event occurred on the 21st of June when the second Doctor Who, played by Patrick Troughton, regenerated into the third Doctor Who, played by Jon Pertwee. Even at the age of 19 I was still a big fan of the Doctor Who programmes and at University there were generally only two programmes, at this time, which ensured a full attendance in the TV rooms. Doctor Who was one, and the other was a programme which started in October and which I will touch on later in this chapter. I thought Patrick Troughton was excellent as the Doctor and brought just the right mix of menace and a touch of comedy to the role during his three years in charge of the Tardis. Jon Pertwee was never to my taste as the Doctor, though.

The second event was the death of Brian Jones, recently ousted from the Rolling Stones, on the 3rd of July. It is believed that his death, in his swimming pool at his home, occurred as a result of heavy drug and alcohol abuse but some people believe to this day that he was murdered, although there does not appear to be any hard evidence to support that theory. Brian Jones was an extremely talented musician, (just listen to his slide guitar on "Little Red Rooster" as an example) and it was he that effectively started the Stones, before Mick and Keith, particularly Mick, assumed the roles as the group's leaders. Whilst Brian was a mainstay of the group in their early days, his importance within the group began to wane once Mick and Keith started coming up with songs for the group to record. Brian was no songwriter and whilst he could not compete with the Jagger/Richards partnership, he most certainly beat them where consumption of drugs and alcohol were concerned and that is saying something when you are up against the prodigious intake of those substances by Keith Richards. Keith, of course, has managed, somehow, to survive all the abuse he could throw at his body but lesser mortals like Brian sadly succumbed to their effect. Whether being ousted from the band also led to his demise we can only speculate, but his death in 1969 was the first major one of the sixties generation of musicians, but certainly not the last.

Also departing from the earth towards the heavens, but physically this time and not spiritually, on the 16th of July, was Apollo 11 and it's three man crew of Neil Armstrong, Buzz Aldrin and Michael Collins. Their mission was to be the first men to land on the moon. I can still remember the thrill of seeing, on our black and white TV, the Saturn V rocket lift off from Cape Kennedy on the first part of it's journey to the moon. It is no exaggeration to say that the majority of the world's population were gripped by this historic venture and it monopolised TV news and newspaper coverage for the whole of the mission. Once the spacecraft left earth's orbit for the moon the news coverage scaled down a little until it reached orbit around the moon on the 19th of July. The actual moon landing took place on the following day when at around 9.30pm in this country, the lunar module landed safely on the moon's surface. I saw the landing covered live on TV and was then mostly glued to the screen waiting for the historic moment when a man would first set foot on the moon's surface.

I have to say that I didn't expect quite such a long wait as in fact transpired. It was not, in fact, until just after 2.30 am the following morning that Neil Armstrong finally started his exit from the lunar module. After seeing coverage of the spacecraft's landing, I had fallen asleep on the couch in our small living room but thankfully just woke up in time to see the grainy image of an astronaut descending the ladder on to the moon's surface and I heard Neil Armstrong utter those famous words quoted at the start of this chapter. I really didn't want to miss this event as, so far as truly historic occasions go, this was probably the most momentous event in man's brief tenure on earth. The first time that man had left his planet and one occasion that would be written in history for all future generations.

It is difficult to emphasise just how important this event was at the time. One giant leap indeed, particularly when you consider that the Wright brothers had been the first to fly in a powered machine in 1903 and the first full crossing of the Atlantic in a plane occurred only in 1919, just fifty years before the moon landing, or almost the time difference between the writing of this book and the actual period which I am writing about. I find that fact quite astonishing. I was never one for putting posters up on my bedroom wall, but I made an exception for the full colour poster of Buzz Aldrin standing on the moon, with the earth as a backdrop. What an iconic image that was.

The moon landing was just the first, but admittedly the most important, part of the astronauts mission. The next part involved the lunar module successfully lifting off from the moon's surface, docking with Michael Collins in the space capsule which was then orbiting the moon and finally returning safely to earth. I remember the lunar launch and wondered what would happen if it's engines did not fire up. Well, the answer was simple, the astronauts would just have suffocated to death in the lunar module as their air supply gradually ran out. Thankfully that did not happen and the rest of the mission, including splashdown in the Pacific, was successfully completed. John F. Kennedy's bold prediction had come to fruition and no doubt in hundreds of years from now this moon mission will still be marvelled at just as we marvel at the feats of those intrepid explorers who made the first transatlantic voyages in their flimsy sailing ships some five hundred years ago.

Back on earth, the summer season in Blackpool was not quite so stellar when compared with the moon mission. North Pier had the Harry Worth show, Central Pier had The Andy Stewart Show (one for the visiting hordes of Scots), the Winter Gardens had "The Student Prince" (an operetta apparently featuring the famous drinking song, again one for the Scots), the Opera House had "The Val Doonican Show" (think of an exciting version of Daniel O'Donnell, yes I know that's a contradiction in terms) and the ABC had the usual "Holiday Startime" this year featuring Cilla Black. However, there was one concert held at the ABC Theatre this summer which was somewhat notorious. This was a one night show starring Scott Walker and held on the 27th July.

Why was it notorious? Well I can tell you why, as I was there that night. Both myself and my girlfriend were, at the time, big Scott Walker fans and as I had never seen him live I was persuaded, by her, to go with her to the second house of the concert. On taking our seats in the circle, Susan pointed out to me a girl she knew who was seated on the front row of the stalls, right next to the stage, who turned out to be her friend Ellen, the one she had previously met at the Beatles' concert in 1964, and who would, unbeknown to me, eventually become my wife. But that is not the sole reason that the concert was notorious, although that may well be reason enough! No, that lay in the "performance" of the star during the second house. Apparently, according to my wife who has regaled me with tales of that day on the odd occasion or ten since we became married (she had actually met Scott Walker at the Imperial Hotel earlier that day having first hid in a linen cupboard in the corridor near to Scott's room, yes she was certainly a committed fan!) Scott was fine during the first house but he liked a drink and the whiskey he had imbibed during the interval between the two houses, mixed with some pills he was taking at the time, led to a bizarre second house performance from him, to say the least.

He came on stage and had only sang about three numbers, which all seemed ok to me, but then, all of a sudden, he lurched into singing "Black Sheep Boy", a song he had performed just a few minutes earlier. This certainly stunned his backing band as well as the audience, ourselves included, and as we were in the middle of Glasgow fortnight, a good many of this audience were made up of fugitives from the Andy Stewart show. They were not best pleased, I can tell you. Now the Scots have a certain reputation regarding how carefully they look after their money and they knew when they were not being given what they saw as value for money and they were not slow to let the singer know it, big time. About halfway through this early encore, when the audience realised Scott was singing the same number again, the shouting started from quite a few members of the audience near us, with some choice expletives thrown in. ("You're f***** drunk", being one of the more polite ones.)

Things looked like they could start getting ugly but unlike the

Scots' previous riot at the Stones concert, there were no easily available missiles this time readily to hand. Good job the seats were all bolted down, I thought. Scott was quickly ushered from the stage and the audience then started filing out in high dudgeon. As we went down the stairs into the foyer there were a number of Scots loudly demanding that they be given their money back. I was all for joining in, but Susan dragged me out, so I missed the Police arriving. I too was not happy at having paid my hard earned money to see this shambles of a concert and decided to get my money back in my own way, I promptly sold all my Scott Walker records. Not a smart move as being original pressings they are probably worth considerably more now on Ebay than the pittance I got for them at the time. Oh the impetuousness of youth.

Another concert taking place this summer, but in the USA and not Blackpool, turned out to be the daddy of all music festivals, Woodstock, where some 32 acts performed over three days before about 400,000 people. Although I didn't see much TV coverage of the event at the time, (there was, as you will know, in our day no such thing as music channels, mobile phone cameras or internet to transmit coverage of such events), I did see the documentary film of the event about a year later and a fascinating event it looked. It was held in upper New York state and the organisers had told the state authorities to expect about 50,000 people attending the event but so many turned up that the security fences which had been erected proved of little use against such numbers and Woodstock effectively became a free festival. Those performing included Santana, the Grateful Dead, Creedence Clearwater Revival, The Who, Jefferson Airplane, The Band, Crosby Stills and Nash and the act which wrapped up the festival, Jimi Hendrix. Jimi had certainly come a long way since his appearance in Blackpool when he shared the bill at the Odeon with Cat Stevens, Engelbert Humperdinck and the Walker Brothers! From Dickson Road to Woodstock in just two short years, but he didn't sing the same song twice did he Scott! Such was the life of a sixties musician. As the sixties were drawing to a close, Woodstock seemed to represent the highpoint of youth cultural events of this decade. There have been many open air festivals and concerts since, of course, such as Glastonbury to name just one, but Woodstock was by far the biggest of those type of events which occurred in the sixties and was a pivotal moment in rock history.

One event I was looking forward to at the end of this summer was my first holiday abroad, once I had completed my second year on the deckchairs. It came about because my parents had taken out a small insurance policy for me when I was very young which had matured earlier this year and gave me the princely sum of about fifty pounds. Not a lot of money nowadays you probably think, but let me tell you that this was quite a handy sum in the sixties and quite sufficient to enable me to book a fortnight in an apartment in sunny Malta in September of this year. My mate, Big Al, had agreed to come with me so, earlier in the year, we had both headed off to a small travel agent at the corner of Abingdon Street and Talbot Road called Exchange Travel and booked our exotic, to us anyway, holiday. Actually, it really was exotic as holidaying abroad was very much in it's infancy in 1969 and normally something only the very rich or very adventurous would do. Furthermore, Manchester Airport was not the huge enterprise it is today so this meant that we had to fly from Heathrow.

We had chosen Malta for a number of reasons. First and foremost it was cheap. Come on, £54 each for a fortnight in an apartment in Malta was very reasonable we thought. Secondly, it was both an English speaking island so no language problems there and also it used English currency so no need to obtain any funny foreign money. Thirdly, you didn't need a full passport, you could visit on a British Visitor's Passport which was valid for one year and which you could easily get from the Post Office over the counter. Finally, as our holiday would be taken in September, we wanted somewhere where sunshine was guaranteed at that time of year. What could possibly go wrong? Hmm, read on. As we were flying from Heathrow this meant that we had to catch a bus from the old (that phrase again) Coliseum bus station at Rigby Road from where our respective girlfriends bade us a fond farewell. We had not been able to take them with us as we had booked the holiday some months beforehand and we didn't know then if we would still be going out with our girlfriends in September, did we? Anyway, why would we need girlfriends with us in Malta as there were bound to be either lots of local Maltese girls or other foreign female holidaymakers, so we naively thought.

Well, things started to go wrong fairly quickly. No surprise perhaps to some of you reading this seeing how this is being written by someone who would later "temporarily mislay" his family's holiday money in Seaworld Florida on the very first day of that holiday and who would also lose his family's apartment safe keys on a windswept beach in Lanzarote which then entailed hiring a Spanish locksmith to spend most of the afternoon drilling into said safe in order to fit a new lock. Yes, it's fair to say that holiday calamities and me are not total strangers to each other.

Anyway, having arrived at Victoria coach station on the early evening of our departure to Malta, Big Al and I caught the shuttle bus out to Heathrow for our charter flight to Malta, which was due to depart at about 2am the following morning. Those were the days when Heathrow still had night flights, probably because there weren't that many flights so they didn't disrupt the neighbourhood too much. We duly checked our luggage in for our flight and naturally headed off to the bar for a pre-holiday drink, not that we had many, as even then Heathrow prices were a little on the steep side. The airport probably thought that anyone who could afford to fly could afford their drink prices. We had been relaxing over our drink for some time when we heard an announcement over the tannoy system, how quaint, saying that if anyone was booked on our Malta flight that they could take advantage of an earlier scheduled flight, if they so wished, as that flight to Malta was virtually empty. This sounded good to us. Why wait at Heathrow until stupid o'clock when we could get an earlier scheduled flight and begin our holiday sooner, or so we thought. So off we went to the new flight check in desk and my only concern at the time was for our luggage, which had already been checked in on our charter flight. Would that now be put on our new flight, I asked? Most certainly, the check in assistant assured us. Great, away we went.

The plane we boarded was a Comet 4 and if it held about 80 people, on this flight there were only about six of us in total, practically one air hostess each. The tannoy announcer earlier was certainly not joking when he said the flight had room for surplus passengers but why hadn't our fellow holidaymakers all joined us, we wondered? We would soon find out. I have to say that I thought the plane was very impressive. This was my first flight and I was thoroughly enjoying the experience until we flew over Italy where far down below us we could see one almighty thunderstorm taking place and suddenly the pilot asked us all to fasten our seatbelts. What was all this about, I thought, as I didn't think we were about to land just yet. I was right, we weren't about to land, we were just encountering my first, and also worst, experience of air turbulence I have ever suffered. I didn't think planes could shake like this one did and it reminded me of some of the scarier rides at the Pleasure Beach, but on those rides you didn't have 30,000 feet of clear air below you. I was somewhat relieved when we eventually landed safely at Luqa airport in Malta in total darkness. Leaving the aircraft we duly headed for the arrival "lounge", effectively a somewhat bare room with what seemed like a decorator's trestle table on one side for passengers' luggage and absolutely nothing, and I mean nothing, else. No one around, just me and Big Al in this deserted warehouse passing as a "lounge". We perched on the trestle table and waited for our luggage....and waited....and waited. Yes, that's right folks, we had landed safely in Malta, but our luggage had decided to stick with the original plan and catch the later flight that we should have been on.

This was a good start to the holiday, we thought. Mind you, had we been sensible and thought things through, we would surely have realised that there would have been no holiday rep to greet us from our scheduled flight when it landed. The rep wouldn't know that we were on the earlier flight and so only turned up for the charter flight, which landed just as dawn was breaking, thankfully with our luggage on board. No, Luqa airport's arrival lounge in 1969 was not a place you would want to spend a night in. Once reunited with our wandering luggage we got on the coach and we were deposited outside the door of our apartment in Sliema, just outside the capital Valletta. We quickly unpacked and then headed out to get our bearings. Valletta harbour was just at the bottom of our street so we decided just to relax on the sandstone area at the side of the harbour. We did a bit of sunbathing as it was very hot and we also decided to have a swim in the harbour. Yes, very sensible and hygienic, I'm sure. What were we thinking? It was refreshing at the time, though.

One thing that immediately amazed me in Malta was how quickly it became dark at night. I had always been used to the day gently transforming through dusk into night. In Malta it was as though, come about 6pm, a shutter came down blocking out all the light. One minute it was daytime and within about five minutes it was night. Very strange. As it was the evening we decided to see what the Sliema nightlife had to offer. It proved to be as exciting and lively as that Wednesday afternoon we had spent some years earlier in Wrexham. Not a disco or nightclub anywhere. Just some cafe's and a few strange looking bars, some of which seemed to have a peculiar liking for being illuminated by a red light. Why red light, we had absolutely no idea. Hey, we were still young and certainly naive. The locals' entertainment seemed to consist of families walking up and down the "promenade" escorting their young daughters and taking in the air. It was only later that we found out that this was a very Catholic island with more churches than you could shake a stick at and there was no way any of the local families were going to let a couple of likely lads like us anywhere near their chaste daughters. We could look, but that was it. Not what we had anticipated, believe me.

Girls seemingly off the agenda we decided to go into one of the bars and we chose one which seemed to be nicely illuminated by it's glowing red light. Now one thing Malta did have going for it was the price of it's drinks. They were phenomenally cheap. We couldn't believe our luck on that score and we decided to try one of the bar's cocktails. Well, we were sophisticated English travellers after all, weren't we? No sooner had we sat down than we realised we were being eyed up by two somewhat heavily made up "young" ladies.

Big Al looked at me and we started debating whether or not we should go over and chat them up seeing as how anyone under 25 on this island seemed to be off the menu. Fortunately, for us, just as we were about to make our move, who should come into the bar all of a sudden but a good part of the American fleet. The sailors were in town and the "young" ladies made straight for the sailors like flies round a jam pot. You could almost hear the proverbial penny drop in mine and Big Al's head as we both realised simultaneously what type of bar this was. This was certainly no ordinary bar we were in! We drank up quickly and exited even more quickly. Mind you, I'm sure the conversation with the "young ladies would have been fascinating, particularly when entertainment rates came to be mentioned. This was certainly something I had never encountered anywhere on Blackpool Prom where the only red lights normally led to Gypsy Petulengro's arcade and her crystal ball.

The next day we were visited by our rep who wanted to know if we were enjoying our stay and she recommended a couple of swimming spots nearby and also sold us a trip to a place where they made Maltese wine. Forget historic sites, this was something we definitely wanted to visit, particularly when she mentioned that we might get to sample some wine free. After she left we decided to try one of the nearby swimming spots which she had recommended and which was within easy walking distance of our apartment. This spot was basically a flattish, rocky sandstone area where you could sunbathe on the rocks and dive into the sea directly from the rocks. The water there was a clear and pristine azure blue and was superb for swimming. Apart from a later holiday in Lanzarote, I have never seen such clear water. We spent a relaxing day at this spot before returning to our apartment.

The next day we decided to try a beach which was a few miles away and this meant catching a Maltese bus. I was somewhat unnerved on getting on the bus when I saw, hanging from the driver's mirror, about thirty religious icons, crosses and a variety of what looked like worry beads together with a picture of the Virgin Mary on the dashboard. This was not something you generally saw on

Blackpool Council's buses I thought. Did he need some sort of heavenly guidance on these roads, I wondered? I soon found out. The car drivers on that island were, in fact, absolute maniacs and drove like they were in some sort of dodgem rally. Not only that, the bus itself looked like it had been around since Henry Ford was a lad and rattled as if it was just about to fall apart. I now realised what the religious icons were for! The beach, when we finally got there, was a small sandy beach adjacent to a bay on which stood the Hilton Hotel. It was ok but nothing to write home about. It was at least more comfortable to lay down on than the sandstone rocks had proved to be.

So passed our first week in Malta. Sunbathing by day and sampling the local bars (those not exhibiting a red light, I mean) by night. Then disaster struck. On about our seventh night the heavens opened and the mother and father of all storms started. Rain came down in torrents. In fact, it rained so hard that the locals started considering whether or not to build an ark. Now I have seen a lot of rain in my time but the storm that hit on that night was the wettest that I have ever encountered. I think that we looked out of our apartment door at about 2am, amidst the thunder and lightning, and we saw that the end of our street was now about two feet deep in water. Oh well, just a passing storm we thought. It would be sunny again the next day, surely. Wrong! The next morning the storm had slightly abated. It was now merely bucketing down compared with the previous night's deluge. Now for those of you who may be interested, Malta's normal September rainfall is about two and a half inches for the whole of that month. We had more than that in about three hours!

Well, it continued to rain on and off for the about the next three days and it is fair to say that Big Al and I were cheesed off by this unseasonal monsoon, to say the least. Stuck in an apartment with nothing to do except play cards and avail ourselves of the cheap drink on offer from a nearby store. Why hadn't we brought our girlfriends with us? We were climbing the walls after three days of this weather, to such an extent that we actually asked the rep if we could fly back early but there were no available flights. We were stuck where we were good and proper. It didn't help matters when she told us how unlucky we were with the weather, as even the locals had seen nothing like this before. Apparently an anti-cyclone had hit the island causing all the wind and rain. Imagine, me being unlucky with the weather! Who would have believed that! Sunny Malta indeed.

As our second week progressed, the weather gradually eased, although not sufficiently enough to enable us to go swimming or sunbathe, and by the time the day of our long awaited flight back home arrived the weather had actually started to warm up again. Typical. The only things which alleviated the boredom of our second week was our trip to the winery, where we found the wine very sweet and not at all to our taste, a visit to a nearby football stadium to watch an evening game, and a day out in Valetta where we went to the cinema to pass the time and also did a bit of shopping. My first excursion abroad had been unusual, you could say. The early morning flight back to London, on the right plane this time, was uneventful save for the view when we were flying over the Alps just as dawn was breaking. Now that was a magnificent and dramatic sight, I must say. So two, somewhat chastened, tired holidaymakers eventually arrived back in Blackpool where we were gratefully reunited with our girlfriends. I couldn't see this foreign holiday lark catching on any time soon if our experience was anything to go by. No decent entertainment in Malta for the likes of us and you would find drier weather in the Lake District too. Why would anyone want to go to a place like Malta when you could have all the attractions of Blackpool to hand and it didn't matter too much if it rained either? Good at predictions, aren't I?

At least I had one thing to be thankful for on my return and I don't mean just being reunited with my then girlfriend. No, shortly after I returned from my foreign excursion the Beatles' released what would prove to be their last proper studio album, "Abbey Road", on the 26th of September. They had considered calling the album "Everest", well they were at the summit of their musical careers, but they couldn't be bothered going all the way to the Himalayas for the album cover shoot so just decided to have their photographs taken on the zebra crossing outside the studios and name the album after the road on which the studio was situated. Prior to the album release, the studio itself did not have a name, merely being known as the EMI studio but ever since the album release the studio has been renowned worldwide as Abbey Road studio. The zebra crossing became quite famous too.

So far as the album itself was concerned, I thought at the time, and have ever since, that it was one of their best and although we didn't know it at the time of it's release, a quite fitting last album from the group that really did change music history. In 1969, of course, we only had vinyl records and when you turned the album over and played side two you discovered that it was a more or less continuous mix of some truly fabulous songs. In addition to side two, the album boasted tracks on side one such as "Come together" and "Something". It still sounds incredibly fresh to this day and is certainly one of my favourites. I particularly liked the symmetry of side two closing with the track "The End", followed by Paul McCartney's brief homage to the Queen, "Her Majesty", which was the epilogue to the album, as just six years earlier the introduction to the first track on their first album, "I saw her standing there" had begun with the 1-2-3-4 count in. The start and finish of their album career bookmarked by those intros and outros, but what an album career they had had. Most groups would have given their eye teeth to have produced just one or two of their albums and the Beatles set the bench mark for all to follow but none have managed to beat them for sheer quality and inventiveness and probably never will.

My summer holiday had ended and with the arrival of October it was back to Liverpool and the start of my second year at the University. This was an important year as at the end of it, in May 1970, I would have to sit the first part of my Law Finals exam. We had to sit one part at the end of the second year and the remaining part at the end of the third year. The two sets of results would then be added up and if you were successful you graduated with the right to append LL.B at the end of your name. I had opted to remain in Roscoe Hall and was now allocated a top floor room in the same K block as I had been in the previous year. Most of the students I knew had similarly opted to remain in Hall but one or two had decided to leave Hall and live in flats. That was something that I would have to consider for my third and final year. For now, I was happy to stay in Hall, where most things were done for you, including the catering.

The one big change this year was that in an evening a group of us started to frequent the student's club, "Greenbank", which was situated between the site of Gladstone and Roscoe Halls and the nearby Derby Hall. This club was in an old imposing detached building and was to become a favourite drinking haunt for me and my friends over the next year or so. Well, it was very handy being but a short walk from our block and it provided welcome refreshment after an evening's study so we would generally go there for the last hour or so of drinking time. They still had 11pm closing times in those days. Apart from this change in routine, the term passed much as the previous ones had done but this term I went home more frequently at weekends to socialise with my girlfriend.

I have not mentioned TV much in the later chapters of this book for the simple reason that I was spending less and less time in front of the TV. I was not too interested in the programmes being shown, save for one programme which started on the 5th of October and was to become most students' all time favourite show, namely the wonderful bizarre world that was "Monty Python's Flying Circus". I think it had just begun to be shown the week before I had headed back to Liverpool for the start of Autumn term and the only reason I watched it at first was because I was intrigued by the name of the programme. A flying circus, what was that all about? Well, from the first show I was hooked as it totally appealed to my sometimes strange sense of humour. I soon found that I was not alone. This was the only programme which guaranteed that the Hall TV room was full when it was shown. In fact, so popular was it in Hall that the second TV room we had, which generally had alternative viewing available for those who didn't like what was on offer in the other room, was commandeered for the overflow of students from the first room. I do remember that on occasions we had to "gently persuade" reluctant viewers in the second room that they would either have to watch Monty Python, or find something completely different to do elsewhere. The sketches resonated with most students I knew and you could guarantee that about five minutes before each programme was due to start there would be a sudden mass exodus from student rooms and a scramble for a prime viewing place in one of the TV rooms. It has always been one of my favourite comedy programmes and some years later I actually found myself getting paid by the Council for whom I was then employed for having to watch Monty Python's "Life of Brian" film and advise the Council whether it should be banned from being shown to the public because of it's alleged blasphemy. I think you can guess what my advice was.

Talking of TV, this was the year that programmes first began being broadcast in colour, on the 15th of November to be precise. Not that it made any difference at my house as we did not possess a colour TV, yet. That privilege would not come until May the following year, just in time for the World Cup held in Mexico. Purely coincidence that. For now, we were still restricted to one good old three channel black and white TV set. Weren't we spoiled?

The sixties decade was rapidly drawing to it's close when the curtain fell on the feelgood factor engendered by the sixties youth culture with the advent of a certain music concert held at Altamont in Northern California on the 6th of December. This was a free concert which featured the likes of Santana, Jefferson Airplane, Crosby Stills Nash & Young and the headline act, The Rolling Stones. Poorly organised, it also had the dubious benefit of having security provided by the local chapter of the Hell's Angels motorbike gang. Not the shrewdest move concert organisers would ever make. About as appropriate as putting Jimmy Saville in charge of a programme featuring kids, oh wait a minute. Anyway, the Hells Angels didn't ask for money for their "services", just beer. A recipe for disaster, and so it proved. As the concert progressed the mood of the Angels, and indeed the mood of the crowd, gradually became agitated and violent. Whilst the Rolling Stones were on stage a scuffle broke out in front of them involving the Angels and a black man by the name of Meredith Hunter who had previously tried to get up on stage and the scuffle resulted in Hunter being stabbed to death by one of the Angels, right in front of the Stones. As the concert was being filmed for a documentary, the shocking incident was captured on footage of the concert. From Woodstock to Altamont in just four short months. The vibe of peace and love appeared to be rapidly disappearing, just as the decade drew to it's close.

With the end of the Autumn term I returned to Blackpool for my second stint as a temporary postman. Well, the work was only for two weeks and hardly taxing. Plus it swelled my impoverished coffers. I was not going to spend this Christmas at home, however, as my girlfriend's parents knew someone who had a pub near Macclesfield and they had been invited to spend Christmas at the pub. They asked if I would like to join them and I jumped at the chance. Come on, Christmas in a pub, what's not to like? From what I can recall, our bedrooms were directly above the pub and the time that we spent there was very jovial indeed. On Boxing Day, one of our hosts asked if anyone wanted to go to watch Manchester United play Wolves at Old Trafford. I gladly accepted his invitation. A football match on Boxing Day was just the ticket to blow all the cobwebs away and it was also a chance to see Bobby Charlton and George Best play. Even though I was a Liverpool fan, I would still go to a game to see the very best players in action and the two mentioned above were two of the very best, excuse the pun. I have long since forgotten the game except that I remember the Wolves goalkeeper was magnificent and the game ended in a 0-0 draw. That would be the last time that I visited Old Trafford for many years. You had to be mad or very brave to follow your own team to that ground in the seventies and eighties, especially if your team was Liverpool! Mind you, the same probably went for opposing supporters visiting Anfield in those days too. Thankfully things are a bit more civilised now.

The momentous sixties decade duly came to it's end on

Wednesday the 31st of December. I cannot remember now exactly what I was doing on that evening but it is likely that I was at a party with my girlfriend. We didn't, of course, realise back then that this New Year's Eve was greatly different from any of the others which had gone before but, looking back now, I believe it most certainly was.

The seventies would prove to be a very different type of decade on many different levels and the music it would produce could in no way stand comparison with the riches we had been able to enjoy in the sixties. Yes, there was still some very good music to come, but the immediate future didn't look too bright because as the sixties drew to a close, the most popular choice of record buyers that New Year's Eve, and the nation's number one, was..."Two little boys" by Rolf Harris. Hardly something to set the pulses racing. I was just waiting for the Beatles next record to come along as both I and all of their fans were in total ignorance that they were actually on the verge of breaking up and that we had, in fact, already seen the last real studio output by the group. There would be one more album from them in 1970, "Let it be", but this was a cobbled together affair, including some of the material they had recorded early in 1969 and it would be the only Beatles' album not produced by George Martin. Effectively, the Beatles finished as a group just as the sixties came to an end. Fitting really. They had come to define more than anything else the spirit and excitement which that decade generated for young people like me who had had the good fortune to have been born early enough to enjoy and savour it's fruits to the full.

When 1960 had ushered in the sixties decade, some ten eventful years earlier, I had been at that time just a boy of ten living in a small mining village in Derbyshire but at the end of the decade, as a twenty year old, I had ended up living and growing up in this country's premier holiday resort, Blackpool, and studying at one of the country's then foremost Universities in the vibrant cosmopolitan seaport and home of my teenage heroes, The Beatles, Liverpool. In between, I had also enjoyed a tremendous time growing up to the incredible soundtrack of the sixties. What a decade to have grown up in. Unmatched since, in my opinion, and I wouldn't have missed it for the world.

So, for the very last time, my music choices for this final year and bringing the curtain down on the sixties are:-

1. Something - The Beatles

2. Get back - The Beatles

3. Crossroads - Cream

4. Suspicious minds - Elvis Presley

5. Who knows where the time goes - Fairport Convention

6. Both sides now - Joni Mitchell

7. Gimme shelter - The Rolling Stones

8. Honky tonk women - The Rolling Stones

9. Pinball Wizard - The Who

10. The Boxer - Simon and Garfunkel

11. Everbody's talkin' - Nilsson

12. He ain't heavy, he's my brother - The Hollies

13. If you go away - Scott Walker

14. My cherie amour - Stevie Wonder

15. Come together - The Beatles

The albums I remember from this year included "Dusty in

Memphis" by Dusty Springfield, "Crosby, Stills & Nash" by the same group, "Unhalfbricking" by Fairport Convention, "Abbey Road" of course, "Led Zeppelin II" by Led Zeppelin and "Let it bleed" by The Rolling Stones. All of these are albums I heard at the time, but an honourable mention must go to one album which I only discovered some time later, "Scott 4" featuring a sober Scott Walker.

Cinema was thoroughly entertaining this year and featured the following films:-

Butch Cassidy & the Sundance Kid - a great western with the inimitable double act of Paul Newman and Robert Redford

Midnight Cowboy - very much not a western (!) starring the great Dustin Hoffman and a young Jon Voight, penniless and adrift in New York

Easy Rider - a hippy sixties film with a great soundtrack and featuring Peter Fonda, Dennis Hopper and an early view of Jack Nicholson

True Grit - John Wayne winning his only Oscar for playing a hard bitten western sheriff

On Her Majesty's Secret Service - the latest Bond film featuring, for the one and only time, George Lazenby as Bond with the beautiful and talented Diana Rigg as his girl.

The Wild Bunch - a somewhat violent, for then, western by Sam Peckinpah.

The Prime of Miss Jean Brodie - a tale of a free spirit of a teacher and her influence on her class of impressionable young girls featuring the brilliant Dame Maggie Smith.

EPILOGUE

"And in the end, the love you take is equal to the love you make".
- "The End" by The Beatles

As this book was always intended to cover just the sixties decade, I think it only fitting that I end the book with a brief resume of what has happened to some of the major participants and the places detailed in the previous pages.

Creswell, where I spent the first two years or so of the decade, has long since lost it's coal mine, as has Whitwell, where my father worked before we moved to Blackpool in 1962. Both were victims of the mine closure programme with Creswell Colliery closing in 1991 and Whitwell in 1986. Blackpool has, sadly, long since lost it's true sixties glamour as the top holiday resort of choice as most people nowadays much prefer the guaranteed sunshine of the mediterranean (well the sunshine is guaranteed as long as I am not there) or more exotic destinations. It has become a short stay holiday venue but still has the "lights" as we locals call them, illuminations to you outsiders, which are well worth seeing and the Pleasure Beach is still going strong. Most of the local places which I frequented during my youth are, however, no longer with us. Derby Baths and the wonderful ABC Theatre being prime examples of civic vandalism. Liverpool has now become a very modern and dynamic city, almost unrecognisable from it's sixties heyday and Anfield is undergoing major reconstruction work as this book is being typed. The old Spion Kop was, however, demolished and rebuilt as a seating area some years ago.

As for the individuals, well yours truly completed his Law degree at Liverpool University in 1971 and qualified as a solicitor on the 1st of April 1974, April's fool day, and totally fitting given what my once honourable profession has now become. I practised in Blackpool for most of my career, specialising in property law, and I retired from the profession at the end of 2014. My old girlfriend,

Susan, and I drifted apart in 1973 but not before she had first introduced me to Ellen one summer's day on the sunroof of Derby Baths and who I would go on to marry in 1976. Our daughter, Anna-Clare, was born in 1978 and she graduated from York University with an English degree and then went on to work in London for Granada TV and MTV before joining my firm in 2007 as it's practice manager. My parents are no longer with us but my brother still lives nearby on the outskirts of Blackpool and seems to specialise in writing books about seventies scooter gangs and their exploits. In fact, he still has a very stylish machine of his own (a dream machine I think he calls it) and with his old scooter mates can be found participating in scooter rallies held each summer.

Finally, so far as the music and the musicians of the sixties are concerned, well that will never die, will it? Motown and soul continue to be played both on the radio and at parties and entertainment venues and just a few opening bars of any of the classics are guaranteed to get those of my generation, who are still able and have two good legs, on their feet and on to the dance floor. The Rolling Stones (aka "the greatest rock n' roll band in the world" or to some, the "Strolling Bones") still continue touring but have not yet reprised their Empress Ballroom gig in Blackpool from 1964, surprisingly enough! As does Bob Dylan, who I did manage to see at the Opera House a couple of years ago. Oh, and that group who my father memorably branded as "the group no one would remember in five years time", The Beatles I think they were called, all went their separate ways in 1970. They still sell the odd record or two I believe. John, of course, was assassinated in 1980 and George died in 2001. Ringo is still alive and kicking as is Paul McCartney, who I was finally fortunate enough to see in concert in Liverpool in 2010 at a small, intimate venue known as the Academy.

I never did get to see The Beatles live, as you already know by now, but that Liverpool gig was the nearest to it I could ever come and on that night, when Paul struck into the opening bars of "I saw her standing there", for one magical moment the years fell away and, for me, I was transported back to the sixties and it was yesterday....once more.

ACKNOWLEDGMENTS

I am indebted to my younger brother Philip who both gave me the inspiration to write this book as well as his invaluable assistance in showing me how to get it printed. My indebtedness also to my wife, Ellen, for reading and correcting my words with surprisingly little censorship! Lastly my grateful thanks and appreciation to all the marvellous sixties artists who gave my generation such a wonderful soundtrack to experience and enjoy during our formative years, particularly John, Paul, George and Ringo who truly did irrefutably change the whole music scene during that memorable decade.

Alan Mumby

Poulton-le-Fylde

December 2015.

Printed in Great Britain
by Amazon